Praise f...

'A pure delight . . . beau... ...ndled with some unexpected, humorous and emotional moments, all thrown into a fast-moving plot. I loved it.'

Lovereading.co.uk

'A page-turner that keeps you gripped until the end.'

Daily Mail

'An enjoyable romantic comedy with some entertaining twists.'

Sunday Mirror

'A really impressive debut. The writing keeps you on edge and has you wanting to read more and more and more! Helen is definitely an author to watch out for.'

Chicklitclub.com

'Explores the vulnerability and strength that accompany pregnancy and motherhood in a distinctive way.'

Novelicious.com

'A light-hearted . . . satisfying read.'

The Lady magazine

'A quick and entertaining read with a number of twists and turns to the story that I couldn't have predicted and a wonderfully satisfying ending . . . Funny, insightful and romantic – an absolute joy to read!'

Onemorepage.co.uk

'I didn't want to put it down! Chandler is an exciting new voice in women's fiction, and this debut makes me very excited for what else she has to come.'

Chicklitchloe.blogspot.co.uk

'A wonderfully written debut . . . Written in a lovely laid-back style that quickly absorbs the reader's attention and provides witty, warm-hearted reading, with regular giggles and loads of fun, the story explores the complexity of relationships, misunderstandings and drama of first babies and second chances.'

Handwrittengirl.com

Also by Helen Chandler

Two for Joy

About the author

Helen Chandler read English at Oxford University
before joining the NHS and working as a general
manager in various healthcare organisations.

She gave up (paid) work when she had a baby, and wrote
her first novel, *Two for Joy*, in any spare minutes she could
get when her daughter was either asleep (rare) or could be
palmed off onto one of her grandparents for a little while.

Other than reading, Helen's main passions are food –
reading about it, shopping for it, cooking it, eating it
and sometimes just thinking about it – and London.

She lives in east London with her husband and daughter.

You can visit Helen's website at www.helenchandler.co.uk
to find out more and read her blog, or follow
her on Twitter @HelenLChandler.

HELEN CHANDLER

To Have and to Hold

WITHDRAWN

HODDER

First published in Great Britain in 2014 by Hodder & Stoughton
An Hachette UK company

First published in paperback in 2014

1

A CIP catalogue record for this title is available from the British Library

Paperback ISBN 978 1 444 78677 4
Ebook ISBN 978 1 444 78676 7

Printed and bound by CPI Group (UK) Ltd, Croydon, CR0 4YY

Hodder & Stoughton policy is to use papers that are natural, renewable
and recyclable products and made from wood grown in sustainable
forests. The logging and manufacturing processes are expected to
conform to the environmental regulations of the country of origin.

Hodder & Stoughton Ltd
338 Euston Road
London NW1 3BH

www.hodder.co.uk

To Thomas, my amazing husband,
cheerleader and best friend.

I

Phoebe lay on her bed, hands clenched into two tight fists, tears streaming down her cheeks as she tried to blot out what had just happened to her and, perhaps even worse, her mother's reaction to it. She had been standing in the corridor at afternoon break, trying to blend into the background as usual. Not particularly easy when your school uniform is burgundy and you take the largest size in it. She looked like a sofa, or so her mum had kindly informed her when she'd skulked out of the John Lewis changing room during the dreaded uniform-buying session.

Suzi Withers had come up to her and touched her arm gently. That had been a shock, for a start. Suzi was definitely one of the in-crowd, not someone who would normally give a girl like Phoebe, who epitomised the out-crowd, the time of day. Yet there she had been with a sickly-sweet smile, faux sincerity dripping from every pore. Phoebe had been instantly defensive. If she'd been a hedgehog she would have curled into a ball ready to spike a potential attacker. Unfortunately evolution hadn't provided teenage girls with this level of protection; a fact which, had Charles Darwin ever seen St Augustine's High School on a wet Thursday afternoon following a period of double maths, might well have caused him to question his entire theory.

'What?' she'd growled at Suzi, studiously refusing to make eye contact.

'Oh Phoebe, I just wanted to tell you, because I know I'd hate it if it happened to me and no one did, but your period must have started, and you've got a big stain all over the back of your skirt. You should probably go and sort it out.'

Phoebe had felt colour flame up into her face. Although she didn't think her period was due, she was very irregular – yet another thing that could be blamed on her weight, according to her mother. This was her worst nightmare. Suzi had smiled again, and asked, 'Are you alright? Sorry, it must be horrible.'

And the thing was, even in the midst of her flaming embarrassment, Phoebe had felt a tiny warm glow that someone had cared enough to tell her, that Suzi was being so unexpectedly nice.

She'd managed to smile back at Suzi, and said awkwardly, 'Thanks, thanks for telling me. I'd better, you know, go to the bog and sort it out.'

She'd walked away then, as quickly as she could without breaking into a run, which she knew from hellish experience in PE classes caused her boobs to bounce up and down in a way that both hurt and provoked numerous ribald comments.

As she pushed open the door to the putrid-smelling girls' toilets, which she normally avoided at all costs, there was a sudden wave of mocking laughter, and the eight or nine girls who formed the core of Suzi's gang were screaming insults at her and sanitary towels and tampons were raining around her ears. It took her a few seconds to process what had happened. She'd been set up. She turned round, pushed past Suzi, who stood in the doorway behind her, her face alight with sadistic triumph, and ran for the school gates, this time uncaring that her breasts were bouncing wildly or that she was going to miss History, which she normally loved. She had just wanted to get home to a place of safety. She had wanted, God help her, her mum.

By the time she arrived home she was out of breath, sweaty, red-faced and tear-stained. Hair had escaped from her usually neat ponytail, but instead of framing her face in pretty tendrils as her mother's would have done, it was sticking lankly and clammily to her face and neck. Her mum had been in the living room, her perfectly slender body encased in leggings and a Lycra crop top, working out to a Davina McCall exercise DVD. She had not been pleased to see Phoebe.

'What the hell are you doing here at half two in the afternoon?'

'Oh Mu-uuumm,' she'd wailed, and flung herself down on the sofa, waiting for the warm enfolding hug that would blot out the rest of the world and make everything OK. Instead, she had got a rather awkward pat, and her mum had asked slightly wearily, 'Go on then, tell me, what's happened now?'

As she had recounted her story, Phoebe, always hypersensitive to such things, had seen pity on her mother's face, but also impatience.

'Oh Pheebs, you do make life difficult for yourself.'

That was a classic manoeuvre. Whatever happened, it was always, somehow, Phoebe's own fault. For not being pretty enough, or thin enough; for being too clever, for being too clumsy; for not being enough like the kind of daughter Liz McCraig had always wanted and couldn't quite forgive Phoebe for not being.

'How is this *my* fault, Mum? You're meant to be on my side.'

Liz had sighed deeply.

'I *am* on your side, that's why I wish you would make a bit more of an effort to fit in, to make some friends. If you didn't always have your head stuck in a book, lost a bit of weight . . .'

Phoebe hadn't stayed to hear any more. A fresh bout of sobbing was only seconds away, and she ran out of the room and up the two flights of stairs to her converted attic bedroom. This was her sanctuary, easily her favourite thing about her life. Her parents had converted the loft of their three-bed south Liverpool Victorian semi two years previously, and Phoebe had begged to have this room for her own. Although it had sloping ceilings and more than its fair share of corners it was a large room, big enough for a squashy sofa as well as her bed, and she had her own tiny en suite shower room. Her father had got a local carpenter to come and build fitted bookcases into the awkward corners, so she had all her books from earliest childhood lining the walls. She had saved her Christmas and birthday money and bought a tiny fridge and a kettle, so she was basically self-sufficient, practically speaking at least. Reaching her room and turning the key in the lock, she felt herself breathing slightly more easily. Then she

4

stood by the door listening tensely for the footsteps on the stairs that would indicate her mum had followed her. After a few minutes there was still nothing. Caught somewhere between relief and disappointment, Phoebe went and put the kettle on. She had recently read a selection of diet tips in one of her mum's glossy magazines, and one of them had been, 'When those chocolate cravings strike, try a diet hot chocolate – virtually calorie-free, but you may just find they hit the spot.'

Phoebe had bought a box of Options on the strength of that, and she made one for herself now. The saccharine warmth was comforting, but just a few sips were enough to tell Phoebe that the public humiliation she had experienced that afternoon could only be erased by far more drastic measures. She went to her secret chocolate stash in a shoebox in the bottom of the wardrobe and chose a Twirl and a Double Decker. She yanked off her hideous school uniform and left it pooled on the floor while she pulled on pyjama bottoms and an old T-shirt of her dad's. Lying on the bed, she ripped the wrappers off and crammed the chocolate into her mouth, waiting for the sweet creaminess to erase her feelings of loneliness and misery. The problem was, as soon as she stopped eating, the negative feelings poured back in, and the tears started all over again.

She went over the mathematics of her situation for the umpteenth time. She was fifteen and a half now, in Year 11 at secondary school. She could legally leave home and school in just over six months' time. Unfortunately, though, the jobs she had seen advertised that seemed suitable for completely inexperienced sixteen-year-olds, and the rents of bedsit flats she had looked at in the local paper, didn't appear to be particularly compatible with each other. And although she disgusted her mother by not being slim or stylish or popular, the one thing she was pretty good at was schoolwork. If she could hang on another two years then she could take her A-levels and escape to university. In fact, only yesterday Mr Hynes, her History teacher, had said she should think about applying to Oxford or Cambridge. Dorothy L. Sayers's *Gaudy Night* and Evelyn Waugh's *Brideshead Revisited* had given her a strong prejudice in favour of Oxford, and she'd had a happy evening fantasising about the dreaming spires and of a world where liking books and reading wouldn't mark her out as a freak. That was the prize, but could she possibly stick another two and a half years at home in order to get there?

At times like this, she doubted it. Her dad wasn't the problem; in fact her dad was great. He understood her passion for books and, as a teacher, he realised how difficult she found it to fit in at her modern comprehensive school. The problem was that he was completely under her mum's thumb, and her mum was a total bitch.

Phoebe clenched her fists. What really made her furious, with herself more than her mum, was that she still had some kind of emotional dependency on her. Like today, her one thought had been to get home to her mum, even though experience should have amply demonstrated that Liz would probably only make things worse. But it was as though Phoebe's subconscious had absorbed society's expectations of what mothers were – warm, caring, sympathetic, loving – and insisted on applying them to her own family, despite all the evidence to the contrary, and every time these expectations were confounded it left her a little more internally bruised.

There was a soft knock on the door.

'What?' Phoebe croaked.

'It's Dad, can I come in?'

Phoebe got up and went to unlock the door. Callum McCraig took in her tear-stained face and swollen eyes and wrapped her in a huge hug before he said anything. Phoebe buried her face deep in her dad's shoulder, wishing she never had to come out again. Eventually he released her, and she went and flopped back on the bed in her nest of chocolate bar wrappings. Callum sat down on the denim-covered sofa and surveyed his daughter with a mixture of love, sympathy and frustration. The frustration was mainly directed at himself as he felt so pathetically unable to find a way to help her.

'What happened, love?'

Phoebe sighed. Suddenly she felt very tired and heavy, and couldn't face going through it all again. She shrugged.

'Same old, same old, really. Some of the girls in my year played a horrible joke on me, I got upset, came home, and Mum said it was all my fault, basically.'

Callum felt a surge of fury against his wife, but controlled it and said gently, 'Mum didn't mean that, I'm sure. She just wants to help you.'

Phoebe felt the tide of hysterical anger rise in her again.

'She doesn't want to help me for *me* though, Dad, she just wants to help me turn into the perfect daughter she always wanted, someone she can dress like a doll and go to the gym with, and be proud instead of ashamed of. You know, this week she asked me if I'd like to go to Zumba with her? I mean, like there's any chance I'm going to do Zumba!'

Here Callum felt on firmer ground.

'Your mum loves you, and she's just trying to think of things you can do together. And honestly, Pheebs, you should do some exercise, it's healthy for anyone.'

Phoebe was shaking her head adamantly.

'No, it's not like that. She wants to do things with me on her terms, she doesn't care what I actually like. I don't mind doing some exercise – I'd like to go on a country walk, like we used to when I was little, out in Wales or somewhere, but she's not interested in that.'

Callum lapsed into resigned silence. Phoebe was too intelligent and clear-sighted for her own good, and he knew that her analysis was pretty much spot on.

'Well, why don't we go up to the Lake District on Saturday, if the weather's OK? We can have a hike, a pub lunch maybe. I could do with a chance to blow the cobwebs away. What do you think?'

Phoebe smiled at her dad. His attempts to cheer her up were pathetically transparent, but still effective. At least he cared enough to try.

'That sounds great, Dad. I'd love to.'

'OK, well, I'll have a chat with your mum about it.'

And then he was gone, his six-foot-three bulk leaving no trace other than a slight dent in the sofa cushions, and a lingering whiff of the Hugo Boss aftershave she had saved up to buy him for his birthday.

★ ★ ★

Callum ran down the stairs two at a time and burst into the kitchen, where his wife was chopping vegetables, thin latex gloves protecting her hands and nails.

She turned and smiled at him, displaying the perfectly even white teeth that had cost her several thousand pounds to achieve. By most standards Liz McCraig was a stunningly beautiful woman. Pencil thin, but with high, round breasts (another few thousand pounds), perfectly straight ash-blonde hair that fell to her shoulders in a shiny curtain, large blue eyes with long dark lashes and a sensuously full mouth. The problem for her was that the modelling world applied a different set of standards, and Liz was forty-two years old. This fact meant that, despite her perfect figure, good looks and previously lucrative career in modelling, she was now finding it difficult to get work.

'How's the drama queen?' she asked him now.

'She's really upset, Liz. It's not easy for her, you know. She's sensitive, and clever and—'

'And fat. She's overweight, Callum, seriously overweight, and that's why she gets bullied at school. And I know you think I'm a hard-hearted bitch, you both think that, but I only want to help Phoebe, and it isn't healthy for her being the size she is. Look at all the stuff about childhood obesity, and lower life expectancy, and type 2 diabetes.'

'I know, I know. But Pheebs hasn't got any health problems, and it's a vicious circle, isn't it? She eats to make herself feel better, but then fits in less well because she's overweight.'

Liz nodded.

'Yes, I know that. But you're an enabler, Callum. I give her a hard time because that's what she needs to give her the motivation to lose weight. All your sympathy doesn't get her anywhere, does it?'

Callum said softly, 'It might make her less unhappy.'

Liz rolled her eyes.

'You just don't get it, do you? I'm sick of being painted as the baddie when I'm the one being the responsible parent. Whatever I try – helping her with diets, making healthy food, suggesting she comes to exercise classes with me – it's all thrown back in my face, and you just pat her on the head and say "Oh dear, poor Phoebe" and she adores you for it.'

She turned and continued slicing onions and mushrooms with such vigour that Callum felt sure she was picturing some part of his anatomy on the chopping board. He sighed deeply. He just couldn't face another argument, and he searched for something conciliatory to say, before hitting on the perfect thing.

'I think you're right, about the healthy lifestyle. So I thought we could all go to the Lake District for the day on Saturday, have a long walk, spend some time together. I had thought of a pub lunch, but we could always take a salad or something if you want to be really healthy.'

Liz groaned inwardly. She liked gyms and studio classes. Clean, neat, organised, with lively music, warm showers and saunas, stylish sportswear, friends to gossip with afterwards. She did not like hiking. In her experience it was cold, wet, uncomfortable, there was no one to see what you were wearing, and the only people to talk to would be Callum and Phoebe, who would go off in their little club of two, talking about books or Phoebe's schoolwork, and leave her completely out of it.

'Hmm, I'm quite busy this weekend,' she prevaricated, but then when she saw the smile beginning to fade from Callum's lips she hesitated. After all, he had been offering her an olive branch of sorts, and she didn't want to alienate him completely.

Liz was under no illusions that she loved her husband, hadn't for years, but equally she had no intention of ending up as a divorce statistic. Her own mother had left her father to 'find herself', and Liz had experienced the consequences of that voyage of self-discovery first hand. A series of grotty rented flats. No spare money for new clothes or treats. Seeing how patronising people could be to a single, middle-aged woman. No, Liz had escaped from that world with her first modelling job and subsequent marriage to Callum, and she had no intention of ever returning to it. Every so often, after a particularly bad row, Callum would talk about moving out, but she knew he never would. She had always told him that, if he ever left, she would ensure she got custody of Phoebe and would limit his access to her as far as humanly possible. That would hardly be an ideal scenario for her – single motherhood didn't appeal in the least – but she knew how much Callum adored Phoebe, and she was certain he would never take the gamble.

There was no point having an argument for the sake of it, and she back-pedalled.

'It's a good idea, though, we'll go one weekend soon, I promise.'

And with that, the fragile equilibrium of their marriage was once again restored, at least temporarily.

2

Ella flung herself into the seat opposite her friend, poured half a bottle of Chenin blanc into her glass and declared melodramatically, 'Sometimes I just think I can't stand my husband, or my kids, or my life for one more day. Is that so wrong?'

Imogen looked at her with a combination of wry amusement and concern.

'Well, not *wrong* exactly. What have they all done to upset you now?'

A succession of images flickered through Ella's brain. Harriet had been teething, so instead of tucking the children up in bed at 7 p.m. and then having a luxurious hour to pamper herself, she'd actually spent the time rocking, soothing, Calpoling, cuddling and, finally, begging her daughter to sleep. Knowing that she had less than five minutes to get ready, the long hot bath became a quick swipe under her arms with the Peppa Pig flannel lying soggily forlorn on the side of the bath. Instead of deep conditioning, her hair had to make do with a quick spritz of Batiste, and when she'd retrieved her make-up bag from under Aidan's bed, she only had time to wave the mascara and blusher in the vague direction of her face.

When she'd finally made it downstairs it was to find her husband sitting at the kitchen table, glass of red wine in one hand and copy of the *Evening Standard* in the other. He'd made all the right noises – he would have looked after the kids, she should let him do more, blah, blah, blah – but Ella knew deep down, in her womb as well as her heart, that she was the only one who could adequately comfort the children when they weren't well.

A flicker of guilt shot through her at this point. She'd felt such an unfamiliar and intoxicating lightness when she set off down the road, unencumbered by double buggy, nappy bag, microscooter, snacks, travel potty and assorted soft animals and board books, but effectively she was abandoning her children. Oh God. What if Greg forgot that Harriet had already had Calpol and gave her more?

'Come on, girls' night out! No guilt trips, remember?' Imogen was laughing at her.

Ella let herself relax into a smile, and took another large gulp of wine.

'How did you know I was guilt-tripping?'

'How about because I'm a world expert in it? And because it was written all over your face.'

Ella took deep calming breaths, as learned in yoga classes a million years ago.

'So, do you want to talk about it?' Imogen asked, patiently.

'Oh, I don't know really. Aidan was possessed by the devil, every single item in every single drawer in the house has been removed and scattered around, and Hattie is teething, so she wouldn't settle. And Greg . . .'

She paused. However irritating she was finding her husband, she was well aware that compared to Imogen's boyfriend, Pete, he was the very model of a perfect partner and father, and she didn't want to test their friendship too far by complaining. On the other hand, Greg was driving her absolutely mad. Better not to push it though.

'Oh well, I've escaped them all now,' she concluded. 'And I haven't even asked about you, how are things?'

Imogen had a very good idea what had stopped Ella launching into her customary stream of complaints about Greg, and she was grateful for her restraint. However sympathetic she felt towards Ella, and goodness knows, being at home on your own all day with two children under three was no joke, she could never really see what the problem was with Greg, always feeling that, if anything, he was the one given the hard time by Ella.

'Me?' She shrugged, resignedly. 'Nothing interesting, as per.'

Ella looked closely at her. Imogen never wore make-up, didn't bother with hair products, and fashion generally passed her by as she was always, depending on the season, in faded jeans, boots and a chunky hand-knit cardie, or ankle-length cotton dress and Birkenstocks. None of this in any way detracted from her natural beauty though; long auburn curls, vivid bluey-green eyes, perfectly clear porcelain skin with just a scattering of freckles across her delicate nose, and full, gently curving lips. Combined with her long legs and naturally slim figure she was head-turning but had no real idea of the fact. Ella tried not to hate her for it, or to be envious of the fact that Imogen was stunning without even trying, whereas Ella needed regular highlights, careful application of make-up and frequent, albeit largely unsuccessful, diets even to hope to pass as passably pretty. None of which had happened much in the last three years, leaving her plump, pale and mousy.

This evening though, Ella noticed with concern that her friend looked tired, paler even than usual and had purple shadows under her eyes. And even though she was the most glass-half-full person Ella had ever met, Imogen seemed slightly subdued this evening.

'Is Pete looking after Indigo?' she probed, gently.

Imogen laughed.

'Come on, is that likely? Pete stay in so that I can go out? No, my next-door neighbour has a fourteen-year-old daughter who's absolutely brilliant with Indigo, and Indigo adores her, so she's babysitting. And her mum's only next door if there are any problems, so I can come out with an easy mind. Easier than it would be if she was with Pete, really.'

She laughed again, to indicate that she was joking, but the laugh was tinged with a slightly bitter note and Ella knew that really it was anything but a joke.

'Oh Immy, you are hopeless. You need to be tougher with Pete. Why shouldn't he do something for a change? You work full-time to pay the rent and put food on the table, you do ninety per cent of the childcare when you're not in work, and all the housework, while he contributes nothing, and yet he won't even let you go out for a couple of drinks with a friend.'

Imogen shook her head sadly.

'No, it's not that he won't *let* me go out, he doesn't care one way or the other, it's just that he sees Indigo as my responsibility. It wouldn't even occur to him to offer to look after her, or even to arrange childcare for her. And he wouldn't have a clue, anyway, how to put her to bed, or what to do if she woke or wasn't well.'

Ella was incensed.

'But she's *his* daughter too. How can he behave like that?'

Imogen had been through all this in her head many times.

'I think it's because he didn't really want a baby in the first place. In his mind, it was my decision to go ahead with the pregnancy, and therefore Indigo is my responsibility. He does love her, but it's more the love of an older brother, or uncle – he has no concept of parental responsibility. He loves it when she's cute, when he can play with her or read to her, but the moment there are any decisions to be made, or any of the tougher sides of parenting come along, he's nowhere to be found. I suppose I'm just used to it.'

Ella was still furious on her friend's behalf. She had known Imogen for more than three years now; in fact, they had met at antenatal classes before Indigo and Aidan were born. Although very different in some ways, the two women had bonded instantly, and had been a huge support to each other through the exhausted haze of early parenthood. During all that time Imogen had seemed more like a single parent, and Ella had marvelled at how she seemed constantly to be defending Pete.

The half bottle of wine she'd just downed in ten minutes flat, on an empty stomach, made her brave now.

'Are you in love with him, Immy?' she asked bluntly.

Imogen shrugged.

'As Prince Charles infamously said, yes, whatever love means. Before Indigo was born we were madly in love, I've never known anything like it. We couldn't keep our hands off each other, but we always had so much to talk about as well. Things have been tough since, he's struggled with being a dad, money's been tight, I'm constantly exhausted, and I guess I do put Indigo first. But like I said, he loves Indigo and she loves her dad. And I hold on to how we used to be, and just keep hoping that when Indigo is a bit older, when we have a bit more cash, we'll sort things out.' She looked very directly at Ella. 'After all, could you honestly say that you are properly "in love" with Greg, in that heart beats faster when he comes into a room kind of way?'

Ella giggled tipsily.

'Oh my God, it's like being at a sleepover when you're fourteen! No one ever asks you if you're "in love" once you're actually married! Is that because it's tacitly assumed that it becomes irrelevant at that point?'

Imogen shrugged.

'I wouldn't know, I've never been married.'

Ella giggled again.

'So, why not, if you don't mind me asking? Why have you and Pete never tied the knot?'

Imogen laughed.

'I just don't think Pete's the marrying kind. Neither am I really, we're just a couple of hippies. I mean, can you honestly see me in a long white satin dress, or a veil? I've never thought you needed to be married to be committed to one another. In fact, I would have said that having a child together is the biggest commitment you can make, although I guess what I've just been saying about Pete's attitude to Indigo slightly proves me wrong on that. But I know he'd never cheat or anything.'

She paused. 'Anyway, this isn't fair. I asked my question first – are you still properly in love with Greg?'

Suddenly Ella didn't feel quite so much like laughing. There was no doubt in her mind that she *had* been in love with Greg; she'd married him utterly certain that he was the only man in the world for her, that they would remain blissfully happy together for the whole of their lives, and that was less than four years ago. The problem was, there was a big difference between the certainty of a childless twenty-four-year-old and the certainty of a twenty-eight-year-old mother of two, and her transformation from one to the other had left her feeling disorientated, unsure of herself and who she was, let alone how she related to her husband. Becoming a mother, and trying to be the best mother she could, had been such a steep learning curve that it hadn't really left much room for anything else. Now that Harriet, her youngest, was nearly eighteen months old and things were stabilising slightly, she was beginning to realise that leaving a marriage unattended for several years inevitably left it, if not dead, then certainly very wilted. However, she wasn't really ready to confront these realities in her own mind, let alone discuss them with her friend, so she just replied lightly, 'Oh of course I am. Would be even more so if he'd learn how to empty the dishwasher occasionally, but yeah, we've been together for so long, I can't imagine life without him.'

If Imogen noticed that her friend had backed off slightly she tactfully didn't mention it, instead just picked up the menu and said, 'OK, well I definitely know I want chips, so I suppose it's just a case of deciding what I want to go with them.'

3

Ella lay in bed, willing herself to relax, but it was no use. Every line of her body was tense, and although rationally she knew she was tired, sleep had never felt further away. It was 8 a.m. on a Sunday. In that dimly remembered country called Life Before Children, this wasn't a time that had ever existed for her. She would have been out late the night before; perhaps just her and Greg, perhaps a large group of mutual friends, maybe with the girls. It could have been a comedy club, a cocktail bar, a local neighbourhood restaurant or even a dinner party, but there was no doubt that she would have been out, she would have gone to bed late, and she would have fallen asleep safe in the blissful knowledge that she could sleep for as long as she needed.

On a Sunday it was invariably at least 9 a.m. before she opened her eyes. She and Greg would often make love, gently, fuzzily, sleepily before lying contentedly in each other's arms, chatting and gossiping about the previous evening. Finally, one of them would summon the energy to get out of bed and pull on an old sweatshirt and track-suit bottoms to nip out and collect the Sunday papers – always the *Observer* and *The Sunday Times* – and some croissants, which they would then bring back to bed. The bedroom in the little flat they'd shared was tiny, but south-facing, so they would pull back the curtains and let the sun stream through the slightly grubby windows. The sun always shone, surely, in Life Before Children. By the time they were finally out of bed, showered and dressed, it would be early afternoon, time to meet up with friends for a pub lunch and a lazy afternoon in a beer garden.

How things had changed. Now the day invariably started at 6 a.m., when Harriet woke up and started crying for her morning cuddle. Ella would often bring her into bed and try to snuggle them both back to sleep, but it rarely worked. Greg would be irritated by small feet pummelling him in the back and would get up, resentment visibly oozing from him as he stormed off to the bathroom. Ella was always left feeling obscurely guilty, although it was hardly her fault. By the time she had given up any hope of Harriet dropping back off, Aidan was also awake, running in with an armful of *Mr Men* books and demanding that she read to him.

By 8 a.m. she was generally knee-deep in Weetabix and exhausted from the battle to wrestle both children into their clothes, clean their teeth and wash their permanently sticky faces. She, of course, would still be in her far from sexy tartan pyjama bottoms and a T-shirt from a university summer school she'd volunteered at around ten years ago. At this point she would gently suggest to Greg that he could look after the children for a while so that she could have a relaxing shower and get dressed in peace, whereupon he would give her a martyred look and indicate that he had some urgent work to do 'so that we can have the rest of the day together as a family'. So Ella would take her shower as she did every morning: as quickly as possible while keeping up a faux-cheerful running commentary and sing-song in order to try to distract the children from killing each other or destroying the house.

This Sunday morning, however, was different. It was Mother's Day, which meant that when Harriet had started whimpering at 6 a.m. it had been Greg (responding to various subtle and not-so-subtle hints during the previous week) who staggered out of bed, whispering to her that he would sort everything this morning and that she should have a relaxing lie-in. And she had tried to relax, she really had. It's just that things had started badly when Harriet's whimpers had ramped up to outraged screams when she realised that it was Daddy, not Mummy, this morning. And then Ella had needed the bathroom, and on her way across the landing had seen through Aidan's open door that he was lying in bed playing with Greg's iPhone, a strictly forbidden and therefore highly desirable activity. Greg was clearly using it as a distraction while he changed Hattie's nappy; had she been in charge Ella would have set Aidan up with a talking book, which was so much more educational.

And now it was 8.30 a.m., and she still hadn't managed to get back to sleep. Ella sighed, and rearranged the pillows once more. As she did so, she sniffed. There was a strong aroma of burning toast, and when she listened carefully she could hear muffled giggles and footsteps on the stairs. Her bedroom door opened, and Aidan walked in and over to the bed. His little face was rigid with concentration as he carefully carried the plate over to her and placed it on the bedside table. When it was finally safe, he visibly exhaled and allowed his features to relax into a smile.

'Happy Mother's Day, Mummy! Hattie's got a card for you, and Daddy's got your tea. He said it was too hot for us to carry. And we've got flowers for you downstairs, but they're a surprise, so I'm not going to give those to you until you come down.'

By this time, Hattie had also toddled in; far more laissez-faire than her brother, she abandoned the card she had been clutching as she tried to scramble into the bed to be near her mummy. Feeling tears prickling her eyelids, Ella pulled them both into bed with her and cuddled them close.

Greg followed his children in, smiling at the picture they presented. He was carrying a steaming mug of her favourite Earl Grey, which he set down next to the plate of toast.

'Come on kiddiwinks, let's leave Mummy to have her breakfast in peace, we've got to go out. We've got some jobs to do, haven't we?'

Much to her surprise the children instantly leapt off the bed; normally they had to be practically prised away.

As the door shut behind them she picked up her plate of toast. The burnt pieces must have been discarded, because there were two perfectly golden slices, spread with the Nutella she loved but hardly ever allowed herself.

Toast, chocolate and a nice cup of tea while snuggled up in bed were quite a good way to block out the empty, desolate feeling that seemed to be overwhelming her more and more frequently these days. As was the bubble bath Greg had run for her, for when she finished eating. She still couldn't fully relax though. Usually Ella had very little time for introspection. From 6 a.m. to 7.30 p.m. she was constantly on the go, coping with the demands of two small children. After they'd gone to bed and she'd cooked a meal and exchanged a few pleasantries with Greg about their respective days, she was completely shattered and was generally asleep on the sofa before the ten o'clock news started.

Now, though, lying submerged in the warm bubbles, she could try to work out what her problem was. Her dominant feeling was slight irritation because she didn't really like having a bath in the morning; it was an evening treat. Greg had only been trying his best to give her a nice day, but somehow the fact that he didn't quite know what she wanted seemed emblematic of the state of their relationship.

But that really wasn't fair. Her main complaint, frequently voiced to Imogen and other friends, was that Greg no longer saw her as a woman, that two children in just over three years of marriage had eroded anything romantic in their relationship and left them with a functional business partnership, based on mutual need, affection and respect rather than love and passion. She had lost her libido completely since Hattie's birth nearly eighteen months previously, and although she and Greg still had sex every couple of weeks, it was brief and perfunctory and she felt that she was submitting to it only because she knew she ought to rather than because of any flicker of desire. Along with her libido she had lost all her self-confidence; whether the two things were related she had yet to work out. One of her problems was that she felt direction-less. Before Aidan was born she had been a PhD student, but despite her best intentions of working while the baby slept, she had yet to complete her doctoral thesis. Of course, becoming pregnant with Hattie when Aidan was only five months old hadn't helped. She had believed the midwife who told her that you couldn't become pregnant while exclusively breastfeeding, and had told everyone, including Greg, that the pregnancy was unplanned, although on some levels she had been absolutely delighted. It had certainly postponed any decisions she needed to make about her doctorate or her future career – with two children under two, no one could expect her to complete her thesis, and they certainly couldn't afford childcare.

Throwing herself into full-time motherhood had been incredibly satisfying in many ways. Aidan and Harriet were gorgeous, perfect, adorable bundles of wonderfulness, and every day she thanked her lucky stars that she wasn't stuck in a soulless office job, paying sixty per cent of her salary in childcare for someone else to enjoy all the pleasures and privileges of bringing up her children. However, now Hattie was a little bit older, Greg had been starting to drop hints that Ella might feel happier and more fulfilled if she returned to her studies, or looked for a part-time job. Maybe he was right, but sociolinguistic feminist discourse, which was the subject of her thesis, no longer seemed the least bit interesting or relevant to her life, or to future employment. A part-time job, however, would have to be incredibly well paid to justify childcare costs, and although Ella had a first-class degree and a master's with distinction from Oxford, and had been within spitting distance of completing a PhD at the London School of Economics, she couldn't help feeling that she had no experience that prospective employers would consider especially useful – most of her paid employment had been in bars or waitressing, and her voluntary work in orphanages in Eastern Europe didn't seem that much more pertinent to gaining gainful employment in east London.

Something definitely needed to change though. She pondered this, washing herself lazily as the water grew colder. As she rinsed shampoo off her hair it came to her: the perfect solution to all their problems. As soon as the idea occurred to her, she felt more positive and energetic than she had done for months. She jumped out of the bath and dried herself, her mind racing ahead at lightning speed. In the bedroom she checked her diary, and a slow smile spread across her face. The timing literally could not be more perfect.

She dressed in a printed wrap dress that Greg had always liked, and pulled on knee-high boots that even had a bit of a heel. She carefully applied foundation to even out her skin tone, blusher to add a warm glow, eyeshadow and mascara to highlight her large deep-brown eyes, which, unlike everything else, didn't seem to have been ravaged by childbearing and motherhood. Once her hair was blow-dried she took a deep breath and looked in the full-length mirror. The woman who stared back at her was a complete revelation. The plump, harassed-looking woman in faded jeans and a grubby T-shirt had been replaced by the person she felt she had once been. Curvaceous, sexy, fantastic cleavage, a sparkle in her eyes. She laughed in delight, and ran downstairs to join her family.

After that, they had a lovely day. Greg had booked a table in Carluccio's at Canary Wharf for lunch, and for once the children behaved impeccably, sitting quietly engaged with the free crayons provided. Ella was able to enjoy a glass of Prosecco and some delicious pasta before sharing a plate of tiramisu with Greg in a distinctly flirtatious manner, without really worrying about her maternal duties. After lunch they strolled through Canary Wharf to the Museum of London Docklands, which had a children's section Aidan and Hattie both adored, and then gave them their tea in the little café there. When they returned home, Greg volunteered to put the kids to bed, meaning that all Ella had to do was lay out the antipasti and focaccia they had picked up in the Carluccio's deli and pour herself a glass of wine.

When Greg came downstairs she was very slightly tipsy, extremely relaxed and full of excited anticipation – a mood that made her wonder if her libido was really dead after all. Greg certainly looked gorgeous in his dark-blue jeans and crisp white shirt. When he stooped to give her a light kiss on the lips, she pulled him down on the sofa, half next to her, half on top of her, and kissed him deeply on the mouth.

'Mmm,' he said at long last. 'This is unexpectedly nice.'

Ella smiled up at him. Her wrap dress was by now unwrapped, her cheeks flushed, and she felt confident, wanton and sexy in a way she hadn't for years.

'Shall we make it even nicer?' she suggested, in her best sex-kitten purr.

'Umm, here? Why don't we go upstairs?'

Biting back her irritation, trying not to let it spoil the mood, she purred again, 'I want you right here, right now.'

'Err, OK.' Greg looked utterly bewildered, as well he might, given that the closest Ella had come to talking dirty over the past three years was to sigh reluctantly and groan 'If you must, I suppose' when he suggested having sex.

'Only thing is though, I need to go upstairs and get a condom anyway . . .'

Ella drew a deep breath. This was her moment.

'No, don't get a condom. Let's make a baby.'

4

It was one of those days that feels more like July than April. Deep, improbably blue sky and blazing sunshine, but even nicer than July because it had the freshness of spring, with blossom on the trees and the scent of springtime flowers in the air.

Imogen and Pete had been bickering all morning.

The flat felt fetid in the heat, smelling far too strongly of the spliff Pete had smoked the night before (the cause of yet another row), the dirty dishes were piled up in the sink and the entire atmosphere, which, on a good day, could just about pull off cheerfully bohemian, was definitely veering towards squalid. Indigo trotted in and out of the backyard, oblivious, or perhaps just accustomed, to the mess, but Imogen felt waves of despair at her life.

Pete was also seemingly oblivious to the waves of hostility coming off her. He was sitting in his boxer shorts in the back garden, smoking and reading the *Guardian*. Every so often Indigo would run up and try to engage him in some game she was playing, and he would smile and ruffle her hair, but refuse to be drawn out of either his seat or his own little world.

And that was another thing that made Imogen seethe with resentment. Indigo, darling perfect eager little girl, was so pathetically grateful for the crumbs of attention he threw her way, and so accepting that this was the way things were. Of course, it wasn't like this with her mother. Imogen could arrive home from work at 6.30 p.m., exhausted and drained from spending all day being creative and sparky and engaging with her class, but woe betide her if she let Indigo sense that she wasn't a hundred per cent present throughout bath-time, or if she failed to pull off a RADA-esque performance for the bedtime story. No matter that Pete's working day had involved a couple of hours spent putting up some shelves, or digging someone's garden, come 6 p.m. he would invariably be down the pub, pint in hand, expostulating on human rights abuses in some far-flung corner of the globe and in the process ignoring the human responsibilities right under his nose.

Imogen could count on the fingers of one hand the number of times Pete had read Indigo her bedtime story, but she could also recollect with perfect clarity the iridescent joy on her daughter's face when he did so. And that was the problem. Every time Imogen thought that sharing her life with Pete was just too much effort for far too little reward, and that she should forget the kind, sexily intense, sparkily intelligent man she had fallen in love with, cut her losses and leave, she would remember how much Indigo adored her father, and realise that she couldn't bring herself to be the cause of her missing out on a relationship with him. Because she was under no illusions; Pete was hardly the most satisfactory father at the moment, but sheer propinquity meant that Indigo saw him, however briefly, most days, and he was always carelessly affectionate to her, but if they lived apart there would be no custody visits, no weekend trips to museums or McDonald's. He would simply move on without a backward glance.

God, her thoughts were as depressing as her environment. Imogen gave herself a mental shake and decided to try to do something about both. She gulped down a vitality vitamin supplement with the last of her green tea, and started running a sink full of hot Ecover bubbles. With *From Our Own Correspondent* in the background she washed dishes, swiped a cloth around the (minimal) work surfaces, chucked the toys littering the floor into a big wooden chest bought third-hand for the purpose and painstakingly painted and stencilled, and then for an encore carried out her specialist manoeuvre, which was cleaning the bathroom while simultaneously showering.

She pulled on a long floaty white dress, twisted her curls up into a loose bun, ignoring the wispy strands that escaped, and marched determinedly into the garden. Indigo's face lit up and she ran across and flung herself into her mother's arms as though they'd been separated for years rather than half an hour. Imogen caught her up and buried her face in her neck, revelling in the evocative scent of sunshine on skin.

'What are we going to do today, Mummy?'

Imogen smiled.

'Well, kitten, I've had an idea, but I just wanted to talk to Daddy about it. Would you like to go on a train ride, and then a bike ride and have a picnic?'

Indigo nodded solemnly.

'Yes, Mummy, I think that's a very good idea. But if we're going to go on a bike ride then we'll need to get the bikes out of the shed first, you know.'

'Yes, well, I think we can manage that. What do you think, Daddy?' She almost, but not quite, avoided a sarcastic emphasis on the last word.

Pete looked up from his paper and grinned lazily at her.

'Do you mean get the train to Gospel Oak and then a bike ride on the Heath? I guess we could.'

'Don't overwhelm me with your enthusiasm, please.'

His face was still maddeningly calm and unbothered.

'Well, come on Immy, it's not a plan to set the pulses racing, is it? I really wanted to go to that new exhibition in Hoxton.'

She gritted her teeth.

'That's hardly suitable for Indigo, is it?'

He shrugged.

'Well, no, I hadn't really thought of taking her, to be honest. Violet and Seth are going, so I thought maybe I'd . . .'

His voice tailed off under her glare. She silently counted to ten before replying.

'And where did I fit into these plans, Pete? As the unpaid childcare I suppose? When was the last time I got to go to an exhibition with friends? Before Indigo was born is when.'

'Alright, alright. Calm down. You went to the pub with whatshername the other evening, didn't you?'

All the calming effects of her cleaning therapy and shower had now dissipated. She could feel sweat prickling around her hairline and under her arms.

'Where do I start? "Whatshername" is, I assume, my best friend Ella. It's over three weeks since I went out with her, or indeed at all, and I had to pay for a babysitter then because you were mysteriously unavailable, and you go to the pub every fu— flipping night, while I sit at home by myself.'

He patted her hand infuriatingly.

'Alright, no probs. We'll go to the Heath. It'll be fun, won't it, Indy-Baby?' He scooped his daughter into his arms, and the tension that had been etched on her little face as she watched the verbal tennis between her parents evaporated.

Imogen sighed deeply. The pleasure she had felt in her plan for a family day out had vanished, but at least they were going. She loaded leftover pasta salad into a Tupperware tub, filled some reusable bottles with water, grabbed the suncream, and they were ready to go.

Three hours later she was feeling slightly better. Indigo was ecstatic at so much time with both her parents' undivided attention, and she and Pete had managed to be civil to each other. The sun was warm, and the Heath was verdant, and all in all life didn't feel too bad after all. Now they were on top of Parliament Hill. Imogen was standing a little way away from the others, gazing down at the panorama of London spread out below her. Although she'd lived in London all her adult life, Imogen still felt like a country girl by instinct and desire; but there was no doubt that London had a powerful allure, and looking at the view before her, Imogen wondered whether a countryside vista, however beautiful, could ever have the sheer vitality of this one.

Her musings were interrupted as she overheard the conversation between Pete and Indigo.

'Could we hold hands and run down the hill, Daddy?'

He was smiling.

'Oh, I think we can do a bit better than that! How would you like to ride down it, really fast, with Daddy on his bike?'

Indigo was too overcome with excitement to actually speak and just jumped up and down clapping her hands.

Imogen strolled over.

'Just be careful, Pete. Put her helmet back on. And you'll need to use my bike, it's got the child seat on it.'

He looked at her in disbelief.

'Oh lighten up, Immy. I'll be fine on my bike, I'll hold her. Yours is far too small for me, it'd be more "dangerous". And as for that bloody helmet, well, we survived our childhoods without them, didn't we?'

'Pete, no, it's not safe without a seat and a helmet. Come on, I'll sort the helmet out, and you adjust the seat on mine and—'

He was glaring at her in real irritation now.

'When did you turn into this uptight, rule-bound person, Imogen? All I get from you is nagging to spend more time with Indigo, and then when I try to do something fun with her you have to start interfering, because of course you always know best. Well, just for once, Daddy's in charge!'

He picked up Indigo from where she was still scampering around with excitement and hitched them both up on to his bike. He sat Indigo on his lap, one arm around her waist and the other hand on the handlebars. She was squealing with anticipation, and he smiled. This was what parenting was about, not all the cotton-wool fussing that

Immy went in for. Suppressing a momentary qualm at quite how small Indigo felt, and blocking out Imogen's protests, he gave a loud whoop and launched them off down the path. He didn't need to pedal at all, and they picked up velocity very quickly. The wind rushed through their hair, and he felt a surge of the freedom that seemed to elude him these days. Indigo was quiet, perhaps slightly scared now that fantasy had become reality.

It happened in a split second. One moment he was escaping all the cares of the world. The next his front wheel hit a stone, he tried and failed to control the swerve with his single free hand, and then he hit the floor, hard enough to wind him, with Indigo underneath him.

He kept his eyes closed, trying to pretend it hadn't happened. Waiting for the screaming from both Indigo and Imogen to start. But nothing. Silence. He opened his eyes. Indigo was lying unfeasibly still, her arm twisted at a sickening angle underneath her. Panic started to set in and he pulled himself up to a sitting position. Indigo flopped lifelessly underneath him and he broke out in a cold sweat.

'Indy? Indy-Baby? Indigo? Are you OK?' Still that silence. The noises of the Heath on a sunny Saturday had receded as though they were under water, and it was just him and his girl alone in a suddenly precarious-seeming world. He was laying her gently on her back and steeling himself to feel for a pulse when there was a flash of white in the corner of his eye, and then Imogen was on the grass next to them. Her face was as pale as her dress, and her red hair looked almost obscenely bright in that context, but otherwise she seemed icily composed. She expertly rolled Indigo into the recovery position, and began following the ABC of resuscitation.

If the accident seemed to Pete to have happened at the speed of light, to Imogen it had all been in agonising slow motion. She'd been angrier with Pete than she'd ever been with anyone when he set off down the hill, and all she could think of was rehearsing what she'd say to him when they reached the bottom. Then she'd seen the bike swerve violently and fall, her little girl out of sight under her father's weight. She'd started to run then, of course, but in that nightmare way of dreams when your feet are weighted, and however hard you try you never get any nearer to your destination.

When she finally reached them Pete was doing nothing and Indigo was lying obviously unconscious and heart-rendingly small and vulnerable. Her yellow gingham dress was torn and a thin trickle of blood showed at the corner of her mouth. An enormous effort of willpower enabled Imogen to recall her first-aid training, and with unspeakable relief she realised Indigo was still breathing and she could feel a pulse. Her hands shaking, she reached into her handbag for her mobile, and as she did so Indigo's eyelids flickered and half opened, and she said falteringly, 'Mamma?'

5

'So, what do you reckon, Dad? Do you think I should apply to Oxford?'

Callum opened his mouth to respond, but Liz jumped in first. She was not enjoying their family day out, hiking around Lake Windermere on a cool, cloudy Saturday, and was resentful of this conversation about Phoebe's academic options, which had largely excluded her for the last half-hour.

'If I were you, I'd think about passing your GCSEs and choosing your A-levels before you jump ahead to considering university. But while we're on the subject, you need to think about money, Phoebe. It doesn't grow on trees, you know, and Oxford would be so expensive, all these tuition fees going sky-high, and then accommodation. If you went to Liverpool Uni you could live at home, and we'd save a fortune.'

Phoebe felt angry tears begin to prick at her eyes and close her throat, and cursed herself. She wasn't unhappy; she was furious, but somehow instead of a searingly articulate response that expressed her anger and frustration she started crying like a four-year-old instead. And threw the most hurtful things she could at her mother.

'Well, my degree wouldn't cost more than your bloody boob job, and facelift, and at least there's an outside chance that it might lead to me getting a job at some point! And I'd rather . . . prostitute myself to pay for my degree than live with you for another three years.'

Liz went white with fury, and her mouth tightened as much as the Botox would allow.

'Well, that would be interesting, wouldn't it? I can't imagine there'd be many takers for that offer.' She looked Phoebe up and down disparagingly.

She had been looking at her daughter with disappointment for over a decade, ever since it became apparent that while the other little girls in Phoebe's class were losing their baby chubbiness to become all arms and legs, Phoebe was, if anything, getting rounder. She was unable to perceive the beauty in her almost turquoise-blue eyes, long golden blonde hair and delicate features, because all she could see was her plus-size figure. Such a pretty face, friends and relatives would say, leaving unspoken the obvious implication, but Liz just felt repulsed at seeing her own beauty reflected back at her as though through the distortion of a fairground mirror.

Callum had been listening with impotent distress to the familiar sounds of his wife and daughter arguing, but at Liz's latest jibe he felt he had to intervene.

'Leave it, Liz.' He spoke quietly, defeatedly, the easy authority that made him a successful deputy head teacher of a large and difficult school seeming, as always, to desert him when it came to his family.

Mild though Callum's rebuke had been, it was fuel to

the fire of Liz's anger. She turned on him, and at first he thought she was going to hit him, her face was so livid.

'How dare you, how *dare* you always, *always* take her side against me? You're supposed to be my husband, and yet you never support me, you let her swear at me, insult me, but if I try and criticise your perfect princess in any way then *I'm* the wicked witch. It's unbelievable. I have no idea why I put up with this.'

Phoebe held her breath, hardly daring to hope. This was the first time she'd heard her parents argue like this, openly in front of her. It wasn't that they didn't argue, they did, constantly, but normally it was when she was in her room and they were downstairs and didn't know she could hear. When she was younger she had crept to the top of the stairs to listen, feeling sick with nerves, terrified that her dad would leave. Now she would listen with growing hope that her mum would.

Callum glared at his wife, sick almost beyond endurance of the constant jibes at him, at the self-centredness that almost amounted to self-obsession, at the cruel streak that caused her to lash out at Phoebe as a displacement activity for her own frustrated ambitions.

'Well, why *do* you put up with it then? You don't have to – leave if it's that bad, if *I'm* that bad. Phoebe and I will be fine. But you won't, will you? Couldn't be that the attractions of living in a nice house, off my salary, outweigh my undoubted deficiencies as a husband, could it?'

Liz smiled coolly, mistress of herself once more now that she had provoked Callum to such an unusually overt display of anger.

'Nice try, darling. But believe me, I'm going nowhere.

And if you choose to leave our marriage, then I think you'll find that most family courts are more than ready to award custody to the mother. And you'd hate Phoebe to suffer the trauma of a broken home, wouldn't you? Imagine only seeing her a couple of times a month, living in some grotty little bedsit . . .' She smiled again. 'Anyway, I seem to have lost my enthusiasm for country walks. I'll leave you two to it.'

And with that she turned and sauntered back towards the car park, cutting an elegant and stylish figure even in her walking gear.

Callum drew a deep breath and looked down at his daughter.

'Come on then, sweetheart, let's hike.'

The two of them had one of the nicest days together that Phoebe could remember. The scenery was spectacular, and the air felt so fresh and clean after suburban Liverpool, and then there was the physical satisfaction of stretching muscles. After Liz stormed off they didn't talk for a while, and then when Callum broke their companionable silence it was to resume the discussion about Phoebe's education and future. He was entirely supportive of Phoebe's ambitions to apply for Oxford. As an experienced teacher he was pretty adept at spotting potential; he knew that it wasn't just paternal bias that told him Phoebe had an exceptional quickness of intellect and maturity of expression for a girl of her age. He was pretty sure that she would gain stellar grades in her forthcoming GCSEs and have no problems ultimately getting into the university of her choice.

Phoebe's eventual departure for university was a date he had been looking forward to for around the last ten years. It was at around that time, then in her early thirties, that Liz had begun to obsess about losing her youth and her looks, and with them her prospects of employment and what she saw as her power. He'd tried to be sympathetic, indeed he *had* been sympathetic, but she was still an outstandingly beautiful woman, and he found it hard to take seriously the near-invisible crow's feet that she claimed were ruining her life. He had never been particularly keen on modelling as a career. Cliché though it was, he found it shallow and amoral at best, downright immoral at worst. Although he could see no discernible difference in his wife's looks, he had tried to encourage her to take the opportunity – especially as by this time Phoebe had started school – to retrain, go back to college, take an Open University course: something, anything that might give her a future not dependent on her looks.

She had been scornful and her angry retorts then had been the splinters that would eventually grow into a wedge between them. She had mocked his commitment to, and belief in, education and belittled his own success as a teacher, calling him dull and boring, saying that he was going nowhere. Liz's income had always been sporadic, months without work, then getting a job that paid half his annual salary for a couple of weeks' work. She'd never hit the big time, much to her chagrin, but she had been a very successful jobbing model throughout her twenties, including a shoot for a Mothercare catalogue while pregnant with Phoebe, which had done much to reconcile her to her changing body shape.

He hadn't been perfect either, and had his own guilt to contend with. Around this period he'd had a girl in his

A-level group to whom he found himself increasingly attracted. She seemed to be everything that Liz wasn't. She was pretty, but in a far quieter and less obvious way than his wife. She was curvy and soft while Liz was pencil slim and with the kind of muscle tone only achieved through daily sessions at the gym. His student had babysat for five-year-old Phoebe on a fairly regular basis, and she was warm and playful and loving, and far more maternal aged eighteen than his daughter's own mother had ever been. She was serious and studious and ferociously intelligent. Nothing had happened: he wasn't entirely stupid, nor entirely lost to his moral responsibilities, either as a husband and father or as a teacher. He'd thought about it though, fantasised about it. Not just sex – although that had undoubtedly come into it, and he salved his guilty conscience by repeatedly reminding himself that she was after all eighteen – but of running away with her, taking Phoebe and forming a new family.

Then one day Liz had told him she'd put an end to the babysitting arrangement.

'I've seen the way you look at her, and I'm not having her in my house minding my daughter and letting you make a fool of yourself over a teenage bimbo, though God knows she's nothing special. Mrs Davies can do any babysitting we need in future.'

Phoebe had been devastated – Mrs Davies, their seventy-year-old neighbour, was very unlikely to pose any sexual temptation to Callum but she was equally unlikely to scoop Phoebe up in her arms and swing her round until she was dizzy, or to play madcap games of football or hide and seek.

In a way Callum had been relieved. He knew he was playing with fire, and it was much easier to remain professional and aloof at school and just get through the weeks until the girl sat her A-levels and left. He missed her hugely, their sparky discussions, her original thinking and witty remarks and sweet smile, but the real love of his life was Phoebe, and he was largely just relieved that temptation had been removed and he could concentrate on ensuring that he had a happy marriage and therefore a stable home for his precious daughter.

Unfortunately that had never really happened. The beautiful, sexy, carefree woman he had married had disappeared, and it now turned out that their relationship had never been built on much more than mutual physical attraction. They had no interests or hobbies in common, their outlook and attitudes to friends, family, work and, crucially, to bringing up their daughter, differed wildly, and ten years later they were strangers sharing a house and a child with varying degrees of suspended animosity. At times things were really bad, and Callum talked about separation, but Liz had made it crystal clear to him that if he ever left her she would fight him tooth and nail for custody of his daughter, and he couldn't bring himself to put Phoebe, or himself, through that much pain.

When, tired but content, they finally arrived back at the car park by the lake where they had parked that morning, a Range Rover sat in the place where their Ford Focus had been, and there was no sign of their car anywhere. Callum sighed in frustration. Why he had imagined that Liz would have kicked her heels by Lake Windermere all day he couldn't think, but although he had been expecting this it was still a nuisance. He sighed wearily, took his phone from his pocket and dialled.

'What?' Liz barked at him.

'What do you bloody think? How the hell are we meant to get home?'

Her voice dripped smug sarcasm as she replied, 'I believe there are things called trains, *darling*. But don't bother coming back here, I need a bit of time to myself. You can send Phoebe home to apologise to me properly, though.'

Callum snorted. Trains! Bloody hell. He doubted Liz had been on one for the last twenty years; she'd have no idea whether they could get back to Liverpool by train or not. Selfish cow. And then to tell him that he couldn't go back to *his* house, that he paid the mortgage on month after month, because she wanted space, but to expect him to send poor little Phoebe home to God knows what reception. Oh no. He could feel the small core of steel that had emerged during their earlier argument growing stronger by the second.

'Fine. Phoebe and I will sort out our own way back to Liverpool, but don't expect either of us to be back home tonight. And you and I need to talk tomorrow, seriously.'

She didn't respond, and after a few seconds the line went dead.

Phoebe looked up at him, eyes wide with anticipation.

'What is it, what's going on, Dad?'

His mind was racing ahead, planning.

'Well, sweetheart, obviously your mum and I are having a bit of a bad patch. We will sort it out, I promise, but in the meantime, your mum wants me to give her a bit of space, and I thought you might prefer not to go home on your own?'

She nodded, gratefully.

'But what are we going to do, Dad?'

'Well, first of all we'll go and find out from Tourist Information where the station is, I suppose . . .'

Just over an hour later, as they sat on the first of the three trains that would allegedly take them back to Liverpool, Callum's plans were complete. Phoebe had texted her one friend from school, Becky, and arranged to stay the night. They'd been to one of the bijou little shops that lined the street of the nearest town and Phoebe had bought pyjamas, the brushed-cotton pink gingham kind that she loved, and new underwear, and then they'd popped into the chemist to buy toothbrushes and other essentials. Callum had previously arranged to meet a couple of friends in the stylish bar of the Liverpool Hilton that evening, and he was sure that one of them would give him a bed for the night. Liz wasn't the only one who needed space that evening. He wasn't sure how she'd expected him to react, but he was well and truly in the mood to call her bluff, and Phoebe was ecstatically happy to play along.

6

'Mamma?' Indigo said again falteringly, and Imogen broke into a cold sweat of relief. She was alive.

'Yes, baby. Mummy's here. I love you, I'm here. It's all OK. Mummy's here.'

'It hurts, Mamma.' Indigo shut her eyes again, as though the effort of talking had exhausted her. Imogen felt tears prickling her eyelids, but this wasn't the time to give in to them.

'I know it hurts, baby. Mummy's going to phone the ambulance to take you to the hospital and they'll make you better. It's going to be alright, darling.'

Pete was totally silent, not meeting her eyes or speaking to Indigo, but she had nothing to spare for him at that moment. She dialled 999 on her mobile.

'Ambulance please. Yes.' She gave the number of the phone she was dialling from, her location and then, voice shaking, described what had happened. The woman on the other end of the phone was calmly and professionally reassuring, and she listened to the instructions, gently stroking Indigo's hair the whole time. Finally she was assured that the ambulance would be there shortly, and hung up.

Now she did turn to face Pete, with vitriol in her voice and in her eyes.

'You idiot! You complete moron. You could have killed her! Would you even have cared, or would that just have made your life easier? No more responsibility – not that you exactly take the responsibility seriously. I can't believe you put her at risk like that.'

Pete tried to break in, but she ignored him and swept on.

'This is just typical of how you've been since we discovered I was pregnant. I don't think you care a damn about me or Indy, and I'm just sick to death of it. We'd both be so much better off without you, d'you know that?'

Pete scrambled to his feet and stood loomingly over them.

'You fucking bitch. I can't believe you. All *you* care about is yourself and Indigo. Oh, and your job, and the flat. Where do I come, Imogen? Fucking nowhere, that's where. I've just about had it.'

He climbed onto his bike and pedalled furiously away, leaving Imogen dazed and bewildered but still icily furious.

Indigo seemed to be lapsing in and out of consciousness, and now that Imogen's initial terror had subsided she started to worry about all the other things that could be wrong with her daughter. Her right arm was horribly twisted, and she could see blood trickling down her head, but after ascertaining that she was in the recovery position the woman in the ambulance control centre had advised her not to try any further first aid.

Only a minute or two had passed since Pete left, but it felt like a lifetime, and she was conscious, suddenly, that despite the bright spring sunshine she was shivering convulsively.

Then there was a voice at her shoulder. She looked up, expecting the paramedics, but instead saw a tall man in his mid-thirties with close-cut dark hair who looked vaguely familiar somehow, and not just because he bore more than a passing resemblance to Barack Obama. His combat shorts and linen shirt strongly suggested that he wasn't a paramedic, and he was holding the hand of a little girl about Indigo's age.

'Hi. It's Imogen, isn't it?'

She looked at him blankly.

'Sorry, I'm Alex, Molly's dad? Molly's at nursery with Indigo.'

Recognition dawned on Imogen.

'Oh, yes, sorry. I'm just in a bit of a state.' She gestured at Indigo.

He looked uncomfortable.

'Yes, I know. I mean, I saw what happened. The accident, and then your partner . . . leaving. And I really don't want to butt in, but I just wondered if I could help at all? We're parked by the lido, if you need a lift to the hospital or anything?'

'Oh, that's so kind, but the ambulance should be on its way. I hope. Oh God.' And then, moved by the kindness and warmth in this man's voice, so different to anything she had ever heard from Pete, she finally dissolved into the tears that had been threatening.

Alex handed her a tissue, wrapped a sweater around her shoulders and then gave her an awkward hug.

'Hey, it's going to be alright. Honestly. Look, she's opening her eyes again.'

Imogen bit back her tears to comfort her daughter

once more, and was still soothing her when the paramedics arrived five minutes later. Things passed in a blur then. They seemed to be doing various checks on Indigo, then lifted her onto a stretcher. The whole time Imogen could feel Alex's arm comfortingly around her shoulders.

They followed the paramedics down the path to where the ambulance had been able to park. As she climbed in, Alex said urgently, 'Look, Imogen, I'll see you at the hospital, OK? I just need to drop Molly at her mum's and then I'll see you there. Royal Free, right?' The paramedic nodded.

Imogen tried to formulate a sentence to repudiate the offer, but somehow couldn't, and then the doors were closing, and she was clutching Indigo's little hand as the wail of the siren started up and they jolted off towards the hospital.

Ella was in the hairdresser's when she got the text from Imogen later that afternoon.

> Horror day. Indy fell off bike, broken arm and concussion. In hosp for observation, but shld b fine. Arrgghh. I've aged 10 years!

She texted back instantly.

> Oh no, you poor thing, and poor little Indy. Nightmare. So glad she's going 2 b ok. I'm in Lpool for weekend, but let Greg know if anything you need. I'll call you tomorrow?xxx

Then she sighed and looked at the glossy magazine open on her lap. Great, one more thing to feel guilty for. This weekend was pushing enough guilt buttons as it was. She'd come to Liverpool for the hen do of a friend from school and had left Greg at home with both children. It was the first time she would be spending a night away from them since Aidan was born, but things were so difficult between her and Greg that she really felt she needed some serious breathing space, and the chance of a weekend of carefree indulgence with friends she saw far too little of was too tempting to turn down.

They'd spent the day in a luxury spa, where she'd been massaged, manicured, pedicured and facialled to within an inch of her life. Now the hen, Angela, and their other friend, Janey, had bullied her into the salon section of the spa and she was sitting waiting for her foil highlights to cook, trying not to think of how much money this was all costing. Later they were off for cocktails and clubbing in town, and she was trying just to focus on the excitement of going out in a new dress and totally unfamiliar high heels, before sleeping for as long as she wanted in a double bed she'd have all to herself, and to ignore the fact that her marriage seemed to be collapsing around her.

And now she felt guilty at not being there for Immy as well. Not for long though: another text arrived.

Don't worry darling, I'm fine. Sleeping at hosp tonight, but we shld be home tomoro. I'd forgotten this was your young free & single w'end. Enjoy, u deserve it. Come round tomoro nite after kids asleep 2 catch up?

She quickly responded.

Great, c u 8ish? I'll bring a bottle. Take care. Xx

and then returned to hedonism and *Vogue*.

A few hours later in her hotel room, Ella literally couldn't believe the woman who looked back from the mirror at her. The hairdresser had totally ignored her murmured 'just a trim' instructions, and her hair was a good six inches shorter, cut into a choppy layered bob that made her look years younger, assisted by the chunky highlights in various subtle shades of chestnut and copper. After the spa they'd hit the shops in Liverpool One, and Ella had been tempted by the special offer on the Clinique counter – buy two products and get a whole make-up bag's worth of samples for free. She had taken time to apply her new illuminating foundation, magic concealer and a delicious palette of coffee, caramel and vanilla eyeshadows. The terrifying gel eyeliner combined with lash-lengthening mascara made her eyes look twice the size, and berry-coloured lip stain was understated but sexy.

She knew her new dress with its vibrant print of splashy flowers was flattering, and she was totally in love with the turquoise patent-leather peep-toe shoes that were a million miles from the Converse she usually lived in. In fact, she felt completely different in every way to the Ella she was the rest of the time. Thinking of the woman who had spent the past few weeks in tears because her husband refused even to discuss the possibility of another baby felt like thinking about a character in a book she had read, utterly unconnected to herself. She didn't know whether it was the new hair and make-up, or the dress and heels, or just that she was back in her home town, but tonight, instead of thinking of herself as a mother and a wife, she felt like an excited irresponsible teenager out to have fun with her friends, and she could hardly wait to get down to the hotel bar and hit those cocktails.

While Ella preened in front of the mirror, Imogen sat with her long legs curled up under her in a slightly scuffed chair next to the hospital bed where her daughter lay sleeping. The nurse had told her that later they would set up a camp bed for her to try to get some sleep on. Although it was only early evening Imogen was shattered, exhausted by the extremes of emotion she'd been through that day. Furious anger, terror, anxiety and relief. It had been terribly stressful in the hospital, seeing the pain on Indigo's little face and being forbidden to give her anything to eat or drink until they knew whether or not she would need surgery. Thankfully she hadn't; the break to her arm was a simple greenstick fracture, and although she had mild concussion and so was being kept in for monitoring, the medical staff had been very reassuring.

Alex had been a bizarrely unexpected tower of strength. He'd arrived at the hospital just as she and Indigo came out of triage and had given her another hug. It should have felt overfamiliar, but somehow it didn't; she was just grateful for the warmth and support. He'd bought her hot coffee and a Mars bar from the vending machine; at first she had felt that she couldn't eat at all, and she usually avoided refined sugars and caffeine anyway, but then suddenly she'd felt almost light-headed with hunger and had devoured it all in about two bites. And he'd been fantastic with Indigo too, playing 'I Spy' with her, somehow following the leaps of logic and imagination that could have been the result either of concussion or of natural toddler idiosyncrasy. His patience and compassion were all the more noticeable given that the only contact she'd had from Pete was a text message sent three hours after he had stormed off: 'How is Indy?' She'd been tempted not to reply at all, but then her own natural compassion had intervened and she'd replied to say, 'In hosp, but fine. No thanks to you.' He hadn't even replied to ask why, or which hospital, let alone turned up to bring her and Indigo chocolate, comfort and distraction.

'Call me tomorrow, and let me know how Indigo is,' Alex had implored as he finally left her when Indigo went up to the ward. And she knew that she would call him, wanted to call him, talk to him, see him again. The one blessing of Indigo's accident seemed to be that she was well on the way to making a new friend. The problem was she had no idea where it had left her already vulnerable relationship with Pete.

7

Ella was already slightly tipsy after two strong and unaccustomed cocktails, and was pouring out the woes of her marriage to Janey.

'He just doesn't get it, at all,' she concluded. 'It's like he's refusing to see that a new baby would be the perfect thing for me, for us, for the family. 'Cos I just can't carry on like we are.'

Janey was looking at her in slight bemusement. 'So, let me get this straight. You love your kids, but you feel lonely and bored and you're always tired, and you feel like life is passing you by, and you think having another *baby* is the solution?' She shook her head. 'Honey, I know I haven't got a husband or kids, so what the hell do I know, but it doesn't sound like a good idea to me.'

Ella's face crumpled in disbelief. Greg's opposition to her baby plan had been vehement, but the only other person she had spoken to about it, Imogen, was far too tactful to voice any overt opposition. True, she had asked her why she thought that a baby would make her feel better, but Ella felt certain of her grounds on this, and she repeated her justification to Janey now.

'No, you don't understand. The thing is, babies are so absorbing, they take all your time and energy and you just don't have space to think about anything else, to regret, or wonder, because they need you so much, they're just so completely dependent. It's an amazing feeling.'

Janey was still looking very doubtful.

'But you've already got two kids! And Hattie's what, not even two yet, is she?'

'Eighteen months,' Ella murmured. 'But it's not the same as a new baby. It just isn't. Once they're walking and starting to talk . . .'

Janey was now gazing at Ella in a way that suggested she could well be certifiable. And being a straight-talking Scouser, she didn't dress up her views in the way that Imogen or some of Ella's other friends might have done.

'Yeah, but you can't keep on and on popping them out! I mean, OK, you have another one now, fine. Three kids is a sensible number, I suppose. But what happens in a couple of years' time when this one starts to walk and talk and you feel bored and lonely again? Do you have another one? Jesus, Mary and Joseph, Ella, you're only twenty-eight – if you have a baby every time you're bored you'll end up with about ten by the time you're forty. And that's not a good idea in this day and age, even if you were brought up a Catholic! And then when you go through the change and can't have any more, what do you do with the remaining thirty-odd years of your life then?' She shook her head decisively. 'No, sorry hun, I'm with Greg on this one. Have another baby if you life, but don't do it as a substitute for deciding what else you want to do with your life.'

Ella's lips tightened. Janey's views were far too similar to Greg's for her liking, so taking them seriously would

mean that she'd have to do some rethinking on her attitude to her husband, which was basically that he was
cruel and insensitive, denying her what she most wanted
and had convinced herself her family most needed, on
totally spurious and unfeeling grounds. She breathed
deeply and took herself mentally to her 'happy place' –
imagining the midwife handing her a tiny towel-wrapped,
scrunchy-faced bundle, of Aidan and Harriet sitting
together on the sofa with their newborn sibling laid across
their knees, of herself gazing down in adoration at a tiny
nursing baby, feeling fulfilled and content once more.

Janey looked in exasperation at the dreamily rapt
expression on her friend's face, sensing that nothing she
had said had got through at all.

'Oh, for fuck's sake! Are you listening to me at all?' She
didn't wait for an answer, but continued, 'I can tell you're
bloody not.' She shrugged. 'Oh well, up to you, I guess.
But if you're going to be up the duff again soon you might
as well get the drinks in now I suppose – same again?'

Ella nodded happily, a few moments of baby fantasies
having completely restored her equilibrium and her
sparkly and excited mood of earlier.

An hour and two more cocktails later, she and the
other girls had given up their plans of moving on to a
club. There was a small dance floor here, the cocktails
were fab, the barmen were fit, and it had started to rain.
Tottering around town in their strappy heels trying to
find a club without a queue didn't seem in the least
appealing. Ella was at the bar waiting to get the next
round in when she saw Janey scuttling towards her,
squealing with excitement.

'Oh my God, Ella! You'll never believe who I've just seen! Oh my God!'

Ella looked at her in tolerant amusement. Janey was a passionate Liverpool supporter, so the most likely reason for this knicker-wetting excitement was that one of the team was in with his WAG.

'Go on, who've you seen? Are you going to embarrass us by asking for autographs?'

Janey grinned at her.

'Oh, I don't think I'm the one going to be embarrassing myself, darling! I've just seen . . .' She paused for dramatic effect. 'Mr McCraig!'

Ella felt the muscles in her legs turn to liquid and clutched at the bar for support. Those four syllables had taken her from a sensible married mum to a crazy teenager so in love she could barely see straight. She could feel her cheeks turn bright red, and her hands were shaking slightly. She grabbed the Grey Goose martini waiting on the bar, Janey's drink as it happened, and downed it in one.

Janey was regarding her with a kind of horrified amusement.

Finally Ella said, 'You are joking?'

'No! Swear to God. He's sitting at a table round the corner with a couple of blokes. Would have thought they'd be a bit old for here, to be honest.'

'He's exactly fourteen years older than me,' Ella murmured mechanically.

Janey laughed.

'God, that doesn't seem that much now, does it? But when we were at school he seemed ancient. To me, anyway. I know it never bothered you! So, shall we go and say hello?'

Ella shuddered.

'Oh my God, no! When I think what I was like at school – how obvious I was about fancying him – I never want to see him again in my life! He won't remember me, anyway.'

Janey grabbed her hand.

'Of course he'll remember you! We all thought he totally had a soft spot for you too! And anyway, don't you want him to see you all grown up with a husband and kids, looking completely hot, and totally over him?' She looked hard at Ella. 'You are, aren't you? Totally over him?'

Ella forced a laugh.

'Of course I'm over him! Hadn't thought about him for years!'

Which was true. She just wasn't about to reveal to Janey that the mere mention of his name had brought all those old feelings flooding back as though it were yesterday.

Janey was pulling at her arm.

'Come on, then! Oh my God, this is going to be hilarious!'

They tottered across the bar, Ella relying heavily on the support of Janey's arm, but reflecting that her shakiness would probably be put down to a combination of booze and high heels rather than the effects of nostalgic passion, or whatever it was.

They rounded the corner. And there he was. At a small table, relatively secluded from the bustle of the main bar, glass of red wine in hand. Callum McCraig. Looking older but, oh my God, just as gorgeous as he always had done. Obviously tall, even sitting down, shoulders to die for, chiselled jaw, brown hair not showing any signs of greying or balding. Her legs wobbled again, but then the Grey Goose seemed to imbue her with confidence suddenly, and she put her shoulders back and sashayed over to reintroduce herself to the man she had once believed was the great love of her life.

Callum was far from having the best evening of his life. It was good to be out with his mates – he and Dave and Tony went back a long way; they'd all been at teacher training college together in the Eighties, and had been passionate student activists as they'd seen the terrible toll Thatcher's policies were taking on their city. They still got together regularly, all now feeling comfortably middle-aged, and although they would complain at length about the coalition's education policies, these days they never felt sufficiently motivated to march or protest, and it was pretty safe to say that their subscriptions to the *Socialist Worker* had been replaced by an occasional glance at the *Guardian* on a wet Tuesday morning break-time.

The Liverpool Hilton was by no means their normal meeting place; comfortable pubs and curry houses in the suburbs of Allerton and Mossley Hill where they all lived were far more usual, but Tony had got a special offer voucher, buy one bottle of wine, get another free, and had persuaded the other two they should break out of their Thursday evening rut and hit the town on a Saturday night for the first time in years. This change, combined with the knowledge that, however temporarily, he seemed to have separated from his wife, was giving Callum a strange sense of dislocation. He knew that he had drunk far more than his share of the two bottles of wine from the special offer, and they were now well into a third.

He hadn't really discussed his marriage problems with Dave and Tony. Oh sure, in a general way they all moaned about their wives and kids, but Callum knew that there was an underlying difference. The others both genuinely loved their wives – they might have arguments about unemptied bins or where they went on holiday; they might regret that their sex lives had settled into a comfortable but unexciting once a week routine; but he could tell that they were basically both engaged in genuine partnerships, sharing their lives and pulling in the same direction.

And that was a million miles away from where he was with Liz. He hadn't had sex with his wife in five years, and it had been extremely sporadic for several years before that. Five years ago Liz had complained that he snored and kept her awake, and suggested that he sleep in the tiny box room that was their spare room. When they'd had the loft extension done, ostensibly to provide more space and privacy for Phoebe, there had been a tacit assumption that he would move into Phoebe's old room, far more generously sized than the box room, and that there would be no further question of he and Liz sharing a bed for sleep or anything else. That wasn't something he could share with his mates. He wasn't even sure how he felt about it himself. Frustrated, often. Tempted, sometimes, when he sensed an interest from a colleague or a woman he met on a lads' night out. He'd never succumbed to temptation though; the image of Phoebe, and Liz's threats to separate them should they ever split up, had always deterred him. Sometimes he had flashes of desire for his wife – after all, she was a beautiful woman – but she had made it very clear that she was simply not interested, and when he thought of her coldness and hostility, the way she treated Phoebe, his feelings of lust tended to wither away.

He knew he had been weak where Liz was concerned, and should have stood up to her and confronted the farce that was their marriage, should have properly defended Phoebe, a long time ago. And he had tried, but Liz was completely intransigent and steadfastly maintained her position – she would fight him every inch of the way for custody of Phoebe, and she would win, and she would restrict his access to her as much as possible. And he knew that there was every probability that she would be able to carry out her threats – she was effectively a stay-at-home mum; certainly her modelling work was very flexible, whereas he had a busy full-time job. From the little he knew about it, it seemed there was always an assumption in favour of the mother. And when push came to shove he never felt he could take the risk, and so always backed down on whatever he and Liz were arguing about, figuring that at least this way he was under the same roof as Phoebe and could see her and talk to her every single day. The problem now was that he wasn't sure how well this strategy was serving Phoebe, as it meant he was basically unable to protect her from Liz. Her happiness and excitement at not having to go home that evening spoke volumes, and Callum was mulling more and more over the feeling that he was going to have to make some kind of dramatic change to their lives; that simply waiting for Phoebe to go to university was not a viable option.

None of these reflections were conducive to a relaxed and enjoyable evening, and Dave and Tony were sharing concerned glances as Callum, unaware of them, stared morosely into his wine glass.

And then his train of thought was interrupted in the least welcome way he could imagine, a loud and undoubtedly intoxicated voice screaming, 'Mr McCraig! Do you remember us?'

He groaned inwardly, and looked up. The blonde woman in a short skirt and low-cut top standing in front of him did look vaguely familiar, but it was her companion who caused his heart rate to quicken and his breath to catch in his throat. More subtly dressed than her friend in a Fifties-style dress, cinched in at the waist with a wide leather belt, shiny chestnut hair framing her face and above all the radiant smile that had remained etched on his brain for ten years – Ella O'Connor, the girl who had at one point seriously threatened his marriage and career, and who he had never been able entirely to forget.

8

Despite, or perhaps even because of, the crisis looming over her family, Phoebe felt happier and more relaxed than she could ever remember. She had occasionally spent the night at Becky's before, but generally tried to avoid it whenever possible because she felt so self-conscious about her body. Being with other people when she could hide herself in layers of shapeless black clothing was hard enough, but pyjamas were a scary prospect, and undressing in front of someone else was just plain terrifying. Tonight though, as an alternative to going home and confronting her mum after the worst row she could ever remember, a sleepover at Becky's seemed a warm and welcoming sanctuary.

Becky was Phoebe's closest, indeed probably her only, friend. At a school where you had to conform with what the in-crowd considered 'normal' to fit in, Becky was a fellow freak on three counts. First, she was Jewish. That meant she didn't eat ham or bacon, that she didn't celebrate Christmas, and that her dad and brother wore yarmulkes on occasion. Not, perhaps, very strong grounds for social ostracism, but when combined with the fact that Becky was clever *and* suffered from acne it became more than adequate justification, and she and Phoebe clung to each other as ports in a storm.

And now Phoebe was curled up on the sofa in Becky's living room, watching *Shrek* with Becky and her little brother, Ben. Theoretically, Becky and Phoebe both considered themselves far too old and sophisticated for *Shrek*, but, aged eight, Ben loved it, and it was such a total and obvious treat for him to be watching it with his sister and her friend that both girls were enjoying it in spite of themselves. Phoebe stretched luxuriously. It was always relaxed and comfortable here. Becky was *so* lucky. Her parents were really warm and friendly, and genuinely interested in her. A bit like her dad really, or like he would be if he wasn't always being distracted by rows with her mum. And Becky had Ben as well – he was so cute, and so much fun, and although Becky said he bugged her sometimes, she obviously adored him really. Phoebe had always wanted a little brother or sister. A few years ago she'd asked her mum if she could have one, and the reply still stung.

'Oh my God, no thank you! One is bad enough! Never again for me, Phoebe.'

Of course, when Phoebe had got upset and asked if she'd not been wanted, her mum had backed down and said that she was only joking. But Phoebe knew that she hadn't been really. It was only this last year or so that Phoebe had stopped hoping for a sibling – she would still have loved one on a purely selfish level, but now that she was counting the days until she could escape from home herself, she hated the thought of another child being stuck there for years to come.

'Beckyyy, I'm *starving*!' Ben interrupted Phoebe's thoughts.

Becky grinned at Phoebe.

'What do you reckon, Pheebs, shall we make some nachos?'

'Yay, nachos, nachos, nachos, nachos!' Ben yelled. He pressed pause on the DVD and then backflipped from the sofa to the floor in one fluid movement.

Phoebe giggled. Her stomach was rumbling in anticipation of nachos; she could almost taste the crunchy corn tortillas and the contrast of the sharply spicy salsa with the unctuous smoothness of sour cream. She had a pang of jealousy as well, though. Becky and Ben both had huge appetites and yet were stick thin. Becky's mum joked that she just couldn't fill them up, and yet she was always making wonderful home-made cakes and delicious meals like lasagne and chilli and roast chicken. Phoebe's mum never joked about food or weight; it was a deadly serious subject. Phoebe never felt full after dinner at her house; more often than not her mum bought ready meals – diet ones for her and Phoebe, Taste the Difference for Callum. When she did cook, it was always a salad or a veggie stir-fry. Liz said, in all seriousness, that she would be thrilled if she could take a calorie-controlled pill for nutrition and never worry about food or meals again, whereas Phoebe felt that her whole life revolved around food, planning from one meal to the next and sating herself with snacks in between.

In the large, cheerful, chaotic kitchen Becky went to the fridge and took out some tomatoes and a bunch of green herbs, then a red onion from the vegetable rack and a jar of chilli flakes from the cupboard. She grabbed a chopping board and started to dice the tomatoes while Phoebe looked on in fascination.

She'd had nachos when her dad took her out to a Mexican restaurant, and occasionally she'd made them herself at home with jars of Doritos salsa and sour cream, but it had never occurred to her that they could be made from fresh ingredients. She knew that Becky helped her parents with the cooking a lot; she said that she really enjoyed it, but Phoebe had never done much more than make toast or occasionally scrambled eggs for herself. Callum hardly ever cooked – the occasional bacon butty on a Saturday morning maybe – and Liz had never encouraged Phoebe's involvement with the cooking she did. Phoebe had learned that she enjoyed food most when it was consumed well away from her mother, else every mouthful was accompanied by a silent barrage of criticism and Phoebe felt that she could actually see bathroom scales reflected in Liz's eyes. School cookery lessons, or Food Technology as it was called, had involved a sandwich project, including analysing its nutritional content, designing its wrapping and writing a marketing plan, but only one week actually making it. And really, how much culinary skill is involved in making a tuna salad sandwich anyway?

Becky glared at Ben, who was zooming around the kitchen making racing car noises.

'Come on, Ben, if you want nachos you can help make them!' She handed him a lump of cheddar and the cheese grater. Ben groaned but set to work, and it was obvious that this was something he was totally accustomed to.

Phoebe asked, slightly shyly, if she could help – she wanted to be involved, but equally Becky seemed to have metamorphosed into someone frighteningly competent in the kitchen, and she felt her own inexperience was magnified in consequence.

Becky smiled her thanks and handed her the green herbs and a sharp knife.

'Could you do the coriander for me?'

Phoebe took the bunch of herbs, gingerly. It smelt fabulous, grassy yet sharp, and as she started to chop it even more heady scent was released.

'I wouldn't have a clue how to make salsa,' she ventured.

Becky looked up from the onion she was now dicing and smiled.

'It's one of Mum's rules,' she explained. 'If Ben and I want to eat what she calls junk food, then we have to learn how to make it from scratch, ourselves.'

'Oh my God!' Phoebe's eyes were round. She didn't know which was most startling – the idea that someone's mum would permit them to eat junk food, or the idea of being taught to cook it from scratch. 'So what kind of thing do you mean?'

Becky thought for a moment.

'Well, nachos is a good example. We love eating nachos while we watch a film on a Saturday night, so Mum taught me how to make salsa. It's really easy. You just chop up the tomato and onion quite small, and stir in a teaspoon of chilli flakes and lots of coriander and a bit of olive oil. If we've got any limes, then I squeeze some lime juice over it. And then we use Greek yoghurt instead of sour cream, and sometimes mash up an avocado to make guacamole too. And it tastes loads nicer than the stuff in a jar.'

Phoebe nodded. This was an entirely new concept for

her. She'd been to dinner with Becky and her family before, of course, and knew that Ruth, her mum, was a great cook, but she hadn't realised just how much Becky knew about food and cooking.

'What else do you make?'

'Umm . . . pizza – we're never allowed frozen pizza, or takeaway. We make the base from scratch, properly, with yeast and everything. And then we all choose different toppings – peppers, mushrooms, chicken, tomato, onion, sweetcorn, pineapple. It's the only way Ben eats any veg normally!'

Phoebe considered again. Pizza would never cross Liz's lips, but when she was out for an evening, Callum would sometimes order a double-pepperoni from Domino's for a treat, followed by a tub of Häagen-Dazs. The cosy family picture conjured up by Becky's description was a million miles from her own experience.

'And what else do you make?'

Becky was slightly bored now, and puzzled at Phoebe's insistent interest.

'Oh God, I don't know. Loads of stuff. Pizza and nachos are what we normally have on a Saturday, or sometimes we make burgers. Or Chinese duck pancakes a couple of times. But that's the fun stuff. My mum also makes me do loads of boring stuff in the week, like peeling potatoes and carrots.'

'Wow.' Phoebe was lost in jealous admiration. She decided there and then that when she had children – always supposing, she thought morosely, that she ever found someone who'd actually be prepared to sleep with her – this was how she was going to bring them up. She'd learn to cook herself, and teach them, and they'd all spend hours in the kitchen making delicious yet healthy food together, and she'd never ever shout at them.

As though reading her thoughts, Becky glanced over. She'd now finished the chopping and was combining the ingredients, with lots of salt and pepper, in a big bowl.

'Thing is though, Pheebs, it's a complete pain sometimes too. Like we're never allowed shop-bought cakes or snacks. Sometimes I just want to come home from school and have a Penguin or a Twix, but instead Mum makes big batches of flapjack or banana loaf cake or raisin cookies and we have to have those instead.'

Phoebe grinned wryly. Given that *her* mum's idea of an after-school snack for her was dry rice cakes or carrot sticks, she didn't feel she had that much sympathy to offer Becky and Ben. Constantly ravenous following her low-cal packed lunch, even after an afternoon-break assault on the chocolate machine, Phoebe would eat her mum's desiccated offerings and then retreat to her room to devour some chocolate bars, or a family-sized bag of Kettle Chips or a box of Mr Kipling Cherry Bakewells. She wondered briefly if she would actually be slimmer if she ate what Becky ate. Was a proper lunch of pasta salad, or crusty rolls filled with Brie and tomato, or a slice of homemade pizza, actually healthier than two slices of 'lite' bread sandwiched together with a scrape of low-cal 'cream' cheese? That is, if the proper lunch meant you didn't need the mid-afternoon chocolate binge? But then she dismissed the idea. Phoebe was self-aware enough to know that hunger was only one of the many reasons she ate, and while she was so unhappy at home she couldn't imagine not using food as her emotional crutch, so surely she'd just be even fatter if her 'official' food wasn't of the low-fat, low-cal, low-taste variety.

Nachos made, the three of them settled back into the two big sofas in Becky's living room and resumed *Shrek*. Phoebe wasn't really watching it any more, though. She was replaying the argument between her parents that morning, and her dad's side of the phone call that followed, and his comments afterwards, and trying to analyse what it might all mean. She wasn't stupid; she knew that her parents' marriage was unhappy, she'd heard the muttered arguments, she'd seen her dad become more and more withdrawn and her mum become more and more brittle, but the idea that they might split up had never seemed more than a distant fantasy. Now, though, she allowed herself to dream. She and her dad leaving, or better still, her mum moving out – then she could even keep her own bedroom. She'd only have to see her mum a couple of times a week, wouldn't have to live with the sickeningly tense sensation of being braced for critical attack, or the feeling that every look, gesture, word or mouthful was being scrutinised and found wanting. And then maybe – Phoebe allowed her fantasy full rein at this point – maybe her dad would meet someone else. Someone relaxed and loving and funny, who would make him happy and would understand Phoebe and listen to her. Maybe Dad would even have another baby, and she would get her proper family after all.

9

When she was little, Ella had owned a snow globe that she loved. In it, two Disneyesque figures, prince and princess, were locked in a permanent embrace. The globe could be turned upside down and shaken, the snow would cascade down around them, but they remained unmoved, immobile and immortalised. Give or take several yards of pink tulle, she felt a little like that princess now. When they'd walked over to Callum he had got to his feet, a huge smile breaking across his face.

'Well, well, well, Ella O'Connor. And . . .' He'd stared hard at Janey, and then attempted 'Jeanette?'

Janey had winked at Ella and grinned at Callum.

'Janey, actually. Janey Morrison. But she's not Ella O'Connor any more, she's Ella Casey now.'

Ella had felt herself blush again, and wouldn't interrogate herself too closely as to why. Her hands were still shaking slightly.

Callum had smiled again, slowly, sexily, and Ella could have sworn that her heart had literally missed a beat.

'I'm afraid she'll always be Ella O'Connor to me.' He introduced his friends, briefly, and then stepped forward towards her. She put her hand out to shake his, but he'd either not noticed or ignored her and she found herself with his arms around her, his stubble grazing the corner of her mouth as he bent down to kiss her cheek. Even wearing her highest heels her head barely reached his shoulder. She could feel the heat of his body and the muscles of his back through his thin cotton shirt. Embarrassingly, her nipples had hardened, and she hoped he wasn't able to feel them through the padding of her bra. And then she was in his arms for far longer, surely, than an ordinary social embrace would dictate she should be, with her head spinning, and the only coherent thought to emerge being her absurd reflection on that long-ago snow globe.

Finally he let her go, and stepped back slightly. She smiled up at him, and knew with clear and confident certainty that she had never looked, or indeed felt, sexier. She could see that reflected in his eyes as he looked her ravenously up and down. She thought perhaps she should feel offended at such a blatant appreciation, but actually she suspected she was looking at him in just the same way.

When she dragged her eyes away she saw that Janey had sat down with Tony and Dave and was flirting outrageously, theatrically with them, and they were responding laughingly in kind. None of them appeared to be taking the least notice of Ella and Callum. Callum pulled out a chair for Ella at the opposite end of the table, sat down himself and poured her a glass of wine. She could feel his eyes on her cleavage, creamily expansive above the deep V-neck of her dress.

They started chatting, and Ella knew she was being sparkling, witty, engaging. Oh yes, and flirtatious. Distinctly flirtatious. They caught up on the previous decade of each other's lives, Ella feeling temporarily old when Callum said that Phoebe, still five in her head, was about to sit her GCSEs. Was a similar age, in fact, to Ella when she had first met Callum.

Her all-girls' school hadn't had a sixth form, but the boys' school next door took girls after sixteen, and Ella had spent the summer after GCSEs talking a lot with her friends about the gorgeous boys they would be meeting in September. Ella knew that she was inexperienced with the opposite sex – she'd had a couple of snogs at the joint school discos, and a bit of a crush on a friend of her brother's. Nothing, though, that compared to what she'd read about, or what some of her friends seemed to feel.

That all changed with her first A-level Politics lesson. Mr McCraig had been the embodiment, she had thought at seventeen, of every Byronic hero she'd ever dreamed of. Tall of stature, broad of shoulder, chiselled of jaw, dark and smouldering of eyes. And so much younger than the middle-aged teachers she was used to. Ella had been smitten at first glance, heartbroken at second when she spotted the plain gold band on the fourth finger of his left hand. Those two moments of elation and despair encapsulated the emotional rollercoaster of the next two years. Not that she let it distract her from her work – the opposite, in fact. She was fired with a new determination to excel academically. Five A grades and an Oxbridge offer would surely mean he'd at least notice her.

And he had noticed her. By her upper sixth year, friends were teasing her that Mr McCraig was just as smitten as she was. In her most optimistic moments she couldn't help but agree. When their eyes met, the bolt of electricity she felt was surely mutual. In class she was feisty and argumentative, witty and scintillating. They sparked off each other, and the rest of the class were basically the audience to their double act. When he'd asked her if she'd be interested in babysitting for his daughter she'd said yes, reacting to the same impulse that keeps your tongue returning to a sore place in your mouth. Although their existence caused her untold nights of misery, she desperately wanted to see his wife, his child, his home.

Of course, she'd hated Liz McCraig on sight. Unfeasibly beautiful, but, to Ella's admittedly biased eye, cold and vain, with a core of hostility only partially disguised by a veneer of friendliness. Phoebe was a delight though, and Ella had fallen almost as much in love with this adorable roly-poly child as she had with her father. And then suddenly the babysitting gigs had stopped, and she sensed a change in Mr McCraig's attitude, a coolness and distance that was entirely new. She had been devastated, barely eating or sleeping, dropping to a size 10 for the first and last time in her life, managing to get through her A-levels on an unhealthy, although ultimately effective, diet of vodka, cigarettes and black coffee.

Things had improved after that, of course. She was young, and away at university with so many new people to meet and experiences to have that it was impossible to remain broken-hearted. For most of her first and second years, though, she had felt too fragile for a relationship and had settled for the odd one-night stand. It was only when she met Greg that she'd really moved on and fallen in love again, and even then she knew in some secret corner of herself that she had never fully obtained closure on her feelings for Callum McCraig.

And now he was sitting opposite her, and she was reminded of those long ago Politics lessons as the conversation and repartee flew between them as though scripted by Richard Curtis.

Ella was interrupted in the middle of a particularly amusing anecdote by Tony and Dave standing up and trying to attract Callum's attention. He dragged his eyes away from her animated face, and gave his oldest friends the kind of vague and slightly unfocussed look that you might give someone sitting opposite you on the Tube who you think you might recognise.

'Callum, mate.' Tony's voice was half amused, half insistent.

'Yeah, you OK?'

'*I'm* fine.' Ironic emphasis on the first person singular. 'But Dave and I are heading off now – it's nearly midnight. Are you coming?'

Ella started and automatically glanced at her watch. It was indeed five minutes to midnight; she and Callum had been locked in conversation for nearly two hours, which had passed like five minutes, and she was conscious that, more than anything else in the world, she did not want him to leave now. She held her breath, waiting for his reply.

'Erm, I think I might hang around for a bit longer, actually. Carry on catching up with Ella.'

Tony looked completely nonplussed.

'Okaay. But . . . how can I put this? You asked if you could sleep on our sofa tonight, which absolutely isn't a problem, but Caroline will kill me, and probably you too,

77

if you turn up in the early hours of the morning and need letting in. So it might be better if we all went together.'

Ella leapt in desperately.

'It's OK, I've got a room booked.' She realised as soon as she said it how that sounded, and blushed, then started to giggle nervously. She seemed to have regressed to her teenage years in more ways than one.

'I mean, if you need somewhere to stay, Callum, you could just have my room, and I could share with Janey. Couldn't I?'

Implausible as this scenario sounded, it provided at least a fig leaf of modesty. She glanced across at Janey, telegraphing a frantic message: don't let me down.

Janey shrugged.

'Yeah, no worries. If that's what you want to do.' She stepped closer to Ella, and asked in a lowered voice, 'Am I allowed to ask why Callum isn't going home?' Tense silence and compressed lips met her question, and she laughed and made an exaggerated lip-zipping gesture.

'OK, I'm not allowed to ask. Fine, I can take a hint.' Then in a louder voice, 'Listen, Ella, I'm going to go and catch up with the other girls, do you wanna text me later?'

Ella nodded, gratefully, and Janey shot her a knowing look before wiggling off. She could tell that whereas she looked at Callum McCraig and saw a tall, reasonably attractive man in early middle age, Ella was still seeing the handsome young teacher she'd had such an overwhelming crush on, and whom she'd endowed with every physical and intellectual virtue, and Janey hoped that an evening of heavy-duty flirting would provide her friend with the closure she'd obviously never quite obtained.

Tony and Dave looked slightly less sanguine at the proposal. Ella had to fight off the urge to start giggling again. This pair of not-quite-middle-aged men looked so anxious and uncomfortable, and were obviously completely flummoxed at their friend's departure from the straight and narrow, yet equally unsure how to herd him back onto the marital path again. Callum wasn't giving them a chance to do anything, though. He stood up, towering half a head taller and seemingly half a foot wider than either of them, and clapped a hand on each of their shoulders.

'Look, guys, it's late, you're tired. Go home, I'll stay here and finish chatting to Ella, crash in her room or whatever, and I'll catch up with you both next week.'

He subtly turned them so they were facing the door, and they seemed eventually to acquiesce in their dismissal.

Ella waggled her fingers in their direction.

'Bye, nice to meet you.'

And then they were gone, and Callum sank back into his seat and smiled that seductive smile again.

'So,' he intoned, in deliberately chocolatey James Brown-esque tones, 'alone at last.'

He is being deliberately corny, Ella told herself sternly. You are not meant to be turned on by this. She managed to smile, and replied flirtatiously, 'I've been waiting over ten years for you to say that!'

His smile faded.

'Oh God, Ella, me too. Me too.' He jumped up again. 'Wait here. Don't go anywhere, I'll be back.'

He headed off towards the bar, and Ella, ignoring his instructions, took the opportunity to retire for a much-needed wee. Call of nature answered, she washed her hands, then took a deep breath and forced herself to confront her reflection in the mirror. Usually by this stage of a night out she looked a horror; panda eyes, red-wine teeth, bird's-nest hair. Now, though, she was struck by how good she still looked. It helped that she'd been too busy talking to drink for the last two hours; and after she had reapplied her lipstick and perfume, and shaken her hair about a bit, she felt pretty confident.

She and Callum arrived back at their table at pretty much the same time. He was holding a bottle of champagne and two flutes. Her heartbeat quickened slightly. She wasn't unaware of where this evening had the potential to go, but she kept on stilling the small voice of her conscience by reiterating to herself that having a drink with an old friend was perfectly innocent. Well, maybe it was. But, put another way, how innocent was sharing champagne, alone, in a hotel bar, after midnight with a man on whom she'd had the biggest crush of her life?

But equally, how delicious was it? She couldn't remember the last time Greg had bought her champagne. Actually, she could. He'd bought a bottle to celebrate their discovery of her pregnancy with Aidan, forgetting that she wouldn't be able to drink any. She'd had a few token sips, and he had finished the rest of the bottle. The following morning they'd had an argument as to whether a hangover or morning sickness was worse. Romantic. But now, this gorgeous man was solicitously pouring her a glass, sending electric shocks through her as their fingers brushed, proposing a toast to 'second chances'. Ella firmly pressed the mute button on her conscience and raised her glass to his.

10

Imogen felt, and knew that she looked, like a limp rag. Even though she had been exhausted the night before, she had only managed a couple of hours' broken sleep on the camp bed next to Indigo in the hospital. It had been too hot, and every couple of hours the nurse had come to do observations on Indigo. These usually woke her up and left her overtired, sore and almost inconsolable, and it would take Imogen all her efforts to soothe her back to sleep again. This morning she had been told that Indigo was fine, just needed to be kept quiet for a few days, and that they could go home.

At that point she'd realised she had no way of getting home. The hospital they'd been taken to, the Royal Free in Hampstead, was a long way from Walthamstow and she had no transport. She supposed she could phone a minicab, but the thought of endless negotiations on the availability of car seats was nearly as unthinkable as risking Indigo's safety again with an uncarseated journey across London. She would have to swallow her pride, phone Pete and ask him to pick them up. She dialled – it cut straight to voicemail. She phoned their landline – it rang out. After repeating this for a few minutes and getting no further, Indigo was starting to get fractious and Imogen felt at her wits' end. Then she remembered that Ella had said she could phone Greg if she needed anything. She tried Ella's number, but that was also cutting to voicemail, unsurprising as her friend was probably enjoying her first lie-in for three years. Desperate now, she phoned Ella's landline and Greg answered after a few rings.

Imogen nearly dissolved in tears when she heard his familiar voice, but managed to hold it together sufficiently to explain the situation to him. Greg was his normal relaxed and laid-back self.

'Alright, Immy, no problem. I'm going to drop Aidan and Hattie at my mum's, and then I'll drive over and pick you up. It's OK, you and Indigo will be home in no time.'

Imogen sank down in relief in the waiting area by the main entrance to the hospital. Her resistance to junk food seemed to have been entirely worn down and she went to the vending machine to buy a carton of Ribena for Indigo and a chocolate bar for them both to share. An unexpected sugar infusion transformed Indigo's mood and the hour until Greg arrived passed surprisingly easily.

Imogen, who had cried more in the past twenty-four hours than in the whole previous year, felt tears of relief starting again when she saw Greg stride in through the big double doors. He looked familiar, and safe and dependable – everything that Pete wasn't. And everything, a little voice whispered, that Alex seemed to be. She shook herself mentally and went over to hug Greg. He held her tight for a moment.

'God, Immy, you poor thing! And poor Indigo. What a bloody nightmare. Come on, let's get you both home.'

He took Indigo's hand and linked his arm through Imogen's and they headed off to the car park.

'I'm so grateful, Greg, and to your mum for having your kids as well. Thank you *so* much.'

He grinned.

'Don't be silly, what are friends for? You'd do the same for us. Can I ask though, where is Pete?'

His tone was neutral, but Imogen was aware that Greg had no particular fondness for Pete. It was mutual – Pete found Greg boring, square, overly conscientious, whereas Greg was singularly unimpressed by Pete's laissez-faire approach to life and parenthood.

Imogen hesitated. Her instinctive reaction, still, was to make an excuse, to protect Pete, but then, when she thought of what he had put her through, how he had put Indigo at risk and then abandoned them, a surge of anger came over her again.

'Pete has . . .' she glanced down at Indigo and then mouthed '. . . *fucked off*, and left me to cope on my own. I had one text message from him yesterday, and now his phone's switched off.'

Greg shook his head and whistled soundlessly.

'Bloody hell, Immy, I bet you're mad. Ella would have my bollocks for kebabs if I tried anything like that with her.'

Imogen smiled, wryly. Ella was always threatening to have Greg's bollocks for kebabs for far more minor infringements than that – half an hour late back from work, forgetting to pick up milk on the way home, losing his dry-cleaning ticket. Yes, such marital pinpricks could be very irritating, but lately Imogen had started to worry that Ella was sweating the small stuff to the extent that she was in danger of overlooking Greg's essential kindness and decency.

As if reading her mind, Greg grinned.

'Of course, Ella half-kills me if I leave the top off the toothpaste, so we are working to slightly different standards here.'

Greg put on a nursery-rhymes CD in the car and Indigo dozed contentedly in Aidan's carseat while Imogen and Greg chatted companionably. When they arrived back at Imogen's, she asked Greg in for a cup of tea. He gently carried the still sleeping Indigo in from the car up to her room and laid her carefully on the bed while Imogen draped a blanket lightly over her.

Imogen could feel her anxiety levels rising again. Indigo hardly ever napped during the day now, and certainly not this deeply.

'Do you think she's OK?' she asked Greg.

He patted her shoulder reassuringly.

'Of course she is. They wouldn't have let her home unless they were a hundred per cent confident she was OK. She's just knackered, Immy – she probably had a broken night, and she's been through a lot. Just let her have a nap, and come down and make us something hot and caffeinated.'

His warmth and positivity was reassuring and Imogen felt her spirits lift a little. Downstairs in the kitchen it seemed that nothing had changed; the dishes she had hastily washed the previous morning were still piled on the draining board, although closer examination showed that they had been joined by a dirty bowl and spoon. As

Imogen took the milk from the fridge she found herself sniffing it as she would if she had been away from home for a few days; the last day had been so emotionally seismic it was hard to believe it was only twenty-four hours since she had last stood here.

As she made the tea, she heard Greg call from the living room, a little awkwardly,

'Erm, Imogen, there's a note for you on the mantel-piece in here.'

She went through, carrying the steaming mugs, and set them carefully down before taking the folded sheet of paper that Greg handed her. She sat down, curling her legs under her, and, in the absence of anything to give her Dutch courage, took a slightly too large gulp of tea. After she had finished choking she looked down at the paper. 'Imogen' was scrawled across the folded sheet in orange felt-tip; Pete's handwriting.

Inside the message was brief:

Imogen,
    I think I'm still too angry to talk to you after what you said yesterday. I need some time out, so going to crash at Seth and Violet's for a while.
    I'll call you.
    P

Great. Imogen's first, probably irrelevant, thought was, 'Who the hell dumps the mother of their child in orange felt-tip?' Absolutely bloody typical. And then anger again. She'd never known she could feel so angry. Yet *he* claimed to be too angry to talk to her, after what he'd done and not done? She screwed the paper up into a ball and flung it across the room.

Greg was looking at her with raised eyebrows.

'Are you OK?'

Imogen laughed, an edge of hysteria present.

'Oh, fine. Just a little *billet-doux* from Pete, saying that he's so angry I expressed displeasure at the way his cavalier behaviour put our daughter in hospital he needs some "time out" and so is buggering off to stay at his mate's.'

'Whew.' Greg looked closely at Imogen. She seemed quite calm. Pissed off, but not tearful. He sighed. This was so not his department. He liked solutions – preferably practical ones; emotional quagmire like this was very much Ella's area of expertise. On the other hand, if he didn't do something to help Immy, then Ella would be furious with him, and he didn't think he had the stomach for another futile row when his wife got home. He was really hoping that a weekend away, a proper break from all the stresses and strains of marriage and motherhood, would have changed Ella's perspective and would allow them to resume a warmer and more loving relationship than they had managed recently. Ever since her crazy baby idea, in fact. The last thing he needed was to wade straight into a row over how he had abandoned Ella's best friend in her hour of need.

Then an idea struck him.

'Look, Immy, you must be shattered. No sleep last night, and all the worry over Indy, and now this.'

Imogen nodded.

'Shattered is one way of putting it, yes.'

'Well, why don't you go and have a sleep? I'll look after Indigo when she wakes up; I can just put on a DVD, or something. You can get a proper rest, and when you wake up, I'll go and pick Aidan and Hattie up, and then when she gets home I'll send Ella round to do the emotional TLC.'

Imogen thought. The idea of lying down in her own bed, letting the world drift away and not having to confront anything for a couple of hours was blissful, but there was the normal maternal guilt to contend with.

'But Indy might not be well when she wakes up – she might need me.'

'Well, if she needs you, I'll call you. You're not going anywhere. But she'll be fine, honestly.' He could sense that her resistance was weak, and pushed the point.

'Look, if Indy has a disturbed night again you'll need all your energy for that, so get some rest now. Everything will seem better after a sleep.'

Despite thinking that she would lie awake, tense and worried, contemplating the car crash her life seemed to have become, Imogen fell into sleep like a stone. She was unaware of Indigo waking, of Greg going in to her, of her giggles of delight when she realised she was going to be indulged with some unscheduled television. Imogen was also completely unaware of the missed call on her mobile, or of the tinny beep that was meant to alert her to the fact that a text message had arrived.

When she woke up, three hours later, she felt she had a new lease of life. Everything that had seemed insurmountable now felt more in proportion; Indigo was OK, and after the trauma of seeing her lying apparently lifeless on the ground, any other catastrophe appeared manageable. After listening outside the living room door for a minute, she decided to take advantage of Greg's kindness for a little longer. She suddenly felt very aware that she was still wearing the same dress she had put on so optimistically the previous morning. White no longer, it was grubby all over, with grass stains on the knees where she had knelt next to Indigo, bloodstains from her cut head, and horribly crumpled from a night tossing and turning in a hospital camp bed. Additionally, the weather had changed since yesterday to the blustery showers that were far more typical of the time of year. Imogen took a long hot shower, luxuriously soaping herself and shampooing her hair; revelling in the clichéd feeling that she was washing away the stresses of the previous day. She towel-dried her hair, then pulled on faded skinny jeans, a long-sleeved white ethical cotton T-shirt, a soft, warm baby-pink cardie she'd knitted herself, and then slipped her feet into her sheepskin clogs.

'Mummy!'

Indigo launched herself off the sofa and into her mother's arms with an exuberance that eased the last of Imogen's concerns about her. Broken arm aside, she seemed completely recovered.

'You look a bit more human now, if you don't mind me saying so.' Greg grinned at her.

'Oh God, Greg, I feel so much better. I didn't realise how totally wiped out I was. You're a lifesaver, you really are. I'm so grateful.' She came over and hugged him.

'Oh, don't be silly. It was nothing. Any time, honestly. Indy and I had a great time, didn't we, angel?'

Indigo giggled happily.

'Mummy, we watched lots and LOTS of *Peppa Pig*!'

Greg looked slightly guilty.

'I found a couple of DVDs, Immy, and I didn't want her to overdo it, so I thought telly might not be a bad thing . . .' He trailed off, aware suddenly that Imogen had always had a fairly militant attitude to television viewing for both adults and children, preferring that they spend their time creatively.

Imogen laughed.

'It's alright, Greg. When you drive halfway across London to rescue me and my ill child, and then look after said child for hours while I sleep, you don't then get a bollocking for letting her watch a bit of telly! Now, listen, you need to go and pick Aidan and Hattie up, and get home before Ella beats you to it.'

'OK then, I'll be off. I'll send Ella round with a bottle of wine after supper, shall I?'

He gave Imogen a brotherly pat on the shoulder, and then bent down to kiss Indigo.

'Now listen, you. No more falling off bikes, hey, and make sure you look after your mummy, OK?'

Indigo nodded seriously.

Imogen's eyes were very soft as she looked first at her daughter and then at Greg.

'Ella's a lucky girl to have you, you know.'

He looked uncomfortable.

'Hmm, I think you might find she doesn't agree with you on that one, Immy.' And with that he was off, leaving Indigo and Imogen to wave him out of sight from the front window.

After an intensive story-reading session, Imogen made an omelette and chips for their tea, bathed Indigo carefully, using the plastic packaging the hospital had given them to keep her plaster dry, and then tucked her up in bed. Despite the long nap, Indigo still fell asleep almost instantly and it was only at this point that Imogen had the time to check her phone.

When she saw she had a missed call from an unknown number her heart quickened slightly. Pete. Phoning to apologise, and asking to come home. It must be. There was a voicemail message, in a huskily hesitant voice: 'Hi, Imogen. Sorry to disturb you. Just calling firstly to see how Indigo is, and secondly to say that I've got your bike. I phoned the park rangers on the Heath, and they were looking after it after what happened yesterday, so I drove over to collect it this morning. I hope you don't mind. I didn't think you needed the hassle, really. Anyway, I've got it, and I can drop it round any time, just give me a call. Oh, it's Alex, by the way. Anyway, better stop rambling now, take care. Bye.'

When she realised the voice wasn't Pete's, Imogen felt a momentary stab of disappointment, but that was erased and replaced by a warm glow at being looked after and being, after all these years, the recipient rather than the donor of a thoughtful gesture.

Then she looked at her text message.

'Hi, hope Indy ok today. Need to talk to you badly, I've done something awful. Ella xxx'

I I

Ella couldn't remember where she'd read about people who'd been unfaithful being branded across their face with an 'A' for adulterer. Was it historical fact from medieval England, or current practice in fundamentalist religious states, or merely something out of a dystopian novel like *The Handmaid's Tale*? No wonder she couldn't remember. Her mind was filled with the murky grey sludge that is the inevitable result of several vodka-based cocktails, half a bottle of champagne and very little sleep. She sank her forehead against the cool glass of the window, averting her gaze from the bacon roll and fruit smoothie on the table. She'd grabbed them at Lime Street station on her way to catch the train, unsure whether saturated fat or vitamin C would prove the best cure for her hangover, and so opting to play it safe with both.

Maybe the sick headache wasn't alcohol poisoning but guilt. God, she felt guilty. Particularly about this morning. Last night, maybe, she could have rationalised, justified to herself. She was drunk; it was a total one-off experience providing closure on a teenage infatuation; what happens in Liverpool stays in Liverpool. But this morning. Cold light of day. Waking up next to a man who was most definitely not her husband, and being instantly wet at the thought of what they'd done the night before. Sneaking into the bathroom to brush her teeth, remove the leftover, caked-on make-up, and brush her hair, then returning to the bedroom as he woke up and gazed at her, at first with incomprehension, then with growing appreciation. And then she'd been in his arms again, kissing like they could never stop, until kissing was no longer remotely enough, and then he was inside her, and she was pulling him closer and closer, deeper and deeper, trying to merge herself with him. And now, despite the guilt, her stomach and groin were filled once more with a sensation of melting chocolate, just from thinking about it, about him. This wasn't good, at all.

She took a mouthful of orange and mango smoothie, then popped two ibuprofen out of their foil packaging and gulped them down with another mouthful. What the hell had she been thinking, and what the bloody hell was she going to do now?

As if to answer her, her mobile rang.

'Hello, you.'

The voice on the other end was warm and intimate and she felt herself melt further.

'Hi, Callum. What can I do for you?'

She was trying, and probably failing, to sound composed and businesslike, but realised too late that she had given him an opening.

He laughed softly, and replied, 'I don't think I should answer that question over the phone – possibly too frustrating when I can't get at you.'

There was confidence and assurance in his tone; the voice of a man talking to his established lover, not a woman he was attempting to seduce. And, thought Ella, why the hell wouldn't he feel confident of her? Last night, this morning, she had been totally abandoned, pretty much literally throwing herself at him. She'd thought her libido was dead, but it had certainly been reanimated last night; she suspected the ghost of it was going to haunt her for the foreseeable future.

She groaned inwardly. Why had he called? She remembered, from pre-Greg days, that men never called. Surely that was the first rule of one-night stands? Sometimes you spent the next few days surgically welded to your phone praying that they would, at other times you spent the equivalent time answering in a foreign accent, preparing to gabble, 'Ella? No, I notta knowa no Ella,' if the need arose. But it never did. It *never* did. That was the whole point. The only way she'd been able to cope at all with what she'd done – what, God help her, she was desperate to do again – was to tell herself repeatedly that she would never hear from Callum again. He was married too, for heaven's sake, and surely all the stuff last night about having been miserable for years, being on a break, surely that had just been him spinning her a line to get her into bed? A fairly successful line, it had to be said.

And now he was on the other end of the phone, presumably waiting for some kind of response from her. When she was at school, she and Janey had read *Circle of Friends* by Maeve Binchy, and had been very taken by Benny and Eve's habit of asking 'What would the wise woman do?' when a dilemma presented itself. The wise woman, who had clearly been taking a sabbatical recently, was quite clear in her view that Ella should feign a signal blackout and hang up the phone. However ...

'I'm not sure this is a conversation I should be having in a crowded train carriage, Callum.' Her voice, to her own ears, was wrong: flirtatious rather than dismissive.

'Get off the train at the next station then, and come back to Liverpool. Or better still, book a room and I'll drive down and meet you.' His voice had an edge of terribly sexy desperation, and it was taking all her efforts of self-control not to pull the emergency cord. As if in response to her thoughts the train began to slow down, finally juddering to a halt at Stafford station. She giggled.

'What's so funny?'

'We've just pulled in to Stafford, which may have saved me from myself. I'm sorry, Callum, but I can't possibly have a romantic assignation in Stafford.'

He laughed as well.

'Really? I would have thought it was right up there with Paris, Rome or New York in a girl's dreams. Thing is, Ella, Birmingham is about equidistant between London and Liverpool, so we're probably going to end up meeting there a fair bit until we get everything sorted out, and I'm not sure that'd be much better than Stafford.'

Now she really did feel panicked.

'What do you mean, Callum, "until things are sorted out"?'

He sounded slightly hesitant.

'Well, I mean, I need to tell Liz today that I'm leaving her. And I need to sort out somewhere to live, and explain things to Phoebe. And you're going to need to talk to . . .' he paused, 'your husband.'

If Ella had felt at the centre of an emotional maelstrom before, that was nothing compared to the waves of nausea,

94

longing, guilt, dread and fear that assailed her now. What the fuck had she done? She got up and walked into the vestibule area, feeling that she had contributed more than enough to the on-train entertainment already.

'Callum.' Her voice, which she intended to be gentle but firm, had an audible shake. 'Callum, no. The last thing I am going to do is talk to my husband. I have two very young children, I have no option but to make my marriage work. I know what happened between us didn't look like that was what I was trying to do. I made a horrible mistake, and I feel unbelievably guilty, but I have to try and put it behind me now, and concentrate on Greg and the children. I'm sorry if I misled you.'

She heard Callum exhale.

'Sorry, Ella. I didn't mean to freak you out. The thing is, I've been so unhappy with Liz for years that meeting you again is just the catalyst for me to change things, not the whole reason. I know your circumstances are different. And I'll wait as long as it takes. But I know – *you* know – we have to see each other again. I'm not letting you walk out of my life a second time.'

Ella's eyes were filling with tears. Previously her guilt had all been focussed on her betrayal of Greg and, indirectly, of Aidan and Hattie. She had assumed that Callum would be dealing with his own guilt, his own branded 'A'. She had never expected that her actions were going to cause him pain as well. She was torn with longing, part of her mind moving at lightning quick speed to imagine taking Aidan and Hattie, moving back to Liverpool, creating a new family (what was it they called it? – a blended family) with her children and Phoebe. Enjoying blindingly good sex every day. And feeling like a woman again instead of a washer of dishes and wiper of bottoms. But set against that, her more rational mind conjured up pictures of her children. Their heartbreaking innocence. Their total dependence on her and Greg for love, stability, happiness: everything.

And also images of Greg. After months of pretty much demonising him, of blaming him for her feelings of discontent, of missing out on life, it took a proposition from another man for her to remember all the good things about him. How he'd brought her ginger tea and dry biscuits in bed every morning of both her pregnancies because they were the only things that made the nausea abate sufficiently for her to get up. How he got her flowers and a card every year, not just on their wedding anniversary, but on the anniversary of them meeting, of their first date, the first time they had sex, the day they got engaged, the day they conceived Aidan. Hattie's conception was the exception, buried in post-partum fug; she wasn't sure either of them could actually remember even having sex, let alone pinpoint an exact date. How he'd chivalrously claimed to fancy her, even at nine months pregnant, and how, when pregnant with Aidan and overdue, and a friend had recommended 'hot curry, hot bath and hot sex' as a way to get things going, he had gone out to the Indian takeaway, bought Radox from the twenty-four-hour general store on his way back and then, as she luxuriated in a bath so hot she was scarlet all over, appeared in the bathroom stark naked with a rose between his teeth.

Why had it taken passionate sex with another man to bring those memories of a happy marriage and a loving husband to the surface? Just exactly what kind of self-sabotage was she indulging in?

The tears were pouring down her cheeks now, and she no longer cared if Callum could hear the sob in her voice as she whispered, 'No, Callum, sorry. I can't do this. I'm sorry.' And she pressed the red button on her phone.

Then she sank to the floor in the vestibule, leaned back against the wall, brought her knees up to her chin and buried her face in her hands as she sobbed and sobbed until her eyes were swollen, her nose streaming, her breath coming in jagged gasps and her buttocks numb. And then, drawing on inner reserves she hadn't known she possessed, she stopped crying. She went into the toilet, splashed water on her face and regarded herself in the mirror.

Despite her misery, she couldn't help an ironic smile as she looked at her dishevelled reflection. If she'd looked like this last night – red eyes, limp hair, grey skin, dry lips and, oh God, more than a touch of stubble rash – then perhaps she would have avoided her present predicament entirely. As it was, she grabbed her handbag and applied moisturiser to the reddened skin around her mouth and chin and neck, concealer to the shadows under her eyes and a brush to her hair. All the while she gave herself a stern talking-to. She was a mother, she could be strong for her children. She had made a dreadful mistake, but it need not have any negative consequences. In fact, she could use it for the good, to strengthen her marriage, improve her sense of happiness with her lot. Change her marriage for the better.

12

Phoebe was lying on her bed in the foetal position, shaking uncontrollably. The dawning optimism she had felt the previous night at Becky's had been replaced by a dark and terrible fear that threatened to envelop her completely.

When she'd arrived home from Becky's a couple of hours earlier, having enjoyed Sunday lunch with the Stein family, she had been more than surprised to find the house empty and quiet. Liz usually went to the gym on a Sunday afternoon and met up with friends for a coffee or smoothie afterwards, but Callum was inevitably to be found sprawled full-length along the sofa with the *Observer* and a large mug of strong tea. In fact, Sunday afternoon was one of Phoebe's favourite times of the week, one of the times she was most likely to venture out of her room into the main house. A time when she could chat to her dad, read the Review section of the paper, feeling self-consciously adult as she did so, maybe put on a DVD or finish her homework. The tension she felt when Liz was around would evaporate for a while, giving her a sense of what a normal life could perhaps be like.

That afternoon, though, the house had been aseptically clean and tidy and devoid of any trace of human presence. Wandering around it, Phoebe had compared it to the family home she had just left, and the contrast could hardly be greater. Where the Steins had a jumble of framed snapshots on every surface, or in large montages on the walls, in Phoebe's house there were just a few professional black and white prints in silver frames. The kitchen was, as every cliché decreed it should be, the heart of Becky's home – a large dresser contained character-fully mismatched china and a collection of miscellaneous papers waiting to be filed; a big noticeboard on the wall held photos, postcards, letters from school, reminders, hospital appointment cards, Ben's artwork – an ever-changing collage of family life; whereas here the gleaming white units and granite work surfaces displayed only one large, perfect glass bowl of fruit.

Inspired by Becky, Phoebe had thought she might take advantage of the empty house to try making some cook-ies. Her mum had a pristine and largely untouched collection of Delia's *How to Cook* series of books, and she was flicking through them in a desultory fashion, trying to find a suitable recipe, when she heard the front door bang. She tensed immediately, listening for either the tap-tap of high heels on the tiled floor or the softer thump of her father's footsteps. Damn, high heels. She shut the cookery book with a snap and, as there was no way to her room without passing through the hall, prepared for confrontation. However, the footsteps stopped, suggest-ing that her mother had gone into the living room, and after a few moments she snuck out, intending to take advantage of her bare feet to make it to sanctuary without attracting notice. When she padded out into the hall she noticed that the living room door was open, and she could see her mother sitting inside, head in her hands, shoulders shaking as though she was crying. She felt instantly uncomfortable and unsure. This wasn't normal; her mum wasn't a crying sort of person. Part of Phoebe, the part that loved her mum and craved her approval, wanted to go in, put her arms around her and find out what was wrong. The other part, though, was the larger part, and this was the part that shrank from the criticism and put-downs that seemed the inevitable outcome of any but the most banal conversation between her and Liz. She hesitated, but fear won over love and she retreated as silently as possible up the stairs.

She'd reached the first-floor landing and turned the corner to her own staircase when she heard the sound of a key in the lock and her spirits lifted: Dad was home. She peeked down through the banisters, as she'd been doing since she was a little girl, and saw Callum walk in and shut the door behind him. He hung his coat on the peg, then took a deep breath and squared his shoulders, as though bracing himself for something. He looked different, some-how. Taller? Broader? More confident. It reminded Phoebe of when there'd been a staff training day at her own school and she'd gone in with her dad to his and seen him at work. Confident, controlled and in command of himself, he'd seemed like a different person to the loving but hesitant man she saw at home, constantly sidestep-ping round her mother.

She watched as he walked into the living room, and then crept down a few stairs so that she could hear what was going on.

'Hi, Liz.'

There was a short silence, then her mother's voice, sounding slightly hesitant.

'Hi. You're back then?'

'Well . . .' Callum also sounded unsure, then asked, 'Where's Phoebe?'

She imagined her mother's graceful shrug.

'I haven't seen her. At Becky's still, I guess.'

'Well, that's good. Like I said in my text, we can't go on like we are, Liz. We need to talk about what happens next.'

Phoebe could feel her heart speeding up. She'd wondered yesterday, when her parents had had the most open row she could ever remember, if anything might change, but she had hardly expected something so definite so soon. Suddenly she felt apprehensive, even scared; five minutes ago she would have said she regarded her parents splitting up as a good thing, now that it looked more likely to become a reality she wasn't so sure. Despite everything, familiarity suddenly had its attractions.

In sharp contrast to the robustness of her words, Liz's voice sounded almost frightened as she replied, 'Oh come on, Callum. We've been round this before. We're both too old to believe in happy-ever-after fairy tales, but we've got a partnership that works, we've got Phoebe, we've got a home, we rub along together. There's no point disrupting all that.'

There was a pause, then Callum's voice, soft but determined.

'No, Liz. No, that's not good enough for me any more. It should never have been good enough; we should have sorted things out before we got to this point. I feel like I'm married to a stranger. And yes, we've got Phoebe, but we don't agree on anything about how we bring her up. I was horrified at how you spoke to her yesterday, and I'm just feeling so guilty that I haven't been doing a better job at protecting her.'

Phoebe leaned forward, straining to hear every word and nuance. It sounded like her mother was trying to talk, but then Callum carried on.

'Wait, Liz. I feel like I've been quiet for ten years, and I want to have my say now. I've not been happy in our marriage, for ages. I've stayed and tried to make it work because I love Phoebe, and more than anything I want what's best for her, but I'm just not sure any more that having us stuck together in a loveless marriage *is* what's best for her – what message are we sending her about adult relationships?'

'Maybe that marriage has to be worked at, that you don't just walk away when you get bored?' Liz's tone was acidic.

Callum snorted.

'OK, because you've worked so hard at our marriage? Constantly belittling me, telling me teaching is a career for losers who can't do anything else, refusing to share a room, or have sex with me? Is that working at a marriage? Not in my book.'

Phoebe fought the impulse to cover her ears; a discussion of her parents' sex life or, thankfully, the lack of it, was not what she needed to hear.

'But what's changed? I don't understand – we've been like this for years, I thought we'd just reached an understanding.'

There was a bang; Phoebe imagined her father's fist striking the coffee table.

'That's bollocks, and you know it! You're well aware I've not been happy, but every time I raise it you threaten to estrange me from Phoebe if I leave. That's not reaching an understanding, that's bloody blackmail.'

Liz's voice was silkily, venomously smooth now, perhaps surer of her ground.

'You can call it that if you like, but it's true, Callum, and it remains true. I will not leave this house – my home, my daughter's home – and if you choose to leave us then you can resign yourself to being a two-hours-a-fortnight father, because over my dead body will you ever live with your precious Phoebe again.'

Silence, and then one word, in a tired and resigned tone.

'OK.'

'What do you mean, OK?' Liz's voice was shrill now.

'I mean, OK. If that's the way you want to play it. I'll get a solicitor, and I'll fight you if necessary. Phoebe's nearly sixteen now, a family court would take her views into account, and I think you might find she'd rather live with me than you.'

Her voice rose almost to a shriek.

'Fuck you! Like hell you'd win! I am her mother, and that is what counts! And where would you live? You can't offer her a home if you're sleeping on a mate's sofa, and your wonderful teaching career isn't so lucrative you can afford two family homes, is it?'

Phoebe felt her world fall apart with Callum's reply.

'Look, Liz. I don't want it to be like this, I'd rather have an amicable split, and make things as easy as possible for Phoebe. But I'm not being blackmailed any more; I'm not sticking around just because leaving is too difficult. I'll stay at Tony's while I get sorted, so obviously Phoebe will have to be here for now, but once I am sorted we should give her the choice. We can't use her as a weapon.'

Phoebe stared fixedly at a loose thread in the beige carpet. In all her imaginings this scenario had never occurred to her – Callum leaving and her remaining. How could she survive this? Surely, surely he didn't mean it? He never kept his resolve when Liz threatened him. Any minute now he would back down. He had to.

Liz's voice was dangerously quiet; Phoebe could barely hear.

'If you go now, I will do everything in my power to ensure that you never live with your daughter or set foot in this house again. Think carefully before you indulge your midlife crisis, Callum, because you have a lot to lose.'

'I'm going to go and pack some things. I'll be at Tony's for a few days. I'll be in touch.'

Phoebe got hastily to her feet and scrambled back up the stairs to the landing. Not quietly enough, as it turned out.

'Phoebe, is that you?' she heard Callum call.

'Go away, I don't want to talk to you!' She ran up the next set of stairs to her room, stumbling slightly and hearing Callum's heavy tread taking the stairs two at a time. She just had to get to her room and get the key turned in the lock, and then she could pretend none of this was happening. Too late, though. Her trip, and Callum's longer legs, had given him the advantage, and he caught up with her just as she reached the top floor. Beside herself with a panicky anger she scarcely understood, she tried to shut her door against him, but he was too strong and forced his way in.

'Go away, leave me alone!' Her voice, to her own ears, was unrecognisable.

'No, Phoebe.' His voice was gentle, but firm. 'Listen to me. You obviously overheard the conversation your mother and I were just having, and I'm sorry about that – it wasn't meant for you to hear.'

'Well, neither of you bothered to keep your voices down! Or even to check whether I was here or not!'

He sighed.

'I know. We got it badly wrong, you shouldn't have had to find out like that. But Phoebe, though I'm sorry about the way you heard it, it's true. Your mother and I haven't been happy together for a while, you probably know that. And I can't manage any longer, I don't think it's healthy for any of us to live like this. I love you so much, and I'm going to miss you hugely, but I need to leave, and until I've sorted things out, you need to stay here.'

'No, Daddy, no!' Phoebe was sobbing now, tears streaming down her face, her voice catching snottily in her throat. 'Take me with you, Daddy, I don't want to stay here by myself. Please let me come.'

'Oh, sweetheart.' Callum's own voice sounded thick with tears and regret now. 'I would if I could, but I don't have anywhere to take you to at the moment; I'll be sleeping in Tony's box room until I get a flat sorted. When I've got somewhere of my own to live then we can discuss what's best to do.'

'Well, I'm going to live with Becky, then. I won't stay here, you can't make me!'

He put his arms around her and pulled her to him. She buried her face in his shoulder and sobbed like a baby, noting somewhere in the back of her mind that he smelt different, like perfume. Not Opium, which her mother always wore, but something light and citrusy.

'I'm sorry, darling, but you're only fifteen. You have to stay here with your mum. But we'll get it all sorted out, I promise.'

Phoebe had wrenched herself out of his embrace then and flung herself on the bed, curling up into a ball to try and protect herself from the hurt and uncertainty and fear. Callum stood watching her for a few moments, hopelessly, racked with guilt but still feeling a calm inner certainty that this was a pain barrier that had to be gone through for a better future for them all. After a while, when Phoebe didn't look up, or further acknowledge his presence in any way, he turned and tiptoed out of her room to go and pack up his belongings and start again.

13

'Mummyyy!'

As soon as Ella inserted her key into the lock she could hear two excited voices and two sets of footsteps echoing on the wooden floor. She took a deep breath to compose herself, then pushed open the door, abandoned her overnight bag, dropped to her knees and opened her arms for Aidan and Hattie to run into. She hugged them close, murmuring endearments, burying her face in their Johnson's-scented hair and generally doing anything and everything she could to avoid making eye contact with Greg, who had followed the children out into the hall. Eventually, though, she couldn't procrastinate any longer. She stood up, lifting Hattie on to her hip, where she nestled in, twining strands of Ella's hair around her fingers. Aidan wrapped his arms around his mother's legs, fastening her to the spot.

Smiling ruefully, Ella finally allowed herself to glance at her husband. He looked so familiar: slightly tired smile, faded jeans, a T-shirt he'd owned since uni days. And he was standing under a lavishly glittered 'Welcome Home Mummy' banner, smiling at her warmly.

'Do I get a hug too?' he asked as he stepped forward.

They kissed awkwardly, the distance between them only partially attributable to the toddler-sized physical barriers.

A few minutes later, curled up on the sofa in their large kitchen-diner, cup of tea in hand, Ella allowed herself to feel a little more relaxed. Here, where everything was just as it always had been, she felt just as she always had, and it was so much easier to see the last twenty-four hours as a mad aberration – almost something that had happened in a film she'd watched – rather than events in which she'd been an active, enthusiastic participant.

The children had already lost interest in the novelty of her return and were crawling round the floor squabbling over pieces of a Duplo castle.

'So, have you all been OK without me, then?'

Greg grinned.

'*We've* been OK, but there have been some seriously dramatic goings-on.'

Ella felt a slight flutter of guilt and apprehension, and then chided herself inwardly for being ridiculous. Greg couldn't possibly know about her 'goings-on', and if he did he would hardly raise the subject in so casual a fashion. She forced a similarly light-hearted note into her own voice.

'Wow, sounds exciting. What's happened?'

Greg's smile faded.

'Actually, exciting probably isn't the word. It looks as though Pete's left Imogen.'

Ella spluttered as a mouthful of tea went down the wrong way.

'Oh my God! What happened? Hang on, Indigo had an accident, she's been in hospital – how can Pete have dumped Immy?'

Greg shrugged.

'I don't know, really. It all seems a bit complicated, but I think Pete caused the accident somehow, and they had a big row about it. I went to collect Immy and Indigo from the hospital this morning, and looked after Indy for a while this afternoon, 'cos Immy was in a bit of a state.'

'Bloody hell.'

Ella was overwhelmed by fresh waves of guilt. Useless friend, as well as callous mother and unfaithful wife. And even more selfishly, her first feeling, though it was quashed almost instantly with sympathy for Imogen, was that now she wouldn't be able to share her own problems with her friend, because it would be all about Imogen and Pete.

She shivered slightly, looking at Greg sitting there, kind and thoughtful and dependable, and contrasted that with Imogen's situation. She smiled warmly at him, got up and dropped a kiss on the top of his head.

He looked surprised and pleased – spontaneous gestures of affection from Ella had been pretty much non-existent recently.

'You are a sweetie to look after Imogen, thank you.'

He shrugged.

'Anyone would have done it.'

'No.' Ella shook her head, adamantly. 'Anyone wouldn't. In fact, even Imogen's own partner didn't. You're lovely, and I'm really grateful. Anyway, I should go and see her, I guess. Do you mind if I go out this evening?'

He stood up and put his arms around her. She tensed before letting herself relax into his embrace and then returning it.

'No, of course I don't mind. I told Immy you'd be round. Do you want to do bath-time first, though?'

Ella nodded.

'Have they had tea? Great, right then, come on kiddi-winks, let's have a race upstairs. 1 – 2 – 3 – GO!'

Even though she was completely exhausted, emotionally drained and still fighting the lingering remnants of a hangover, Ella enjoyed the ritual of bath-time. During the normal working week she'd find herself dreading it, nursing an increasing resentment towards Greg for not being home in time to share the burden and resentment towards the children for arguing, messing, not settling, keeping her from the glass of cold white wine that seemed to start calling her name earlier and earlier these days. Now though, after a night away, she could appreciate it once again; and because she was Fun Mummy, blowing bubbles and raspberries and splashing, rather than Nagging Mummy, trying to reduce the bath experience to the bare minimum cleanliness required, the children were giggly and cuddly rather than whiny and demanding.

After a run-through of Julia Donaldson's greatest hits, the children were both snuggled down looking completely angelic, and Ella found herself wondering, not for the first time, if the fact that she experienced her most overwhelming feelings of love for her children when they were asleep made her a bad mother. She was certainly a grateful one – their unexpectedly early sleepiness meant that she had time to grab a quick shower and pull on a warm and comforting jumper dress in ultra-soft grey wool, some leggings and her flat slouchy boots. With her face washed clean of make-up and the grey-tinged hangover finally receding to reveal her usual rosy glow, she felt much more her normal self.

When she went downstairs, Greg was waiting for her. He handed her a bottle of Pinot Grigio, a large bag of Kettle Chips and a family-sized bar of Dairy Milk.

'I picked these up on the way home for you to take with you tonight – never say I don't know the way to a girl's heart! And I've booked you a cab, it should be here in five minutes.'

He was trying so hard. Had been trying for weeks, probably, but Ella had been too self-absorbed to notice. All she could think of was what he'd said to her when she tried to seduce him with the idea of a third baby.

'No way, Ella. Absolutely no way. It's not just that *I* don't want a third baby, although God knows I could do without the sleepless nights and the cost, but it wouldn't be good for you.'

She'd shouted at him then, asked how he dared to presume he knew what was best for her better than she knew herself.

He'd replied calmly, 'Because I know *you*. You're not happy now, Ella, and it's because you've got no focus, no direction. It wouldn't matter to me if you *wanted* to be a full-time mum, that's the right thing for lots of women, but I don't think it is for you. Something's making you miserable, and I don't want to believe it's me. I think it's the fact that you don't feel fulfilled, but you don't know what would fulfil you, and you're scared. And now you've decided that if you have another baby you can put off thinking about it for a while, but it won't work.'

She had been furious, irate. She'd called him insulting, patronising, sexist, cruel, heartless. Everything she could think of. And he'd taken it coolly enough, but she knew, deep down, that throwing the most hurtful things she could think of at him had had an effect. She was always the overtly emotional one; when she lost her temper she would stamp and shout and throw things and cry, and she'd done all that and more. Greg was quieter, hardly ever vocalised his feelings and had made stoicism into an art form, but he was actually very sensitive underneath it all. When he was hurt he would simply withdraw, and that was what he'd done after this argument. Normally after the initial flash of anger she would revert to being her usual self and coax Greg out of his sulks, but this time she just hadn't had the willpower to do so.

Instead, it was probably Greg who'd come round first and started making friendly overtures to her. Perhaps that would have worked, and their usual equilibrium would have been restored, but with dreadful timing her period had started, and this oh-so-tangible reminder that she wasn't having the baby she suddenly desperately wanted had sent her off into another rage, icily cold this time, and she had rejected Greg's attempts at reconciliation out of hand.

Now, though, guilt and regret blended to make her feel a sudden overwhelming affection for her husband. She went and hugged him tightly.

'I do love you, you know.'

Greg smiled down at her.

'I know, sweetheart. And I love you too.'

The warmth of his body and strength of his arms triggered a small jolt of lust in her; a pale shadow of what she had felt for Callum, but nonetheless she ran her hands over her husband's bottom in a speculative fashion. His hold on her tightened, he bent his head as though to kiss her, but then the moment was interrupted by an insistent tooting from the minicab outside, and regretfully Ella loosened his grip, grabbed her coat and her goodies and headed for the door.

'I'll be back by elevenish, I hope. I don't want to be too late tonight.'

She blew him a kiss and left her warm, snug house for a cold, rainy evening and an overwhelming scent of synthetic pine, courtesy of the minicab driver's air freshener. As she sank back into the faux-leather her phone bleeped to let her know that she had a text message. She was expecting it to be Imogen, but instead it was Callum:

I've just left Liz. Staying with a friend for a few days while get sorted. Was pretty grim telling Phoebe, but I feel better now than I have for years. Thank you for showing me that there's another way. Can we talk soon? Callum

Ella read the message through three times before pressing delete. She felt more confused, guilty and bewildered than ever.

14

As Imogen ran round the living room, gathering up piles of newspapers, tracking down dirty cups, plumping cushions, there was a knock on the door.

Damn, Ella was early, and the place still looked a tip. Oh well, Ella would understand, would probably help her clear up.

She flung the door open, still holding a week's worth of newspapers she intended to put straight into the recycling bin outside. She was about to launch into a combined explanation and apology when she glanced up and saw that the tall figure in the doorway was most definitely not Ella. Her overtired synapses connected sufficiently for her to recognise Alex, and she blushed. He was shifting from one foot to the other in an uncomfortable way, then made a move as though to kiss her cheek but was thwarted by the pile of papers.

'Hi, Alex. Sorry, I was just on my way to dump these papers . . .' She gestured with her chin in the direction of the big wheelie bin for recyclable waste.

'Oh right, yeah, sorry, I'm in the way.' He moved to one side but, flustered, Imogen moved that way too and they spent a moment in an awkward parody of a dance before Imogen made it to the bin. The evening air cooled her hot cheeks and she took a couple of deep breaths, trying to work out why she felt so nervous.

Alex was still hovering on the doorstep, so she gathered her wits and her manners and asked him in, murmuring automatic apologies about the untidiness of the living room.

'I've brought your bike back.' He waved his arm. 'It's in the car, shall I get it?'

'Oh that would be great, thank you, I really appreciate it. Can I get you a drink while you do?'

He smiled a little shyly.

'Wouldn't say no to a cup of tea. If you don't mind. I mean, if you're not busy.'

'Oh no. I mean, my friend's coming round in a bit but, erm, no.'

He took on a slightly crestfallen air.

'Oh, if you've got a friend coming round then I won't stay. I'll just grab the bike and leave you to it.'

Imogen flushed again. Suddenly it was very important to her that Alex didn't just vanish.

'No, no, please stay and have a cuppa. It's the least I can do. I mean, after everything you've done. And my friend won't be here for another half an hour or so.'

'OK then.' His smile was warm and genuine this time. 'Milk, no sugar, nice and strong, please.'

He pulled the door shut behind him, leaving her to make the tea, slowly and thoughtfully. Yesterday, even though he was almost a complete stranger, she had felt totally relaxed with him and he had made the whole ordeal of Indigo's injury a hundred times easier to cope with. Now, she didn't even seem to be able to achieve the level of conversational ease she managed effortlessly with old ladies at the bus stop, or people who served her in shops. She felt flustered, on edge. The problem was that without the dramatic intensity of the hospital setting she felt she couldn't resume the same level of easy intimacy, but having had that she couldn't easily return to the friendly but unemotional register she would normally use for parents of Indigo's friends. Maybe it had been a terrible mistake, asking him in. Oh well, she reflected, at least Ella should arrive to rescue her before too long.

In actual fact, though, the knock on the door that announced Ella's arrival proved to be a disappointment. It had only taken a few minutes for the sense of awkwardness to dissipate totally and Imogen and Alex had begun chatting again like old friends. They seemed to have covered an amazing amount of ground as well – careers, life and relationship histories, feelings about parenthood. It was one of those conversations where neither of you seems to be able to talk quickly enough to convey all the information; where you can't wait to hear what your companion will say next. All Imogen's tiredness and anxiety seemed to have lifted and she realised that she couldn't remember the last time she'd enjoyed a conversation this much. So when they were interrupted by Ella, Imogen's initial reaction was one of guilty disappointment.

Alex immediately stood up, saying that he must be going. He kissed her cheek gently and she flushed yet again, murmured something disjointed, and opened the door to her friend.

Ella had been expecting a tearful and distraught reception, had been prepared to administer copious amounts of wine, chocolate and sympathy and to selflessly put aside her own personal crisis to offer both shoulders for crying on. What she had not been prepared for was Imogen to look glowing – almost radiant – or for the presence of a handsome stranger. Ella felt slightly wrong-footed, unsure how to proceed. She looked from the man to Imogen and back again and raised her eyebrows pointedly.

Imogen flushed deeper as she caught Ella's look of slight disapproval.

'This is Alex. Alex, my friend Ella. Alex was just dropping my bike off, he helped me out when Indy had her accident yesterday.'

For some reason, Ella's own far-from-clear conscience made her want to prick at Imogen's. Granted, her (newly single) friend had been enjoying a quiet cup of tea with a Good Samaritan, whereas she'd been re-enacting some of the less painful scenes of *Fifty Shades of Grey* while her innocent husband looked after their children, but somehow Ella felt she wanted to tar Imogen with the same brush.

'You're a quick worker, Immy! When did Pete leave?'

Imogen frowned, unsure why Ella was being so uncharacteristically difficult.

'I think you've got hold of the wrong end of the stick,' she said gently. 'Alex is the dad of a friend of Indigo's from nursery, he happened to be passing when Indy had her accident and he's been very helpful, but that's all there is to it.' She turned to Alex.

'Thank you so much again, for everything. I'm so grateful. I'll see you at nursery, I guess, on Tuesday?'

He nodded.

'Yes, I'll see you on Tuesday. And it's no trouble at all, I'm glad I could help, and that Indigo is OK.' He smiled at Ella. 'Nice to meet you, Ella. Have a good evening.'

And then he was gone, leaving nothing but a half-drunk cup of tea and a slightly uncomfortable silence between the two women.

They stood and looked at each other for a moment, Imogen with a calm dignity that made Ella feel ashamed and regretful.

'How is Indigo?' she asked at last.

Imogen's features relaxed into a relieved smile.

'She's OK, thank God. She's got a broken arm, but it's a straightforward greenstick fracture, they said, and shouldn't cause any problems in future. And the concussion is very mild. But, God, when I think what could have happened . . .' She closed her eyes, in a vain attempt to blot out the picture of Indigo's tumble from the bike, but it was no use. She started shaking and tears crept out from under her closed eyelids.

Ella breathed her own sigh of relief. This was more what she had expected, more what she felt she could cope with. She took Imogen in her arms, murmuring soft reassurances to her, just as she would Aidan or Harriet. She stroked her pink woollen back until she felt the sobs subside slightly, and then she led her to the armchair, sat her down and tucked the bright crocheted throw from the arm around her.

'Hang on, I'll be back in a second.'

Ella went quickly into Imogen's kitchen, which she knew as well as her own, and grabbed two wine glasses.

Thankfully the bottle Greg had bought was a screw-top, and she wrenched off the cap before pouring two generous glasses. More alcohol probably wasn't the best idea for her after the excesses of the night before, but she needed something.

Imogen had stopped crying, and took the glass and a grateful gulp.

'Sorry about that. I thought I was all cried out.'

Ella shook her head.

'Don't be silly, you've nothing to be sorry about. I'm sorry you're having such a rough time, you poor thing. All the worry of Indigo's accident, and then Pete walking out. Bastard.'

Imogen smiled faintly.

'Yep, pretty much textbook bastardism. But, do you know what? I really don't want to talk about him now. It's been such a mental twenty-four hours, I just can't think straight. I need to get a good night's sleep, and then I can try and process what's happened. Let's talk about you instead. Did you have a good time in Liverpool? Your hair looks fab, by the way. What awful thing have you done?'

Imogen glanced across at her friend, ready to be entertained by a tale of too much money spent shopping, or too many cocktails drunk. To say she wasn't expecting what followed would be an understatement.

Ella took a deep breath. She knew, rationally, that the fewer people who knew about her and Callum the better – Janey, of course, was well aware, and had been amused and somewhat impressed by Ella's uncharacteristic wildness. But the seductive appeal of confession was too strong. She thought for a moment, composing her story, deciding how best to explain her spectacular fall from grace.

'I met someone. A guy who was one of my teachers in sixth form, who I had the biggest crush on. Seriously, he was the love of my life.'

Imogen smiled.

'At eighteen! What was he like now? He must be quite a bit older than you, is he bald and paunchy?'

Ella allowed herself to wish, for a brief moment, that Callum *had* grown old and fat. But the idea was so far from the truth that it seemed ludicrous.

'No – unfortunately. He's still absolutely bloody gorgeous.'

Imogen still wasn't getting it.

'Ooh, sounds like someone still has a little crush! Did you talk to him?'

Ella was exasperated.

'I didn't just talk to him, Imogen, I slept with him! That's the awful thing.'

Imogen paused, her expression of teasing amusement freezing, then fading, as she realised that Ella was serious.

Ella sat tensely, waiting for she hardly knew what. Empathy? Approval? Forgiveness? Although Imogen wasn't the person she had wronged, Ella felt obscurely that if she could make her understand what had compelled her to behave in such an outrageously immoral and out of character way, then that would provide some kind of vindication or justification. However, judging by the look of mounting anger on Imogen's face she wasn't going to get it.

'You did *what*? Please tell me you're joking, Ella?'

Ella shook her head, almost imperceptibly.

'Oh my good God. You stupid, stupid girl. What the bloody hell do you think you're playing at?'

A cold, sick feeling developed in the pit of Ella's stomach. She tried to summon some anger of her own to help her.

'You don't understand, Immy. I loved him so much, I don't think I ever got over him, really. And things with Greg have just been horribly difficult recently, and Callum treated me like a person, like a woman, not just a household function . . .' Her voice tailed off as she heard the clichés spouting. It was impossible to convey the depths of passion and longing that had swept her along last night, especially to a sceptical audience.

Imogen was not impressed by the faltering explanation. She was staring at her as though she disgusted her.

'You stupid girl,' she repeated. 'Honestly, Ella, you might have met the person you imagined yourself in love with when you were a teenager, but you're not a teenager now, you're a grown-up, a mother, and you have responsibilities. You also have a lovely, loving husband, and if things have been difficult between you recently then it's probably because you've been making them difficult, treating Greg like dirt.'

Ella got to her feet, stumbling slightly, desperately trying to hold back the tears.

'I can't believe this! You're meant to be my friend, Imogen. If I can't talk to you, who can I talk to?'

Imogen still had that look of icy disdain.

'You don't want a friend, Ella. You want a mirror. And it strikes me that's been the main problem with you and

Greg, too. He dared to disagree with you. I don't want to get into who's right or wrong about you having another baby, that's just for the two of you, and there are obviously pros and cons, but you've gone off in a fit of pique and slept with another man just because your husband didn't automatically fall in with your wishes, and that makes you seem like a spoilt child.'

Ella couldn't speak through the ache in her throat. Her pride was hurting too much to admit any truth in what Imogen was saying, and all she could think of was putting distance between them.

'Fine,' she eventually managed to choke out as she made her way to the door. 'Thanks for your understanding. I just hope now that you can treat this as the confidence it was intended to be, despite your disgust for me as a friend and a person.'

Imogen put out an arm towards Ella to try to stop her.

'Oh come on, Ella. Sit back down. Of course I'm your friend, yours *and* Greg's, and I just can't bear to watch you doing something that will hurt both of you, and the kids—'

But she got no further. Ella had whirled round and vanished into the night, slamming the door behind her.

15

Ella stumbled down the street with hot, angry, guilty tears pouring down her cheeks. She sank down on a conveniently placed, although rather damp, garden wall at the end of Imogen's road and considered her options.

She could phone a cab and go straight home, manufacturing some kind of explanation for Greg as to why her evening out had been curtailed. She could find a pub and sit with her book for a couple of hours before returning home at the expected time. Or, a little thought-gremlin whispered, she could use the time to phone Callum as he'd asked. Surely she owed him that much, she reasoned to herself. A proper conversation to end whatever it was they'd started. After all, she couldn't leave things as they were, and when else would she get a chance for a proper talk?

Without giving herself time to consider further, she took out her phone and dialled.

Callum answered within a couple of rings.

'Ella. I'm so glad you've phoned.'

'Hi. Where are you at the moment?'

He laughed ruefully.

'I'm hanging round outside my mate's house. I haven't exactly got much privacy, so when I saw it was you I slipped out.'

Ella laughed as well.

'Snap! I'm sitting on a very cold and uncomfortable wall at the end of my friend's road. I was meant to be spending the evening with her, but we had, shall we say, a bit of a disagreement, so I thought I'd use this window to call you.'

'I'm so glad you did. It's been quite a day, hasn't it?'

Ella could feel her buttocks going numb, so she stood up and began walking as she listened to Callum's description of his conversations with Liz and Phoebe. Her heart ached for him as she heard his voice thicken with tears when he recounted Phoebe's reaction. Any memory that this conversation was meant to be about ending their fledgling relationship vanished as she sympathised, advised and counselled. As he started to sound more positive, she launched into a graphic description of her argument with Imogen and now it was his turn to console her.

Mutually comforted, they moved on to more neutral topics, the time flying as they shared stories and anecdotes and got to know each other better and better. At one point Ella glanced down at her watch and saw to her amazement that over an hour had passed. Thankfully the rain had stopped before she'd left Imogen's, but she was freezing cold and wished fervently that they were curled up on a comfortable sofa together rather than pacing cold and solitary streets.

She sighed, and Callum, sensitive to her change of mood, asked instantly, 'What's the matter, Ella?'

She was about to respond and then realised that if she was about to break things off, then confessing she wished they were sharing a sofa was hardly the best way to start. Of course, sharing eighty minutes of conversation that flowed seamlessly from the deep and meaningful to the light and sparkling probably hadn't been the best way either, but she couldn't do anything about that now.

'Oh, Callum.' She paused, weighted down with misery. Never in her whole life had she felt so torn. 'Callum. We can't do this. I'm married. I'm happily married. I have children. Last night shouldn't have happened, and nothing else can happen. We can't talk again after this.'

Callum's heavy silence crossed two hundred miles. He had been leaning against a garden fence, but he straightened up at this point and prepared to fight for his happiness. And her happiness; he had to believe that. He pictured her – all curves and sweetness, but with that razor-sharp intelligence and wit just below the surface, and the warmth and compassion that stopped her ironic take on things slipping into bitterness. No, he wasn't going to let her go.

'Ella. Darling, darling Ella.'

Her heart turned over at the intensity in his voice. She knew that having said her piece she should hang up, but she couldn't.

'This is messy and difficult, and God knows I wish we could have met in different circumstances, but we didn't. This is the hand we've been dealt, and we have to find a way through somehow. But, hand on heart, can you honestly say you never want us to see each other again?'

It wasn't a rhetorical question; he paused, waiting for her answer. And she couldn't lie to him.

'No,' she whispered at last. 'No, I can't say that's what I want, but we don't have a choice.'

'But sweetheart, we do. There's always a choice. I know you have children, but they'll be OK. I'll do anything, everything to make you and them happy. And honestly, it's better for children to have parents who are happy apart rather than miserable together. Believe me, I wish I'd seen that more clearly years ago.'

'Callum, my marriage isn't like yours and Liz's. We're not unhappy. I love Greg. We're good together.' As she spoke she wondered, briefly, who she was trying to convince.

Callum tried to ignore the dart of pain it gave him to hear her declare her love for another man.

'Thing is, Ella, if you love Greg, if you and he are so happy, what were you doing in bed with me last night? What are you doing spending an hour and a half with me on the phone now, wandering the streets, rather than going home to the husband you claim to love?'

It was, thought Ella, a bloody good question, and the answer did not spring immediately to mind.

Callum sensed his advantage and followed up on it.

'You're not that kind of person, Ella. You're not the kind of woman to cheat on her husband, carelessly, meaninglessly, just because. I *know* you. It meant something to you.'

Ella didn't know where to go with this. He was right. She had never cheated on anyone in her life before, had never in her wildest imaginings thought that she ever would.

'God, Callum. I can't deny that I'm attracted to you. I can't really explain what happened last night. It was just like a compulsion. But it's lust, at the end of the day. And that's all well and good if I was single, but I'm not. It doesn't mean anything other than we had a strong mutual attraction, which we should never have acted on. It's not a reason to ruin my husband's and my children's lives.'

She sounded more determined than she felt, and Callum was hit by a wave of despair. Maybe he should tread more softly now.

'It's not just lust. And I think you know that deep down. But I'm not going to pressure you into doing something you don't want to do. Maybe we should say goodnight now. But I can't promise, I won't promise, not to contact you again.'

Of course now, perversely, Ella felt disappointed. She didn't want to stop talking to Callum. It wasn't as good as seeing him, being in his arms, being in bed with him, but it was better than nothing. And she had been anticipating an impassioned declaration of love, not this seemingly calm acceptance of her decision. However, she could scarcely say as much.

'OK. You're right. Goodnight.' She managed to stop herself adding 'my darling', but he could hear the love and longing in her tone and felt encouraged once again.

'Goodnight, lovely Ella. We'll talk again soon.'

On a cold, dark street in Walthamstow, east London, Ella dialled a cab and prepared to return home to her unsuspecting husband.

On a cold, dark street in Mossley Hill, south Liverpool, Callum tucked his phone into his pocket and let himself back into his temporary home. He was well aware that there were significant challenges ahead, but that awareness did nothing to quench the spark of hopeful happiness inside him.

Perhaps he would have felt less positive if he could have seen his daughter. Just a few streets away from where Callum was settling into the narrow single bed in a tiny box room, Phoebe was still lying curled in the foetal position in her attic bedroom.

She had locked her door after Callum left, and was determined not to leave her room, knowing that she just couldn't cope with seeing her mother that evening. Dinner had therefore consisted of a family-sized bag of crisps and a handful of chocolate bars, chomped mechanically and largely untastingly. She was all cried out, but couldn't stop shivering, so she pulled on some thick fleecy pyjamas and curled up miserably on the bed, wrapping around herself a thick blanket knitted for her by her grandmother.

Even though she was completely drained and exhausted, sleep just wouldn't come. Her mind was spinning, replaying scenes from the past couple of days – her row with her mum, her parents' argument in the Lake District and their overheard conversation that afternoon, and then her final talk with Callum before he left. She was also desperately trying to think of solutions that didn't involve her having to live on her own with Liz, but was no closer to finding them.

Her rational self knew that her threats to go to Becky's were not going to happen. She was pretty confident Becky wouldn't mind, but she also knew that, however fond of her Mr and Mrs Stein may be, there was no way they would allow her to move in with them against the wishes of her parents. And her most optimistic assessment of the situation couldn't see a feasible way of her sharing Tony's spare room with her dad. So she lay awake, turning various schemes over in her mind, praying to wake up the following morning and find the whole nightmare had been a dream.

★　★　★

A few days later, Phoebe was in very much the same position, having got up, gone to school, then returned straight home to put on her pyjamas and lock herself in. Two floors below, Liz was seeking oblivion in a bottle of vodka. Never normally a heavy drinker – she was very well aware of the deleterious effects it had on the skin and the figure – she nonetheless felt that there were some situations that called for a stiffener, and your husband of nearly twenty years walking out on you surely had to count as one of these. She'd phoned a couple of her friends and had enjoyed the obligatory 'all men are bastards' conversations. Of course, they'd offered to come round and keep her company, but she'd declined, saying that she needed to be there for Phoebe.

In actual fact she had only made the most cursory attempts to talk to her daughter since Callum left. Once or twice she'd gone upstairs, knocked softly and called Phoebe's name through the door. There had been no response and she had hesitated each time, before telling herself that Phoebe was probably asleep and that there was nothing to be gained by waking her. She wasn't disappointed, feeling that her self-esteem had received a serious enough blow recently; she wasn't sure she could cope with the hostility Phoebe would undoubtedly spew at her when they finally spoke, and, in fact, she had gone out of her way to make sure that she stayed in bed until Phoebe had left for school each morning and that she wasn't around at the time she was due home.

She was feeling completely shell-shocked. Although under no illusions about the happiness of her marriage, she had never actually envisaged it coming to an end, had not wanted it to come to an end. It wasn't Callum himself she wanted, it was the status of marriage – being single in your forties was no joke. Callum might not be her dream man, but she considered herself too old for dreaming and he was attractive, presentable and solvent. She enjoyed the lifestyle of a married woman and his steady, if not stellar, income enabled her to live in a comfortable house in an area she liked, without having to worry too much about the erratic nature of her own earnings. She didn't want to be a single parent in the least, acknowledged, if only to herself, that she felt completely out of her depth with Phoebe, but she had never thought it would come to that. Merely threatening to withhold Callum's access to his daughter had always been enough to bring him to heel in the past, and now that had changed she was unsure what cards she had left to play.

Just as Liz was reflecting on the inevitability of her being the guilty party in Phoebe's eyes – after all, it couldn't be her precious father – the doorbell rang. Liz didn't bother getting up – after all, there was no one she wanted to see right now – and after a short pause, Callum let himself in with his key.

His lip curled rather scornfully when he saw the bottle of vodka on the table next to Liz. He guessed that Phoebe would be upstairs on her own and it irritated him that Liz would rather sit here indulging in her own self-pity than make an attempt to reach out to her daughter.

Liz barely looked at him. On Sunday she had been convinced, or at least had pretended to be convinced, that moving out was just grandstanding on Callum's part. Seventy-two hours later this certainty had ebbed away and she was trying to force herself to contemplate a very uncertain future.

Callum was the first to speak.

'Hi. I've just come back to collect some more clothes and a few bits and pieces. Is Phoebe OK?'

Liz shrugged.

'Define "OK". Her father's just abandoned her, but other than that she's fine.'

Callum gritted his teeth, already exasperated when he'd only been in the same room as Liz for a matter of moments.

'Don't start, Liz. I haven't abandoned Phoebe, I never will. You're the one who's threatening not to let me see her. I've just called time on our farce of a marriage. Can you really and truly say you've been happy all this time?'

Liz paused. Instinctively she wanted to go on the attack again, complain that they'd been perfectly happy until Callum left, but some strange compulsion drew her into an unplanned and unfamiliar honesty.

'No,' she admitted. 'No, it hasn't been easy, for a long time.'

Callum sat down opposite her. She still wouldn't meet his eyes, and instead looked down at her hands as she twisted and untwisted her fingers.

'Where did we go wrong?' he asked softly.

She hesitated.

'When Phoebe was born, I suppose.' She continued quickly before he could interrupt her. 'I never really wanted a baby. I did it because that's what you did, what everyone was doing, but it wasn't really what I wanted. And although I loved her, I do love her, you know, I've just never felt that comfortable as a mother. I wanted to make a success of my modelling career, and they didn't seem compatible. And it was so hard when she was a baby, stuck in the house all day with her crying – and then you'd walk through the door and pick her up, and she was suddenly all smiles. It's always been like that. You two adore each other, and I'm the odd one out. I never feel you make any effort to include me.'

Callum was silent. It was years since he'd heard Liz talk so honestly, with such evident emotion. Suddenly, he could see something of her point of view. He'd been so used to blaming her, for being difficult and cold and emotionally closed, that he'd never really stopped to consider how his own behaviour could have contributed. He couldn't feel regretful, not now, with the tantalising image of a new life with Ella before him, but he did feel sad that it had taken them fifteen years to have this conversation.

'So why did you stay, then?' he asked, eventually.

'I don't know. Security. Stability. It's not like I wanted anyone else.' She looked at him. 'I've never wanted to leave you for anyone else, Callum. Not for want of offers, and I guess there's been the odd – moment, shall we say, but I've never been in love with anyone else. I suppose I didn't see the point in disrupting all our lives for no real purpose. I mean, who's *really* happy, anyway?'

It had never occurred to Callum that Liz might have cheated on him. Typical male arrogance, he supposed. Suddenly, he wished she had overtly admitted to an affair: that would have meant he could have an entirely clear conscience about his own feelings for Ella, both now and all those years ago.

'Have *you* met someone else?' Liz was asking him now. 'Is that why this sudden change?'

He hesitated, fatally, trying to compose an answer that was both truthful and conciliatory. Unfortunately, when your wife asks you if you've cheated on her the only acceptable response is 'No, of course not' within a split second of the question leaving her mouth. When Callum failed to answer immediately, Liz put her own correct interpretation on his hesitation and suddenly the relative calm of their discussion was over.

She glared at him, eyes narrowed with disgust.

'I see. All this rhetoric about our unhappy marriage, but like a typical man you only actually do anything about it when you want to shag someone else. Well, Phoebe's going to love this, isn't she? Not only has her father abandoned her, but she's being replaced as number one in his affections by some bimbo.'

The fleeting sympathy Callum had felt for Liz vanished instantly.

'It's nothing like that, and you bloody know it. Nothing and no one could replace Phoebe for me, as you're well aware. Don't you dare even hint that to her!'

Liz poured herself another generous measure of vodka and smiled sweetly at Callum.

'Don't dare? And who exactly, my dear husband, is going to stop me?'

16

Imogen opened her eyes slowly and stretched. It was several weeks since her long-term partner had abandoned her to life as a single mother and during that time she had received one brief text message from him, and no communication at all from her so-called best friend. It would have been easy to turn her back on the world in self-pity, but that was a luxury she couldn't afford. She still had to go to work and present an interested, interesting, vibrant front to her class of exuberant Year 1s and their parents. She still had to cook and launder and clean and shop. She still had to care for her daughter, with all the stories and cuddles and mess that entailed. In other words, she had to get on with things and not indulge in anything as selfish as feelings.

It was hard going, although in many practical ways Pete's absence hadn't had much impact on their day-to-day routine. Imogen had known on one level that Pete didn't contribute much to the running of the household or childcare; this time without him had demonstrated that her workload was exactly the same, just with fewer dirty socks and overflowing ashtrays. Imogen still had to get up at 6 a.m. to get herself showered and dressed and ready for school before Indigo woke up at 6.30. Then the mad dash to drop Indigo at nursery and get herself into school by 8.15 a.m., trying her best to avoid the head teacher, who felt staff should be in by 8 a.m. at the latest. And then rushing after school to make sure that Indigo wasn't the last child at nursery, incurring psychological scars in the long term and crippling fines in the short term.

The one bright spot on her horizon was Alex. She smiled to herself as she thought of him. He understood the pressures of being a single parent, of always being the responsible one. His daughter, Molly, was the same age as Indigo and he had been managing almost entirely by himself since she was six months old. His wife had walked out, saying that she felt stifled and trapped by marriage and motherhood. Alex suspected she was suffering from post-natal depression, but he had been completely unable to reach her, or to persuade her to have a relationship with her daughter. In fact, they'd had no communication whatsoever for six months, and she didn't see her daughter during that time. Just after Molly's first birthday she'd got back in touch; asked if she could see her. Alex had been initially reluctant, terrified that she would disappear again and break Molly's heart, but she had eventually persuaded him. Their marriage had been damaged beyond repair, but after a lot of talk and compromise they hammered out a co-parenting strategy that worked for them. Molly spent Saturday afternoon to Monday evening at her mum's, and lived with Alex for the rest of the week. So he really understood what it was like, managing on your own.

Alex and Imogen got on incredibly well together, and Molly and Indigo were each other's new best friends, so, although it was only a few weeks since Alex had really come into her life, the four of them had already fallen into a comfortable routine. At least twice a week they would all eat together in one or the other's house after they'd picked the girls up from nursery, and they'd had a couple of Saturday morning visits to the park.

The girls were begging to be allowed a sleepover, and Alex seemed keen as well, but Imogen had reservations. She didn't feel comfortable about Indigo spending the night away from her, especially after her accident and all the disruption of her father's departure. But neither did she feel entirely happy about spending the night in Alex's spare room. He had taken great pains to emphasise that it would be the spare room, and she certainly wasn't afraid that he was going to try to seduce her. The thought of spending a relaxed evening in Alex's warm and friendly living room, maybe sharing a bottle of wine, being able to talk properly without the children interrupting, well, that was more than appealing. In fact, maybe part of the problem was that she was scared to admit how appealing it was.

Within forty-eight hours of Pete leaving she had decided that he wasn't coming back, even if he wanted to. She had been unhappy with their relationship for a very long time and had only held off taking any action because she felt that Indigo needed a family; that an inadequate father was better than no father. Now she had completely changed her mind. It wasn't just that Pete's irresponsibility had put Indigo's life at risk, although she could still feel the bile rising in her throat when she thought about that. Nor was it the fact that he had then tried to blame her for their subsequent argument. No, it was a realisation that Pete was never going to take his parental responsibilities seriously, and that at some point he would walk away from them entirely. She suddenly had an overwhelming conviction that it was far better for Indigo to grow up used to having a loving and stable relationship with her mother, and a more casual and ad hoc relationship with her father, than for Imogen and Pete to paper over the cracks and pretend to be a family only for the whole house of cards to come tumbling down, perhaps at a time when Indigo would be even more upset by it than she would be now. In fact, the impact on Indigo so far seemed to be minimal; Pete had been such an insubstantial presence in her life there wasn't really much for her to miss.

At this point in her thoughts, Imogen glanced at the illuminated figures on her alarm clock. 5.58 a.m. She must have been awake for over half an hour already, running through the same thoughts, which seemed to be on an endless loop these days. She needed to get up and get ready. One of the main reasons for the treadmill nature of her life was the fact that she lived in London. That meant firstly that rents were sky-high and there was no possibility of her ever being able to buy her own place, and secondly that the commute to and from school via Indigo's nursery took the best part of an hour, so she was permanently chasing her tail and barely got the chance to spend any time with Indigo during the week. But what if she moved? It was only a couple of weeks ago that this circuit-breaking thought had occurred to her. It had never been an option when she was with Pete. He loved London and city life as only an escapee from a small village can, and there was no way he would ever have considered moving. But now? She only had herself and Indigo to please. She had applied for a couple of jobs, and reflected on the possibilities they offered as she showered. The more she considered it, all the time she shampooed her hair and shaved her legs, the more the idea had to recommend it. She would move back up to Yorkshire, where her family lived. Housing was so much more affordable there; she might even be able to buy a small house or flat of her own. Her parents would help out with childcare. They'd be by the sea and a few minutes' drive from beautiful countryside. By the time she was dry and dressed, Imogen was on the point of booking the removals van.

While Imogen was lying in bed thinking, Ella was already up and out, jogging. She seemed to have a limitless supply of energy at the moment and was making the most of it by setting her alarm for 5.30 a.m., pulling on scuzzy old leggings, a moth-eaten T-shirt and some trainers and going straight out for a run. She could run for half an hour through the peaceful, undisturbed springtime morning before getting home to grab a quick shower before Hattie and Aidan (and Greg) were awake and demanding breakfast.

Being already awake, dressed and ready for the day by the time the children woke up made a huge difference as well. Instead of four separate bowls of cereal being consumed at different times, hers generally standing up while she loaded the dishwasher, she was setting the table the night before and all four of them were eating together. Sometimes Ella was sufficiently organised to boil eggs for everyone, and then they really did look like the perfect 1950s family, going to work on an egg. She and Greg had a chance to chat about their plans for the day before he left for work, and the children were much better behaved sitting eating with both parents.

After Greg left for work she would be bubbly and fun, keeping the children in fits of giggles and making the process of getting them washed and dressed much less painful. After they'd dropped Aidan off at playgroup she would take Hattie to the swings, to storytime at the library or to the mums and toddlers group. When she had both children again in the afternoon she'd arrange play dates, or take them to soft play, or brave the Tube into town to take them to the Science Museum.

Not surprisingly, the children were relishing this new improved mummy and consequently were much easier; Ella felt that she could actually enjoy them. After a couple of years in the shadows Ella was living in glorious Technicolor, and she couldn't understand why she had found her life quite so difficult and demanding before. After the children were in bed she'd pour herself a glass of wine and potter happily round the kitchen rediscovering her Nigella and Jamie books, instead of slumping on the sofa and calling Greg to grab a takeaway on his way home. Sometimes she even stayed awake for the ten o'clock news.

Just a couple of weeks of this new lifestyle had caused her to drop a few pounds and, according to the numerous compliments she was receiving from her various mummy friends, she was positively glowing. Even her house looked like the Ikea adverts – gleaming surfaces, plumped cushions, vases of fresh flowers. How ironic that it had taken a night of wild passionate sex with another man to enable her to make the most of her idyllic family life.

She hadn't spoken to Callum or Imogen since that Sunday night. Imogen she was trying not to think about. Ella knew that the onus was on her to phone and apologise, but she felt that the conversation would go places she wasn't ready for and so she was pushing the problem under her (immaculately vacuumed) carpet. Callum was another matter. They were in contact via text or email several times a day. Ella's official position was still that there could be no romantic involvement between them, but there could surely be no objection to them being friends? And so their electronic correspondence was, after a fashion, innocent. Certainly not erotic or overtly sexual, yet the messages were imbued with an intimacy and warmth that told a subtly different story.

It was certainly a bizarre side-effect that meeting Callum again should have breathed new life into her marriage and brought her to a new appreciation of her children. It made a big difference that she and Greg were able to chat over breakfast, then share anecdotes about their days with a glass of wine and a delicious home-cooked supper, and they were getting on better than they had done for months. Another side-effect of Ella's manic energy was that she had no time (and even less inclination) for any form of introspection or self-examination. She felt happier and more vibrant than she had done since before Aidan was born, and she just wanted to enjoy that without looking too closely into the reasons why, or thinking too much about the future.

17

Slowly, over the next fortnight, Phoebe's distress had turned to anger. She was no longer lying awake crying; now those 3 a.m. moments when sleep eluded her were all about plotting her best course of action. How she could best seize back control of her life while showing her parents that she was not to be messed with.

Funnily enough, she was arguing less with her mother. Liz seemed to have retreated into her own little world and was no longer a daunting presence, ever hovering at Phoebe's shoulder with calorie-counting and criticism. She made no attempt to cook meals, or check that Phoebe was doing her revision, or even where she was at any given time. They were leading parallel existences under the same roof, though in fact, Phoebe was under that roof as little as possible, spending every waking moment she wasn't in school at Becky's.

Daniel and Ruth Stein were more than tolerant of the additional face at their table.

'Poor girl. My heart goes out to her, it really does,' Ruth commented to her husband one evening after Phoebe had finally, reluctantly, departed for home.

Daniel nodded.

'I know. What exactly is going on with her parents?'

His wife shrugged melodramatically.

'Search me! I've tried asking Becky, but all she says is that Callum McCraig has left – moved into his friend's spare room, apparently – and Phoebe is barely on speaking terms with her mother.'

Daniel looked thoughtful.

'We need to be careful – we don't want to get too mixed up in this, it sounds like it could be messy. And we mustn't come between Phoebe and her parents, whatever we may think of the way they're behaving.'

Ruth nudged him, affectionately.

'I know that, you old fusspot! That's why I told Becky that Phoebe couldn't stay the night here. She was all for her moving in with us, and we can't allow that. But there's no way I'm letting that poor child go home to an empty house every night, eating God knows what junk food, when she could be here with us, eating properly and at least experiencing something of proper family life, even though it's not her own. Plus, it's nice for Becky having her here. And they're helping each other revise as well.'

He grinned, somewhat reassured as well as amused by the anger in her tone.

'OK, well, I don't disagree with you. Tell you what, though, I pity Callum and Liz if they bump into you – they're going to get a real piece of your mind, aren't they?'

Ruth carried on wiping down the worktops with abnormal viciousness.

'They certainly will. Whatever their marital situation may be, it's no excuse for derogating their responsibilities as parents, and I'll tell them that to their face if I get the chance.'

Becky had been listening surreptitiously to this conversation, and reported it all back to Phoebe, but it didn't seem to get them much further. Becky was very taken with a case she had read about whereby an American girl had divorced her parents, but Phoebe was full of objections.

'I haven't got enough money for a lawyer. They're really expensive, everyone says so.'

Ruth Stein was a paralegal, so Becky felt she knew what she was talking about here.

'Not necessarily. You could get someone who does no win, no fee.'

Phoebe looked doubtful.

'But what are the grounds? And can children even do that in this country?'

'Well, the grounds would be unreasonable behaviour, of course.' Becky was very certain of this. 'I mean, come on. Your dad walked out on you, and you've only seen him for a couple of coffees since, and he won't answer any of your questions about what's happening, or why, or where you're going to be living. And your mum . . .' Becky paused, sensitive to the fact that there is a world of difference between patient listening while someone complains about their parents and giving unbridled vent to criticism yourself. Becky liked Callum and couldn't understand why he was acting so strangely now, but she disliked and feared Liz. She was cold and always seemed disapproving, though whether of Phoebe, Becky, their friendship or just life in general was unclear. She proceeded tentatively. 'Well, your mum isn't acting like a mum, is she? She never cooks, she doesn't know where you are, she's not really talking to you.'

Phoebe nodded, thoughtfully. She was furious with both her parents and eager to take some kind of dramatic action, but didn't really buy this whole divorce idea. For one thing, she couldn't actually believe it was possible. And for another, however angry she might be right now, she had enough self-awareness to know that deep down she loved her dad, at least, and didn't want to divorce him.

She did, however, have her own ideas as to what she could do to make her feelings about the direction life had taken very clear, and she began to outline these to Becky now.

For Callum, the combination of his night of passion with Ella ending years of celibacy and his absolute conviction that she was the answer to his problems, the woman he was meant to be with, his future, was keeping him riding high on wave after wave of endorphins. Nothing could subdue his overwhelming energy and optimism for long.

Of course, he knew Phoebe was unhappy, but he was also utterly convinced that this was a clear case of omelettes and eggs, and that what he needed to do was sort things out with Liz as quickly as possible, so that he and Phoebe (and Ella) could get on with the rest of their lives. The practical elements of this sorting took every spare minute, not leaving him much time to actually talk to Phoebe. They'd had a couple of coffees together, but she had been sullen and withdrawn, seemingly uninterested in, or unconvinced by, his cheerful reassurances that it would all sort itself out in the end, so he found himself slightly avoiding contact until he had some more positive news to share with her.

His plans were progressing. He was still sleeping in Tony's spare room at present – not a wholly desirable situation, and one which he suspected was proving even less pleasing to Tony's wife, Caroline, than it was to him. However, every moment when he wasn't at work had been spent badgering estate agents, and he had been working his way through viewings of theoretically suitable rental properties.

Unfortunately for Callum, sixteen years as a homeowner had sheltered him from the reality of twenty-first-century renting. Flats described as two-bedroomed could, he discovered, in actual fact turn out to have a large cupboard that someone had managed to squeeze a single bed into, with a sofabed in the living room. A property that was palatially sized would probably have other major problems – bathroom tiles black with mould, or furniture that Noah had got rid of when he decluttered the ark on the grounds that it was shabby and out of date. One of the main problems was that Callum was so limited by location; he was determined that the divorce would be disruption enough and that Phoebe should not have to move school, or live too far away from her friend Becky.

Callum's parents had died within a few months of one another two years earlier and, as an only child, he had inherited their house. He'd cleared it and sold it and the money was sitting in a bank account, intended as a university fund for Phoebe. Frustratingly, his research had shown that he was about twenty grand short of having enough to buy a nice little two-bed terrace, and the bank had been uncompromising in their refusal to allow him to take out another mortgage, even such a comparatively small one, when he was still solely responsible for the payments on their family home. He had also reflected that such a small house wouldn't be appropriate when (he never allowed himself to think *if*) Ella and her two children moved in, so he was forcing himself to be patient and trawl through the uninspiring flats as an interim solution.

He'd been to see a solicitor, to instigate divorce proceedings and take advice on how to obtain custody of Phoebe, and as a result was becoming very familiar with terms such as 'residence orders', 'ex-marital home', 'contact' and 'conciliation'. Conciliation was the biggie. His lawyer was very keen to impress upon Callum that this was by far the best option for agreeing Phoebe's future, and while Callum agreed with his head, in his heart he just couldn't envisage Liz allowing things to happen in that way.

However, one thing was abundantly clear: a residence order required a residence, which was why Callum found himself pacing up and down outside yet another south Liverpool property waiting for the estate agent to show up.

When she finally did, Callum felt rather encouraged. She was totally different from the identikit twentysomething men with their overly sharp suits and overly gelled hair. This was a woman in her late forties, whose long caramel blonde hair was held up in a twist by a tortoiseshell clasp. Her smile was warm, friendly and genuine and her denim A-line knee-length skirt, fitted white blouse and red leather ballet pumps were definitely veering towards the casual end of the smart-casual spectrum.

They shook hands, introducing themselves, and then the agent, Mandy, pulled out a set of keys from her large, tan leather tote bag and opened the front door. This in itself was a pleasant surprise and a good start. On at least two separate occasions Callum's time had been entirely wasted by agents who turned up without the correct keys and had seemed surprised and vaguely affronted that it was not then possible to conduct the viewing.

The front door itself was painted bright turquoise, with a stylish brushed-chrome letterbox and knocker. Mandy ushered him into the narrow hall and his immediate impression was positive. The house smelt airy and clean – far from being a given, he had discovered – and the white walls and seagrass matting were smart and modern. To his left was a wooden door, and he opened it and went through into the living room. It was a lovely space – a large bay window meant it was flooded with natural light, and the sanded wooden floorboards and original wrought-iron fireplace gave it character. It was a good size, too. There was only one small flaw so far – the room was completely bare.

'I didn't realise this was an unfurnished let!'

Mandy looked anxious.

'Oh, I'm sorry. Is that going to be a problem? It does seem to be for a lot of people, I think that's why it hasn't gone, and she's had to put the price down.'

Callum thought for a moment. The price, although slightly higher than some of the properties he had viewed, did seem rather low given the massive improvement in quality.

'What's the story with it, then?' he asked. 'How come it's unfurnished? It's the first one I've seen that is.'

Mandy hurried to explain.

'Well, basically, Ms Kalton, the owner, has moved in with her partner, and taken her furniture with her. This was her own residence until a couple of months ago. Between you and me,' Mandy lowered her voice, even though no one else was around, 'I should think she'll be selling it quite soon, she only wants a six-month let, and I reckon that's just to wait and see if things work out with her relationship.'

Callum nodded his head slowly. If the rest of the house was as nice as this then he was definitely interested, and perhaps a six-month let wasn't a disadvantage – by that time he would hopefully have persuaded Ella to sort things out with her husband and then they could look for somewhere together. In the meantime, although he had imagined somewhere furnished, how much of a trial would a quick trip to Ikea be? It would be worth it if it meant he could provide a decent home for his daughter, and there was a lot to be said, after all, for not having to sleep on someone else's grotty mattress.

The rest of the house didn't disappoint. The kitchen and dining room had been knocked together to form one bright and spacious room. The cupboards were all painted a soft sage green, and the worktops were light maple wood. He was relieved to see that Ms Kalton had evidently had no sentimental attachment to her white goods and had left them all behind on her departure to her love nest. Upstairs there were two decent-sized bedrooms, both with fitted wardrobes – another furniture cost saving – and the bathroom was obviously newly fitted, with stylish slate tiles on the floor, a deep claw-foot bath he knew Phoebe would adore and a walk-in power shower.

OK, there was no garden to write home about – it was very much a backyard, with barely space for a few tubs of geraniums and perhaps a small table and two chairs – but actually he wasn't really interested in gardening and escaping weekend lawn-mowing duty was something of a plus. The fact that it was within walking distance of Phoebe's school, her friend Becky's house *and* Calderstones Park, should they need a fix of green space, seemed to more than outweigh the lack of garden.

Without giving himself too much time to think, he put an offer in writing for Mandy and signed the various bits of paper that authorised deposits, credit checks, references and all the other administrative requirements.

Half an hour later, Callum left the house and walked down the pleasant Victorian terrace with a spring in his step, mentally composing his furniture-shopping list. Mandy had promised to process everything at double-quick speed, and had been confident that he should get the keys within the next week to ten days. The crucial first step to building his new life had been taken.

18

Greg clicked send on his final email of the day and then with a sigh of relief shut his computer down. He glanced at the clock. 7 p.m. already – no way he would make it home for bath-time tonight. He was sad not to get to see Aidan and Hattie, but based on the evidence of the previous few weeks, at least being late wouldn't mean he would have to run the gauntlet of his wife's fury. Greg was a qualified solicitor and headed up the legal department of a large chain of department stores. Ella couldn't seem to grasp that a well-paid job, with a high level of responsibility, didn't necessarily finish on the dot of 5.30 p.m. to fit in with his children's bedtime routine, although she had been much more understanding recently.

With Aidan's birth, the Ella he had fallen in love with had seemed to disappear. That Ella, his Ella, had been loving and spontaneous and carefree. She could be caustically, sarcastically amusing, but never normally at his expense. She had also been independent and strong-minded, full of quirky opinions and passionately held views. Becoming a mother seemed to him to have diminished her as a person. There were still glimpses of the old Ella from time to time, and his love for her had increased as he saw the infinite tenderness and patience with which she was raising the children, but there was no doubt that their relationship had suffered as a result of parenthood. The patience and tenderness Ella showed her children were utterly absent from her treatment of him – he felt exposed to constant criticism and in a lose-lose situation. If he tried to help with Aidan and Hattie then he would inevitably break one of Ella's unwritten rules and be branded useless, but if he didn't help, or was working long hours, then he was treated to Ella's martyred 'I may as well be a single parent' routine.

He had wondered if she was suffering from a form of post-natal depression, but had got very short shrift on the one or two occasions he had tried to broach the subject, and he hadn't felt sure enough of his ground to pursue it. Whatever the cause, he hated to see her so unhappy, yet felt impotent to help. Her suggestion they should try for a third baby, though, had driven him over the edge. Much as he loved the two children he had, the thought of supporting Ella through another pregnancy and then coping with months of broken sleep, tears and emotional outbursts (and that was just Ella, never mind the baby) filled him with abject horror. Her proposal had also strengthened his growing conviction that what Ella lacked was a project and focus, that what she needed far more than another baby was a career.

Since her weekend away in Liverpool, however, she had been a changed woman. He marvelled at just how much difference a weekend away from the responsibilities of the children – and a chance to have a proper catch-up with her friends – could make. She was literally glowing and her energy levels were through the roof. In some ways Greg's life had never been better – she was like a walking embodiment of *Good Housekeeping* magazine. Every meal was home-made and delicious, the children were behaving angelically, the house gleamed. Greg hadn't been subject to a single outburst of temper – when he helped with the children she thanked him politely, when he had to work longer than expected she took the news calmly and cheerfully. Things were pretty well perfect. And yet . . .

Despite all these manifold perfections, Greg couldn't help but feel that he and Ella were less emotionally intimate than they had ever been. He had no real idea what was behind her new Stepford Wife persona, and, although they talked a lot about what they had been up to that day, the children, the house, mutual friends and all the rest of it, there was some sense that part of Ella was entirely absent from these discussions. He just couldn't work out what was going on, but had the strangest feeling that his marriage was more vulnerable now, with Ella skipping around the house all vibrant radiance, than it had been in those theoretically darker days when she snarled rather than smiled and was inevitably in bed, alone, by 9 p.m.

Greg gave himself a mental shake to dispel these disquieting reflections, stood up and was just pulling his jacket on when his colleague and friend, Mark, put his head round the door.

'Alright, mate? Don't suppose you fancy a quick pint, do you? Lucy's at her mum's with the twins this week, and I'm at a bit of a loose end.'

Greg was about to automatically refuse, then reconsidered. He'd missed seeing the kids that night anyway, and maybe he should take advantage of Ella's ongoing good mood to have a drink with his friend. He and Mark had hardly seen each other since the birth of Mark and Lucy's twin girls just over a year earlier. Four children under three between them was hardly conducive to any kind of a social life, and ten minutes over a couple of plates of chips in the canteen was about as good as it got. The thought of a cheerful pub, a decent pint and some good uncomplicated company was suddenly too tempting to turn down.

He nodded.

'Yeah, I'd like that, actually. Let me just phone Ella and check she doesn't mind.'

Ella sounded positively enthusiastic.

'Oh yeah, you should. Great idea. Give Mark my love, and we must arrange to have him and Lucy and the girls over for Sunday lunch one day soon.'

Encouraged by this response, Greg mooted the idea of grabbing a bite to eat with Mark too, and that suggestion was also graciously received.

Half an hour later, pints of London Pride in front of them and a double order placed of steak pie and chips, Mark and Greg were putting the world in general, and the line-up of the Spurs defence in particular, to rights. Greg was feeling relaxed and comfortable, and conscious of just how much he missed this kind of companionable evening. It was only later, after the cholesterol fest was consumed and the third pints were well under way, that he found himself putting his concerns about Ella and their relationship into some form of words.

'Ella's been acting a bit weird recently,' he heard himself saying.

'Weird in what way?'

Greg paused.

'Weird as in really cheerful all the time, and doing loads of exercise, and being really bouncy, but it's like it's not quite real.'

Mark was looking uncomprehending and Greg scrunched up his face in frustration at trying to express what he meant.

'It's kind of like she's putting on an act. She's just too happy, and everything seems too perfect.'

Mark considered.

'That doesn't sound so bad. I wouldn't mind it if Lucy was permanently cheerful – permanently grumpy is more what I get. Lack of sleep doesn't suit her.'

'That's just it.' Greg seized on this. 'Ella always has been quite grumpy since we had the kids – well, you know what it's like, it's hard work all round. But since she went on this hen weekend a few weeks ago she's like a different person.'

Mark mulled this over, yet to be convinced that this could be considered a real problem. Then something struck him.

'You don't mean you think she's seeing someone else, do you?'

Up until that moment, Greg had no notion that he thought any such thing. However, his subconscious had clearly been busy because Mark's words were met with instant internal recognition, and he found himself nodding.

'Yeah . . . I think that's maybe what I am worried about. She just looks so – glowy. And seems really happy, but totally disconnected from me. I guess I am scared that it's someone else who's making her look like that.'

'Bloody hell.' Mark was silenced, unsure how to proceed. What was he meant to do? Reassure Greg, and pooh-pooh the idea? After all, it did seem unlikely; he didn't know Ella well, but when he'd seen her she'd always been coaxing organic baby food into a child's mouth, or discussing breastfeeding positions or NCT nearly-new sales with Lucy; she hardly seemed a femme fatale type. And even if he had thought she was a scarlet adulteress, he'd hardly endear himself to Greg by sharing that thought with him.

'I'm sure it's nothing, mate. After all, where would she get the time? She's with the kids all day, and presumably she hasn't suddenly started going out in the evenings?'

Greg shook his head, but then a vision of Ella as she'd looked when she'd returned that evening a few weeks ago, supposedly from Imogen's house, came to him. Does an evening comforting a friend over her relationship break-down really make a woman look lit up from within? And then there was the frequency with which Ella seemed to be checking her iPhone recently and the extra little spar-kle about her when she had done so.

Even as Mark concluded definitely, 'No, I reckon you're barking up the wrong tree. She's just not the type,' Greg was inwardly promising himself he would get up to some detective work and find out exactly what was going on.

After Greg's brief call to say he was going out with Mark and would be late home, Ella paced up and down the kitchen, barely able to contain her excited anticipation.

She had a whole evening to herself and therefore a golden opportunity to phone Callum.

Her mood had been so strange over the past few weeks. On some level she knew that the amazing high she was experiencing only usually comes in the initial stages of falling in love. However, because she was directing all of this endorphin-driven energy into her home life and restricting contact with Callum to the platonic and electronic, she was able to convince herself that she had put an ill-advised one-night stand behind her and was now concentrating on being a good wife and mother. A few emails exchanged with an old friend could hardly endanger that.

Now, though, the butterflies in her tummy told a different story, and she knew that she was utterly unable to resist hearing Callum's voice. Oscar Wilde's aphorism about being able to resist anything except temptation floated into her head, and she smiled sardonically. All this time she'd been congratulating herself on how well she had behaved in not contacting Callum, when actually it was just that she was always with either Greg or the children and so lacked the opportunity. The fact that she hadn't phoned before also rather exposed the fiction of the 'platonic' nature of their relationship; after all, she'd never felt the need to wait for Greg to have an evening out so she could call Janey or Imogen.

Still, she knew no power on earth could stop her dialling Callum's number, memorised almost unconsciously so that she didn't have to have it saved on her phone.

Half an hour later, Ella arrived at the conclusion that phone sex was definitely underrated. Any pretence of a casual chat had vanished the second she heard Callum's voice. Through their emails and texts they had been in and out of each other's heads for weeks, and as soon as they spoke in person their talk was all of their intense physical longing. If they had been able to meet up in person, Ella had no doubt they would have been in bed together within moments; they were scarcely less passionate over the phone as their words tumbled over each other breathlessly.

Finally, they calmed down enough to have something resembling a normal conversation. Ella was recounting some anecdote about the school-gate politics at Aidan's playgroup when Callum cut across her somewhat abruptly.

'I've found somewhere to live.'

Inexplicably, Ella felt her heart rate speed up.

'Oh, have you?' She tried hard to keep her tone light and casual, in contrast to the tension in his voice.

'Yes. It's really nice, actually. And a bedroom for Phoebe, so she won't have to live with Liz any more. Only a six-month let, but that's probably a good thing because everything's so uncertain.'

Ella gulped.

'Uncertain with Phoebe and custody, you mean?'

Callum didn't back down.

'Well, yes, partly. But I really meant with you and me, Ella.'

She felt slightly sick and shaky now. She knew what needed to be done, but actually doing it was quite another matter. Her eyes fell on a photo of Greg with the children, taken on the beach last summer, and a wave of guilt washed over her, stiffening her resolve.

'There is no you and me, Callum. There can't be, I've told you that.'

The anger in his voice when he replied took her aback. 'No, Ella, I'm not having that. You can't phone me like you did this evening, we can't talk like we just have, and then you pretend nothing is going on. You do have feelings for me, you know you do, and I'm not going to let you get away with pretending otherwise. You need to face up to what's happening and decide what you're going to do about it.'

She was silent. He was right. She knew he was. God knows what sort of a game she thought she was playing. This last couple of weeks she had been keeping up the charade of a happy marriage while taking all her emotional sustenance from another man. It wasn't fair on anybody and she knew that she had to make a decision one way or the other. It should be a no-brainer, of course. Aidan and Harriet were what really mattered and she loved them more than anything. But since meeting Callum again she'd felt as though she had come out of the dark tunnel she'd been in since Aidan's birth, and she just wasn't sure if she had sufficient resolve to leave the sunlit uplands Callum had shown her to return to the shadowy world she seemed to have been in for so long.

He broke in to her reflections.

'Please, Ella, just think about it, get your head sorted out, and make a proper decision.'

She nodded, realised he couldn't see her, and then murmured

'Yes, OK. I'll think about everything.'

There was something of the old tenderness in his voice as he wished her goodnight, but then he was gone, and the house resounded with silence.

19

'I'm sorry, Mrs Barry, but we are trying very hard to promote healthy eating, and Chiara's packed lunch wasn't really appropriate today.'

Imogen pressed both hands to her temples in a vain attempt to soothe her tension headache as she tried to let Chiara's mum's defence of a can of Diet Coke, a slice of cold takeaway pizza and a Mars bar for a six-year-old's packed lunch wash over her. She loved teaching for the kids' sake, but the parents could be a complete nightmare.

Finally, she managed to get rid of the woman, pressing the brightly coloured school guidelines on 'Healthy Lunches, Healthy Children' into her hand as she left, still muttering obscenities under her breath. Imogen glanced at her watch and grimaced. Only twenty minutes to go until Indigo needed to be picked up from nursery, a ten-minute cycle ride away, and her wall display was barely started. Twelve minutes later, there was a wonderful frieze of the solar system decorating her classroom wall and she'd given up any hope of finishing her paperwork, just thrusting a pile of it into her cotton shopping bag to do at home after Indigo was in bed, and heading out to the bike rack at the back of school at a brisk trot.

As usual, she weaved frantically through the heavy traffic, risking life and limb, trying desperately to control her stressed and panicky breathing with meditation techniques. She was still several streets away from nursery when a glance at her watch showed it was 6 p.m. already. She groaned and was about to pull on to the pavement to call the nursery and grovel, yet again, when she remembered. It was OK. Alex was picking Indigo up with Molly tonight and both girls were going back to his house for the eagerly anticipated sleepover. Alex had asked her if she wanted to pop over and have a bite to eat with him, before either spending the night in his spare room or heading home, depending on how well Indigo seemed to have settled. She exhaled and felt all the tension evaporate. Just for a moment she let herself bask in this unaccustomed sensation of not having to do every last little thing herself, of someone looking after her for a change. Then the traffic started to clear and she made her way in the direction of Alex's place, feeling a far greater degree of excited anticipation than she would have admitted to.

Alex glanced around the room. The girls had been fed and were now curled up on the sofa watching *Charlie and Lola* with their pre-bed beakers of milk. The flat was immaculate. It was far too warm for a fire, but he had lit three pillar candles and placed them in the fireplace and a couple of tea-lights in glass ramekin dishes sat at either end of the table, which was laid for two. He'd taken the afternoon off work to get everything ready and the air was scented with freesias from the vase on the kitchen counter and the veggie lasagne he'd just put in the oven. He didn't allow his thoughts to dwell too much on the possibilities of the new Egyptian cotton sheets he'd bought in Marks & Spencer's that lunchtime and placed on his double bed with care – the futon in the spare room had been made up as well.

God, he couldn't believe he had Imogen coming round for a proper evening together. Just a couple of months ago she had seemed utterly unobtainable – the gorgeous but permanently stressed and distracted Julia Roberts lookalike whose daughter went to Molly's nursery and who never seemed to see him, however often he tried to catch her eye.

He'd spotted the three of them together on the Heath that day; had watched covertly while he and Molly picnicked nearby. Her partner had been messing around with Indigo and she stood a little apart, gazing at the view. There was something about the wistful vulnerability in her gaze that had really caught at his heart, and he could sense his feelings for her deepening, from a vague crush on a beautiful woman that brightened up the school run into a serious attraction. He'd noted with interest the dispute that developed between her and her boyfriend, although on the surface he seemed totally engrossed in a debate with Molly about which Mr Man he'd most like to be. He'd then watched with horror as Indigo's dad had scooped her up and careered off down the hill with her balanced precariously on his bike. When the inevitable fall happened he'd dashed over to help but, although he'd caught the end of the blazing row the couple had engaged in, his thoughts had been totally altruistic – Imogen was simply someone in trouble and he just wanted to help in any way he could.

That had been true in the hospital too; his heart had ached for her distress, but that was the result of parental solidarity rather than any romantic yearnings. He'd got to know her a lot better, though, during those hours in A&E, and everything he found out convinced him further that she was exactly what he was looking for in a woman. Returning her bike had been an act of kindness, sure, but it was also a deliberate ploy to try to turn their tenuous camaraderie into a friendship with the potential for more.

The last few weeks had been about building that friendship, and earning her trust, but tonight he was optimistic that the time might have come to take things to the next level. The doorbell rang and as Indigo leapt up yelling 'Mummymummymummymummymummy' he took a deep breath and went over to the door to answer it.

Greg flicked listlessly through the channels, but nothing held his attention. He wasn't used to being in the house without Ella and, if he was honest, he didn't really like it, but this evening was the first meeting of a book group Ella had joined, so she'd skipped off shortly after putting the children to bed. The freezer was stuffed with delicious home-cooked food – ratatouille, curry, chilli – which he could easily defrost, but he'd looked at the neatly labelled Tupperware tubs with lacklustre eyes and phoned for a pizza instead.

Since he'd allowed himself to vocalise to Mark the secret worry that Ella might have met someone else, the idea had been taking up more and more headroom. It wasn't that he didn't trust her – well, it wasn't that he didn't *want* to trust her – but some atavistic instinct was screaming at him that his marriage was under threat and he was paralysed by indecision as to how to proceed. The one thing he felt sure of, as he lay awake night after night mulling things over, was that he loved Ella and didn't want to lose her. But he had no idea how best to go about preventing that.

Suddenly, his attention was caught by Ella's laptop, neatly zipped into its floral Cath Kidston case, balanced precariously on the arm of the sofa. Well, he always thought of it as Ella's computer, because he had a work laptop that he tended to use, and so the family computer had devolved to Ella in order for her to maintain her Facebook and eBay habits. But it had been a joint purchase, he reasoned. She'd left it out in full view, he reasoned. There was nothing wrong in him using it, he reasoned.

Glancing furtively around, even though Ella wasn't due back for at least an hour and the children were fast asleep, Greg pulled the laptop towards him.

Ella walked home from the pub where the book club had been held feeling very thoughtful. She'd never especially fancied a book group, however de rigueur they seemed to be for the middle-class London mummy. She had little enough time to read and when she did she was normally too tired to concentrate on anything remotely highbrow: she just wanted a good, entertaining story with characters she could relate to. True, her choices were unlikely to appear on the Booker shortlist, but that wasn't the point – they dealt with the things she actually cared about – relationships, friendships, motherhood – in a way she could cope with when she'd only had five hours' sleep. The frothy pink covers irritated her, or perhaps, more accurately, the patronising glances she detected from the playgroup mums when she hosted the regular coffee morning and she saw them clocking the fact that her bookcases didn't exactly scream 'intellectual', irritated her. 'But I've got a first-class degree!' she wanted to scream. 'And a master's. And I was studying for my PhD. I am clever, honestly.'

It had been very tempting when her friend Tanya had contacted her to say that she was setting up a chick lit book club; this, combined with the fact that her newly soaring energy levels meant that the prospect of an evening out seemed appealing rather than horrific, had led to her going along that evening. It was, however, rather an unfortunate coincidence that they'd started with *Playing Away* by Adele Parks, a novel considered groundbreaking when it was published for its gritty exploration of female adultery.

Ella had never read it before and she had been gripped by the realistic characters and page-turning scenario. She'd also more than identified with the heroine, Connie: both with her excruciating guilt at betraying her husband and with the irresistible compulsion that led to her maintaining the affair.

The discussion at the book group had been the real eye-opener though. She'd kept a fairly low profile, terrified of inadvertently letting her secret slip, but the topic had certainly inspired some strong views. To a woman, however, they were united in their conviction that you wouldn't sleep with another man unless your marriage already had real problems: unless you'd already fallen out of love with your husband. None of them seemed to consider it possible that you could love two men at the same time. And none of them thought it was particularly believable that Connie's husband could discover her infidelity and yet be willing to give her a second chance – a viewpoint that Ella found rather sobering.

She pondered deeply as she meandered her way home through the balmily twilit streets. *Was* it possible to love two men at the same time? The consensus this evening was that it wasn't. She was as certain she loved Greg as she was certain of her own name – he was, recent events notwithstanding, the person who knew her best in the whole world, her best friend, the father of her babies – so where exactly did that leave her feelings for Callum? And, more importantly, if her friends were right and being cuckolded was the marital sin no man would ever forgive, how could she possibly make sure that Greg *never* had any opportunity to find out what she'd done?

Greg was sitting frozen in his position on the sofa when he heard Ella's key in the lock. He suddenly galvanised himself and thrust the laptop away from him and under a cushion. He'd been sitting there for over an hour, shocked to his core. He'd thought on one level that Ella was maybe seeing someone else, but when confronted with what looked uncomfortably like the reality of that situation, he realised that he hadn't really believed it. Maybe he'd suspected she had a bit of a crush on someone – there were a couple of stay-at-home dads whose names occasionally cropped up in conversation, and he'd wondered if she was having a bit of a flirtation. Which was upsetting enough – feeling that another man could give Ella her verve and sparkle back when he'd failed so completely – but he had felt the situation was retrievable. He wasn't so sure about this now.

Ella came in, full of warm and loving feelings towards Greg and a determination that she would make their relationship better than ever and that he would never suffer through her brief fall from grace. She was puzzled to find him sitting motionless on the sofa; the room was almost entirely dark but he had made no move to put on a light.

'Hey, what's the matter? Have you got a headache . . . ?' Her cheerful greeting froze on her lips as he turned to look at her and, despite the gloom, she was shocked at the depth of pain in his eyes.

Greg looked at his wife, as beautiful and vibrant as he'd ever seen her. His heart contracted with a mixture of love and anger. Once again he was unsure how to proceed, but his mouth had taken on a mind of its own and, to his dismay, he heard his own voice, slightly cracked, asking, 'Ella, who the bloody hell is Callum McCraig?'

20

Imogen woke up with a start, unsure for a moment where she was. It took her a couple of seconds to realise that she wasn't alone, and then another couple to remember that she was with Alex, in his bed. She shifted position slightly so that she could see his sleeping face and was shocked at the wave of tenderness that washed over her. Last night had been so unexpectedly lovely. Of course, modest as Imogen was, she couldn't help but have had some idea that Alex was attracted to her, and she had been flattered, but she had also felt that, being so recently out of a long-term relationship and with plans to move away from London, this was not the time to think about a new boyfriend.

Last night though, they'd eaten the delicious veggie lasagne and salad he'd made, and then Gü chocolate soufflé with fresh raspberries and cream, which he'd bought because he remembered her saying that raspberry and chocolate was the flavour combination she just couldn't resist. And she'd felt so looked after. He'd really thought about what she would enjoy, what would make a memorable evening for her, and she'd been extremely touched. She felt so relaxed as well, partly by the G&T and half bottle of Pinot Noir, but mainly by the pleasure of being with someone she found so easy to talk with; someone who seemed to be on her wavelength. Living in a way that minimised her impact on the earth's resources was incredibly important to Imogen. She was vegetarian, she recycled and composted, she never bought anything new when she could upcycle, or buy second-hand, or make it herself. Whenever possible, she walked or cycled rather than drove. She generally only bought locally grown seasonal produce from a local organic veg scheme, her tea and coffee were Fairtrade, her cleaning products Ecover and her washing line-dried. This shared commitment to an ethical way of living was one of the things that had drawn her and Pete together in the first place. Recently though, Pete's absolute commitment to the environmental cause, and indeed any other left-wing, right-on cause he came across, had begun to grate, largely because it was so completely at odds with his utter lack of commitment to his own child and to their shared family life.

Attending a Greenpeace meeting or a pub-based discussion with his eco-buddies was an excuse for missing out on anything and everything – from the little Christmas show at Indigo's nursery, or an anniversary dinner Imogen had lovingly prepared, through to innumerable bath-times. It was also frustrating that Pete, despite fairly dazzling academic achievements, refused to get a proper job that would enable him to make a contribution to the family finances – arguing that big corporations were immoral, the public sector was subject to the whims of politicians he almost entirely disagreed with and that he could best contribute to society by using his considerable talents for the benefit of the voluntary sector. Pro bono. He did some gardening and carpentry work to earn a little cash in hand, but it was noticeable that their own flat and garden rarely benefited from his skill in these areas, and it was the landlord of the local pub who was the main recipient of the income generated.

Looking back and contrasting him with Alex, Imogen could barely believe she'd put up with Pete for as long as she had. Alex obviously cared about ethical and environmental issues but there were no two ways about it: Molly came first, above and beyond anything else.

When Imogen had unexpectedly become pregnant and had decided to keep the baby, Pete had warned her that he would not allow parenthood to change his lifestyle. She'd agreed in principle, quietly convinced that the joy of holding his own child in his arms would change his mind. It hadn't. Meeting a man who was the polar opposite, who had taken on the role of a single parent while simultaneously continuing to run his own IT company and who still made time to cook for her, and listen to her, and be there for her, was an intoxicating novelty.

Alex seemed able to make an effort to do his bit without refusing point blank to allow his daughter to eat a mini-box of Smarties she'd been given at nursery because he didn't approve of the policies Nestlé pursued in the developing world. Imogen didn't particularly approve of Nestlé's policies either, but Pete had taken his stance despite Indigo's intense disappointment at the withdrawal of her promised treat and it had been left to Imogen to soothe and comfort her.

She was aware, thinking of the contrasts between Alex and Pete, that she couldn't stop smiling, but equally she was plagued with a reluctance to commit due to her doubt and uncertainty as to where the future lay for her and Indigo. She forced her sensible self back on duty and gently stroked Alex's arm to wake him.

He was instantly wide awake and smiled warmly at her.

'Wow, being woken up by a beautiful naked woman is a pleasant change to being woken up by a stroppy toddler telling me she's had a "little accident". Good morning!'

Imogen giggled in spite of herself, and said her piece.

'I think it's best if I get up and dressed before the girls are awake and realise where I've spent the night. I know they're innocent at this age, but I don't want them putting two and two together.'

He looked quizzical.

'Don't you? Don't you think they'd approve, or be pleased?'

Imogen sighed.

'Alex, we obviously need to talk about what happened, but now's not the time – we need to sort things out without the input of two matchmaking three-year-olds.'

He lazily stroked down her shoulder and cupped her breast. Imogen could feel her resolve weakening as her nipple hardened, but the garish red glow of the alarm clock behind Alex informed her that it was already 6.15 a.m. and, Saturday morning or not, she knew that Indigo could wake up at any moment. She might have adapted remarkably well to her father's absence, but Imogen was certainly not going to ask her to cope with finding her mother naked in bed with her best friend's dad. She kissed Alex lightly on the mouth – whether by way of promise or apology neither of them could quite decide – and slid out of bed, pulling Alex's bathrobe round her on her way to the bathroom.

Ella had woken at 5 a.m. and hadn't been able to get back to sleep, even though for once the children had been dead to the world. She'd lain in bed tossing and turning for a while before giving sleep up as a bad job. She slipped on a light kimono, took her mobile phone from the bedside table and padded quietly downstairs. Although it was still very early, the sun was streaming in through the patio doors, so she made herself a cup of tea and took it out to sit at the garden table. The sun was warm on her back, a light breeze carried the scent of the deep pink climbing roses she'd planted, and the birds were revelling in their dawn chorus. It should have been idyllic, and Ella closed her eyes and tried to relax and focus on the beauties of nature rather than her own overwhelming guilt and regret. If she'd been drunk or high on love and happiness since meeting Callum, she was now experiencing the most crashing emotional hangover of her life.

Ella was a sorter and a fixer. She solved her children's problems with maternal omnipotence, she was the first person her friends turned to with their own emotional crises and she was the model daughter and daughter-in-law, able to help with anything from recommending a plumber to booking a cheap flight. But this problem, one entirely of her own creation, she had no idea whatsoever how to solve. She felt that her life's happiness, and that of her children, was hanging by a thread, but instead of galvanising her into action, this knowledge simply paralysed her with fear.

She looked at the time on her phone. Barely 7 a.m., but Imogen and Indigo were notoriously early risers and she decided to take a punt. She needed to eat a massive slice of humble pie and it wasn't going to get any more palatable the longer she left it. She took a deep breath, wiped her slightly sweaty palms on her kimono and then dialled.

Coincidentally, Imogen was also in the garden when the phone rang. In her case the garden was Alex's and she was keeping a lazy eye on pyjama-clad Indigo and Molly scampering happily in and out of Molly's playhouse, while Alex rustled up pancakes for breakfast. Despite all her misgivings about what having had sex with Alex might mean, she was suffused by a deep calm and contentment, and instead of thinking seriously about her options for the future she was just revelling in the sensuous pleasures of sunshine, children's laughter and the scent of cooking pancakes.

An argument with her erstwhile best friend was the last thing she felt she needed, and she almost didn't take the call, but, despite her hurt at the way Ella had just disappeared from her life for several weeks, she did miss her, and knew that at some point bridges would have to be built.

'Hello, Ella.'

Her voice was cool but not hostile.

Ella didn't pull any punches.

'Imogen, I've been such a cow. I'm so, so sorry. You were right, and I knew you were really, which is why I reacted so badly. But I got it completely wrong, and I feel awful. Especially as you were having such a tough time with Pete and Indy. I'm a crap friend, but I will make it up to you, if you'll let me. Please?'

She finally paused for breath, and Imogen felt the small icy place in her heart, which had been there since Ella stormed out, melting. She had never been any good at holding a grudge, and Ella sounded really distressed.

'Don't be silly. Of course we're still friends. You did upset me, but I've really missed you. Hey, it's OK . . .' She could hear that Ella was fighting back tears.

'I don't deserve you, Immy. Or Greg. I've messed up so badly, and I don't know what to do.'

'Shush, it's OK. It's OK.' Imogen considered and then offered, 'Shall I come round to yours this afternoon? Hopefully the kids will play and we can chat. How about that? Or will Greg be there?'

Ella's voice was bleak.

'No, I don't think Greg will be here. I really need to talk to you, thank you, that would be great. Aidan and Hattie have really missed you and Indigo. And, oh God, I haven't asked about you. What's going on with Pete? Is Indy OK now?'

Imogen could see Alex gesturing from the kitchen window, indicating that breakfast was ready, so she extricated herself from the conversation.

'Indy's fine. And I'm fine too, but we'll talk properly later. I've got to go now, but see you twoish.'

21

It was past midnight when Phoebe finally put out her light, and she was asleep within moments. Her life might have been falling apart around her ears, but she had taken a calm and rational decision that she wasn't going to allow her parents to ruin her academic chances, and so she had been focussing all her efforts on her GCSE exams. There were only two more exams to go – English Literature and Religious Education, both of which she felt fairly confident about, and when they were done she was going to put her slowly maturing plans into action.

She'd continued to spend most evenings at Becky's house, and they'd tested each other to distraction on French irregular verbs, the periodic table and the life cycle of a frog. Ruth Stein was spoiling them both rotten, arguing that food for the body was food for the brain and cooking up endless delicious treats to keep them going. Funnily enough, despite this Phoebe wondered if she'd lost a little weight; her school skirt was feeling slightly loose around her waist. It would be odd if she had when she'd been indulging in large helpings of amazing food every dinner time, followed by a mid-evening treat such as a brownie, or a piece of carrot cake, or a bowl of ice cream. On the other hand, spending so much time with the Steins meant that she had far less time on her own and, therefore, fewer opportunities for raiding her private, bedroom snacks stash.

After she and Becky had revised themselves into a stupor they would discuss code-named Operation Make 'Em Pay. Finally, Ruth or Daniel would decide it was bedtime and one of them would drive Phoebe home.

Liz McCraig seemed to be treating Phoebe as a flat-mate rather than a teenage daughter. She rarely made any enquiry about where she was going, or with whom. She would ask casually how the exams were going on the odd occasion that they bumped into each other, and Phoebe smiled ironically at the contrast with Becky's parents, who had their daughter's exam timetable printed out and stuck up on the fridge. They'd colour-coded it in bright high-lighter pens according to how hard Becky found that subject and, therefore, the level of TLC she would need before and after that exam. When each exam was completed there was a ceremonial crossing out with thick black marker pen. Phoebe doubted her mother even knew when her last exam was, although hopefully within a few days Operation Make 'Em Pay would ensure that the date was engraved on her memory for ever.

Callum was slightly better – she got a text message from him before each exam, wishing her luck, and he'd phoned a couple of times to see how they had gone. He'd made no effort to see her though, no offers of help with revision, no apology for leaving her without so much as a backward glance, or mentions of a plan for the future. When they spoke on the phone he said all the right things about the exams: not getting too stressed, getting plenty of sleep etc, but he sounded distracted and distant and she could sense that his thoughts were elsewhere.

None of this made Phoebe happy, but her steely determination not to let it mess up her exams had led to her closing down her softer emotional responses and, instead, channelling her anger and hurt into her plans for the future.

The Ella who had been Imogen's closest friend for over three years lived in a charming Victorian house full of original features, eclectic furniture and an abundance of the brightly coloured plastic that any parent of an under-five is all too familiar with. Her house was cosy and welcoming, but generally not even on nodding terms with minimalist. Which was why, when Ella ushered her in that afternoon, Imogen did a double take. The furniture was, she supposed, familiar, but she could see so much more of it now that it wasn't concealed under a layer of Playmobil and Duplo. The wooden floors gleamed and there were large vases of elegantly arranged fresh flowers dotted around.

The women went through to the garden. That too was transformed. Most of the pocket-sized lawn was covered by an enormous sandpit, but the small patio area was bursting with colourfully planted troughs and pots. The table in the centre was laid with scones, jam, cream and a large chocolate cake.

Imogen gasped in amazement, but was distracted from making any comment by Indigo demanding to have her shoes taken off so that she could join Aidan and Hattie, who were playing in the sand. Once Indigo was barefoot, suncreamed and had run off to join the others, Imogen was finally free to sink down into a chair and accept the glass of home-made lemonade Ella offered.

'Bloody hell, Ella,' she commented at last. 'Don't get me wrong, I'm not saying that you were a slob before, but it's like you've been taken over by the love child of Paul Hollywood and Kirstie Allsopp. The house and garden look amazing. And what's all this?' She gestured at the sumptuous tea. 'Normally you might crack open a packet of HobNobs, and now it's like afternoon tea at the Ritz.'

Ella made a flapping gesture with her hands.

'Don't be silly, you haven't even tasted anything yet! But I wanted to treat you, to say sorry for how I behaved. And I guess I'm just using housework as a displacement activity – I have no idea how to sort out any of the metaphorical mess I've caused, so I take my mind off it by endless actual cleaning.'

Imogen laughed.

'Well, as displacement activities go, it's not a bad one. Less destructive than drink or drugs or eating disorders.'

Ella shrugged.

'Maybe, but it's not really going to solve anything, is it? Although, speaking of eating disorders, would you like some cake?'

They munched in companionable silence for a few moments and then Ella asked, 'So, you said you were fine. Has Pete moved back in, then?'

Imogen snorted. 'No, thank God!'

Ella raised her eyebrows, and Imogen hastened to explain.

'We've split up for good. He's seen Indigo twice in the last month, and I've had a couple of practical conversations with him on the phone, but basically he's out of our lives, and it's the best thing I've ever done.'

Seeing that Ella was stunned into silence, she continued, 'Do you remember, a few months ago in the pub, and you asked me if I was really in love with Pete?'

Ella nodded, sombrely.

'Well, I said that I was, and I thought at the time that it was true, but since he left I've seen that really I fell out of love with him years ago. Probably when he was so unsupportive after Indigo's birth, I suppose. But because I *had* loved him so much, and because I was fixated on the idea that Indigo needed a father, I just ploughed on, and didn't let myself question what my own feelings were. Now I just feel so . . . free. Light. I've still got all the same responsibilities, to work and to Indigo and all the rest of it, but I haven't got the burden of resentment against Pete for leaving me to deal with all that by myself.'

Ella nodded again. She could absolutely see where Imogen was coming from, and as an outside observer of their relationship she had seen with total clarity just what a one-way street it was and how Imogen had been diminished by it at times. She was still amazed, though, at the difference in her friend. Always beautiful, Imogen now seemed positively radiant and the almost imperceptible air of strain that had previously hovered around her had totally vanished.

'I'm so pleased, Immy. He really didn't deserve you. And Indigo is so much better off with you, loving her and putting her first, and being happy, than with you ground down by an unhappy relationship with a father she hardly sees anyway.'

Imogen nodded confidently and let her eyes drift over to where Indigo and the other children were laughing and shrieking and giggling.

'I know. I just feel completely convinced now that it's the right thing for me and Indy.'

She looked across at Ella.

'So, what about you, Ella? When you asked me if I really loved Pete, I asked you the same question about Greg, and you didn't properly answer. Are you in love with him?'

'Oh yes. I really am. I love him so much, Imogen. I've been thinking about a quote – was it Germaine Greer who said that a successful marriage involved falling in love many times, but always with the same person?'

Imogen shrugged and Ella continued.

'Well, anyway, that's what I think I've done. I thought I was falling in love with Callum, but actually that was just an infatuation, and realising that I've risked losing Greg has made me fall in love with him all over again. But in the process, I've been so stupid I might just have made him fall out of love with me.'

And with that, Ella burst into tears.

Imogen regarded her friend as she sobbed and snuffled. She felt enormous compassion for her, but she had also been horrified that Ella would betray her husband, seemingly so easily and lightly, and she couldn't help but feel she needed to go through this remorse for her marriage to have even a chance of working in the future.

'So, what exactly has happened, then?' she asked at last.

Ella blew her nose violently, took a large gulp of lemonade and began to tell her friend the whole sorry tale.

'So, when Greg asked you who Callum was, what on earth did you say?'

'Oh God, it was awful. I didn't know what he knew, or how he'd found out, so I had to hedge. I said that he was a teacher at my sixth form who I'd bumped into at the hen do. Part of me just wanted to confess, but I was terrified he'd leave me.'

Imogen felt that he would have been entirely justified, but kept that reflection to herself and simply asked, 'So, what did he know? How had he found out about Callum?'

Ella shuddered.

'Well, it wasn't as bad as it might have been. He'd seen my emails, and there were loads from Callum. As we were talking my mind was spinning, trying to think if there'd been any incriminating ones, but I didn't think there had. I'd told Callum that we couldn't see each other, and though I know we shouldn't have been in touch at all, the emails could just have been between platonic friends.'

'Why was Greg so upset, then?'

Ella shrugged.

'Our marriage hasn't been all that great for a while. I hadn't stopped loving Greg, but I was so wrapped up in myself and how exhausted I felt that I didn't have any energy left to spare for him. I resented him, I suppose, for having a life outside us and the kids when I didn't, and didn't see how I ever could have, and that coloured everything.'

She glanced over at the children, but they were happily tipping sand from one bucket to another, totally absorbed and oblivious to their mother's state of nervous collapse.

'The baby thing was the last straw. I felt he wasn't listening to me, that he was ignoring my needs, patronising me.

I'm not trying to justify what happened with Callum, but that's the context. Anyway, the upshot of it is that I hadn't been very nice to Greg for ages. After I slept with Callum I felt guilty, I suppose, but also weirdly energised, and so in a funny sort of way we'd been getting on better than ever.'

Imogen was puzzled.

'But that's good, surely?'

'Well, yes. Except that Greg put two and two together, and luckily didn't quite make four, but realised that the improvement of my mood coincided with the emails from Callum starting. He didn't suspect I was having an affair as such, or if he did he didn't say anything, but he was really hurt that I'd been looking outside our marriage for support and friendship from another man. He assumed that was all there was to it, and I've let him continue with that assumption. But he's been so cold and distant since, and hardly ever at home, so I'm not sure what he's really thinking, or if he still loves me, or if he's gearing up to leave.'

Imogen thought for a moment.

'So where are things going from here?'

Ella laughed, humourlessly.

'What, with Greg, or Callum?'

'Well, I meant Greg. But both of them, I suppose. You're not still seeing Callum, are you?'

Imogen didn't attempt to hide the shock and disapproval in her voice and Ella was quick to issue a disclaimer.

'No! God, no, I haven't been in contact with him since . . .' Her voice trailed off at the guilty memory of that phone call.

'Since what?'

'Since we were . . . talking on the phone and he issued me with an ultimatum – he wanted me to tell Greg about him and then leave, take the kids with me, and move up to Liverpool to be with him.'

'Bloody hell! So he was really serious about you?'

Ella nodded, uncomfortably.

'Looks like it.'

'So, presumably you told him no, and you haven't spoken to him since?'

Ella shifted in her seat.

'Not exactly. I couldn't think straight. I just burst into tears and hung up, and haven't been in touch with him since.'

'Bloody hell, Ella! You're my friend, and I love you, but oh my God you've been making a mess of things. What the hell do you think you're playing at?'

Ella started to cry again.

'I know, I'm a complete bitch. I hate myself, but Immy, I don't know what to do to sort it all out again, you've got to help me.'

22

Ella had vowed to herself, and to Imogen, that the lies and deception had to stop. But when the two women had discussed it, Imogen had also been adamant that Ella had no choice but to speak to Callum and end things properly. It had been nearly two weeks since their last conversation and he'd made no attempt to contact her, so Ella was hoping he'd realised himself that their doomed affair was over, but she knew Imogen was right and she needed, for everyone's sake, to draw a clear line under it.

Which was why, instead of meeting Imogen in the pub at 7 p.m., as she'd told Greg, she was in fact sitting on a quiet bench, warm in the evening sunshine, outside the local church. She really was meeting Immy later, but had adjusted the timings to provide an alibi for the conversation she was about to have.

She realised as she dialled Callum's number that this was only the second time she'd ever dumped someone, and the last time had been over ten years previously. The thought did nothing to quell the morris-dancing butterflies in her stomach. Nor did the happily hopeful expectancy in Callum's voice as he answered.

'Hi, Ella. It's so good to hear from you.'

Ella gathered her resources – pictured the anger and hurt on Greg's face caused by the thought of her having a secret email friendship, pictured her lovely children who adored their father and deserved to grow up in a happy home – and plunged in.

'No, I'm sorry. I don't think it probably is good to hear from me.'

Callum's voice changed. He was obviously trying to maintain a light and flirtatious register, but the fear was audible.

'Believe me, talking to you can't ever be anything other than good.'

'No, Callum. I'm phoning to say that you're right, I can't have it both ways. I'm sorry if it's not what you want, but we must never see each other again, and, after this conversation I don't want us to have any more contact at all.'

There was a moment's silence.

'But why, Ella? How can you do this? We'd be amazing together. I love you so much, you know I'd do anything, anything at all to make you happy.'

Ella's heart ached, but she realised it was mostly with guilt and compassion rather than love. She didn't want to hurt Callum, and she bitterly regretted having put herself in a position where she had to, but she knew with utter certainty that when it came to a choice between hurting Callum or hurting Greg, there was no contest.

'I'm so sorry, but what will make me happy is doing my best to make my marriage work. I love Greg, I really do. I thought I was falling in love with you, but in reality I think it's just that I never properly got over you when I was a teenager. I needed closure. But Greg saw our emails – I know they didn't say anything that incriminating, but just the quantity and the implied intimacy was enough to upset him – and it's made me realise that I just can't risk losing him.'

Ella stared hard at a small piece of peeling green paint on the bench, seeing it blur as she tried to blink back tears. Her transformation from mild-mannered, people-pleasing mother of two to heartbreaker adulteress had been so sudden and dramatic that she felt she was suffering from the emotional equivalent of the bends.

'Please, Ella. Don't do this. I can't bear it. Before I met you again I'd given up all belief in love and relationships, and then being with you showed me what it can be like. You can't take it away again. Is there anything I can do to change your mind?'

Ella wedged her phone under her chin and massaged her throbbing temples with her fingers. This was so much worse than she'd imagined.

'But the thing is, Callum, you now know that there's a possibility of a happy relationship. You've ended a dreadful marriage, and in time you will meet someone who is free to be with you. Maybe at a different time, in a different place, in a different life that could have been me, but that's just not how it is.'

Wincingly aware that sincerity didn't necessarily overcome banality, Ella ploughed on anyway, determined to get through, say what needed to be said and then never have to speak to Callum again.

'If you do care for me, Callum, I know that you'll respect my wishes, and not contact me again. I truly do wish you all the best for the future, but this really is goodbye.'

She waited a moment, but there was still silence on the other end of the phone, so she hung up and rather shakily walked the short distance to the pub, where a good friend and a strong vodka and tonic awaited her.

Within seconds of Ella sitting down, Imogen's phone began to ring. She pulled it out of her bag and answered.

'Oh, hi, Greg. Do you want Ella? Yup, she's right here, hang on.'

She passed the phone over.

'Hi darling, what's up?'

Greg sounded slightly shifty.

'Hiya, sorry to disturb your night out. I did try your phone first, but it was cutting to voicemail, and I needed to speak to you because, umm, because . . . because I thought I'd put a load of washing on, and I can't remember which side you put the Persil and which side you put the fabric conditioner.'

Ella's eyebrows rose sky-high. Her surprise was not that Greg couldn't remember exactly how to load the washing machine; rather it was that he remembered what the box with the round glass window in the corner of the kitchen was actually for. This was possibly the first time in nine years together that Greg had voluntarily decided to do a load of laundry, but his desire to do so now was seemingly so strong that he'd call her friend to get hold of her rather than wait an hour or two until she got home, or send her a text message.

She kept her voice neutral, however.

'Sorry about that, I guess I mustn't have had reception. The Persil goes in the left, and conditioner in the right, but don't use conditioner if it's towels, 'cos it makes them less absorbent.'

'OK, then. Thanks. You have a good evening, see you later.'

'Bye, see you later.'

She passed Imogen's phone back to her and they exchanged glances.

'Are you thinking what I'm thinking?' Imogen asked eventually.

'What? Checking up on me? Yup, it looks like it. Thank God I'd arrived and you could pass the phone straight to me, hopefully that's put his mind at rest.' She giggled suddenly.

'Poor Greg, not only has he got a nightmare of a cheating, lying, unfaithful wife but he's now got to do a load of laundry to cover up his own lies. Life really doesn't get much worse than that.'

Imogen tried to look severe.

'Ella, it's not funny, you know.' But even as she spoke a little bubble of laughter was welling up and started to escape, and suddenly they were both convulsed, unsure what exactly was so funny, perhaps responding as much to the release of tension as to anything else. As they laughed together, any lingering strain in their friendship was alleviated and Ella reflected that, continuing her diving analogy, laughter with a good friend was probably the nearest equivalent to a decompression chamber.

'Sooo anyway,' broached Imogen a little later, 'I have a bit of a dilemma of my own going on.'

Ella was instantly alert.

'Are you thinking of taking Pete back? Seriously, Immy, I don't think you should. I know you want what's best for Indigo, but you have to think of yourself as well.'

Imogen laughed at Ella's vehemence.

'No, relax. There's no way on earth I'm taking Pete back – even though I think he may have been hinting at it the other day. He's still staying with his mate Seth, and Seth's girlfriend Violet, and I wonder if they might be starting to get the teensiest bit pissed off with him. But no, this dilemma is nothing to do with Pete.'

Ella turned expectant eyes on Imogen and prepared to listen.

'Do you remember the night we had the row?'

Ella blushed and nodded.

'Well, you remember Alex, the guy who was there when you arrived?'

Ella squealed, 'Oh yes! He was yummy! A dead ringer for Barack Obama, I thought. It's not a dilemma at all. You should totally sleep with him!'

Imogen smiled calmly.

'Oh yes. I already have. Several times, actually.'

Ella gasped.

'No, the dilemma is what I do next.'

'In what way? He seemed really nice. Isn't he? Oh no, he's not married, is he?'

Imogen shook her head.

'No, he's divorced, and a single dad to Molly, who's Indigo's best friend at nursery. And he is nice, absolutely lovely, in fact. The problem is that, after Pete left, I decided I'd had enough of London.'

Ella tried to protest, but Imogen continued.

'I know, I know. It's an amazing city, there are fantastic opportunities, it's one of the cultural centres of the world, I have loads of friends here, blah, blah, blah. But also,

Ella, it's incredibly expensive, especially for houses and nursery places, it's noisy and dirty and overcrowded, commuting is hellish, and it's miles away from my parents and my sister. Pete would never have remotely contemplated leaving London, and so I'd never really considered it as an option, but when he'd gone, I started to think seriously about it.'

Ella was aghast.

'But where would you go?'

Imogen took a deep breath.

'Well, I've been offered a job, a promotion to deputy head as well, in Hull. Starting in September.'

'What? Oh my God! Are you going to take it?'

Imogen shrugged helplessly.

'I just don't know. On one hand it seems a no-brainer. It's a great job, in a lovely school. I'd be really close to my family, so they could see more of Indigo, and help out with childcare, and I'd get to spend more time with them. I know Hull doesn't exactly have a glam reputation, but there are some really nice parts, and it's on the coast, so Indigo could have lots of bucket and spade time, like I did growing up. And another huge plus is the prices. I could buy an absolutely gorgeous three-bedroomed place with a huge garden, and the mortgage payments would still be less than the rent on my grotty little basement flat here.'

Ella stared hard at her.

'So what's the problem, then?'

Imogen appeared faintly embarrassed.

'Well . . . Alex, I suppose. But that's really stupid. *I'm* really stupid for even taking him into account.'

'Why's that?' asked Ella softly.

'Because I've only known him a couple of months. Because I only slept with him for the first time last week. Because we're not even a proper couple. Because the person who matters is Indigo, and I need to do what's right for her.'

Ella was thoughtful.

'Well, yes, maybe. But, don't forget, it was trying to do the best for Indigo and ignoring your own feelings that led to you staying with Pete when you probably shouldn't have done. And you must feel something for Alex, or you wouldn't be hesitating so much over this job.'

Imogen nodded miserably.

'It's just such bad timing.' She sighed, and then found herself admitting to Ella what she'd barely even admitted to herself. 'I know it's far too early to say this, I've only just come out of a long-term relationship, it's probably a rebound thing . . . but I could really see myself falling for Alex. He's so lovely. Really kind and considerate, and treats me so well. He's an amazing dad. And he's pretty bloody gorgeous too. And spectacularly good in bed.' She smiled, ruefully. 'Actually, it sounds like I've already fallen for him, doesn't it?'

Ella grinned.

'Just a bit, love! Do you think he feels the same about you?'

'Heaven knows! Isn't that always the sixty-four-thou-sand-dollar question? But, if I had to, I suppose I'd say yes, he does really seem to like me. We just get on so well. But there's a big difference between liking me and wanting to uproot his life and his daughter's to move two hundred miles for me.'

Ella had hugely appreciated Imogen's help and advice about dealing with Callum and getting back on track with

Greg, but suddenly she relished feeling like the grown-up one who could support and advise.

'But Immy, there's no need to be so all or nothing. Obviously it would be a mistake for him to move to be with you at the stage you're at now. And, by the same token, it would be putting an enormous strain on a fledgling relationship for you to give up this chance of a dream job and lifestyle for him. But there is such a thing as compromise, you know.'

Imogen glanced up from the beer mat she was systematically shredding.

'But what's the compromise?'

Ella was busy tapping away on her iPhone, and didn't reply immediately. Then after a few minutes she said, 'Trains! It's only two and a half hours from London to Hull, that's easily doable for a weekend. You could take the job, move, and see each other at weekends. Take it in turns between Hull and London. You could rent instead of buying at first, and if you don't like it up there, or things get serious with Alex and it seems like London is the place to be, then get another job back down here.'

Imogen pursed her lips.

'You make it all sound very simple. Jobs don't grow on trees, you know.'

Ella made an impatient gesture.

'Imogen Daniels, you're a fantastic and extremely experienced teacher. The number of school places needed in London seems to be expanding exponentially, and schools are having to do likewise. You would easily get another job in London if you wanted one. But I think the first thing you need to do is have a proper talk with Alex.'

23

Callum gazed despairingly around the room. Cardboard boxes covered the floor. There hadn't looked to be that many when he transported them from his old home – some books, some CDs, a couple of photo albums, the small TV from the spare room – but now they seemed utterly unmanageable, the prospect of finishing unpacking them totally unachievable. Thankfully, common sense had prevailed and he'd used the services of a local handyman who specialised in putting together flat-pack furniture for the cack-handed and/or busy, so at least he had a bed to sleep in (or would when he'd put sheets and a duvet cover on), a sofa to sit on, a small dining table and chairs and a bookcase, on the off-chance he ever did get round to unpacking.

Just an hour earlier he had been full of grand plans for this first day in his new house. He'd get unpacked and sorted and then pop to Sainsbury's to stock up on some basics. It was only a couple of days until Phoebe's last exam, and he wanted to have everything ready so that he could ask her round, show her the house that he hoped would soon be her home, and cook her a celebratory supper. True, he wasn't famed for his culinary skills, but one of his new purchases had been a Jamie Oliver cookbook and he was optimistic that some of the recipes would be within the scope of his limited capabilities.

Now, reeling from the conversation with Ella, his buoyancy was at an all-time low. He decided continuing with his homemaking project was simply not an option; nor was facing a busy supermarket. Thankfully, Mandy, the estate agent, had left a bottle of sparkling wine in the fridge as a welcoming gesture. The irony of popping a theoretically celebratory cork in his current mood was not lost on him, but the need for an alcoholic drink was overwhelming. He fought with the cardboard packaging on his brand-new pack of Ikea wine glasses, succeeded in freeing one and poured himself a brimming glass. That disappeared in a few gulps and he helped himself to another. Leaving the house seemed out of the question, but he had no food in whatsoever and had missed lunch that day due to being called upon to adjudicate in a nasty dispute between two Year 10 boys. He spotted a leaflet that had come through the door for a local pizza and chicken joint, looked at the number and dialled.

Then he flopped on the sofa and stared blankly ahead. For ten years he had lived a sort of half-life. He had a close, positive relationship with his beloved daughter, but had always been uneasily aware that he was letting her down by not addressing the problems of the relationship between her and her mother. He was good at and largely enjoyed his job, but his marriage was farcical. There was no warmth between them, no sex, barely any companionship. He stayed married, and stayed faithful, not through love or virtue or fidelity but through fear that not doing so would cost him his daughter. His life had been one of stasis.

In the few weeks since meeting Ella again, he had experienced more emotion, more excitement, more sensation than in the previous ten years combined. He'd managed to conduct an illicit affair, end his marriage, leave one home and acquire a new one. He'd had hopes and plans for the future, which had seemed very close to being fulfilled. And now – nothing. Anger flooded him. How *could* she end it, just like that? How could she claim to love her husband more than him, when he'd seen the passion in her eyes, heard it in her voice, felt it in her kisses? He knew in his gut that Ella was making the same error he'd made, staying in an unhappy marriage for the sake of her children. But he could show her what a terrible mistake that was. He reached for his phone, picked it up, started to dial, but then stopped and let it fall from his hand. She'd begged him not to contact her again; he couldn't turn into a stalker. A dimly remembered quotation floated into his head. If you love something, let it go. If it doesn't return to you, it was never truly yours. That's what he needed to do now. Let Ella go. Give her space. And hope and pray to the God he barely believed in that she would come back to him.

As if on cue his phone rang and he snatched it up, his heart thumping. It wasn't her, of course. The name flashing up was Phoebe's and Callum pressed the reject button. He felt guilty, of course he did, but there was no way he had the emotional resources to deal with her now. He would get through this evening, somehow. Pouring yet another glass of wine would be a good start. And then he would make it up to her in the next few days. When her exams had finished. Then he would spend some time with her, talk to her, persuade Liz to let her stay with him. But now he just needed peace, solitude, alcohol and pizza.

As Phoebe heard the phone cut to voicemail and realised that her beloved father was now not even taking her calls, she flung the phone across her bedroom in anger and frustration. It clattered against the wall and flakes of the carefully chosen raspberry-coloured paint floated gently to the floor. Worried, she jumped up and ran across to it – now was not the time to break her phone, of all things. Luckily, it had survived better than the paintwork, and she picked it up caressingly and laid it on her bedside table. For a few minutes she sat on the edge of the bed, knees drawn up to her chin, staring at it, willing it to ring, yearning to hear Callum's voice cursing modern technology and apologising profusely for having accidentally hung up on her.

It didn't ring. As she'd known, really, that it wouldn't. She shuddered. That day's English Literature exam had covered Angela Carter's *The Bloody Chamber*, and one of the questions had been: *To what extent does Carter subvert the 'happy ever after' of the traditional fairy tale to depict a darker and more adult reality?*

Phoebe hadn't been able to resist reflecting on her situation, feeling that all her life she had been waiting for the happy ever after to happen. Her mother had been the wicked witch, the bullies at school the ugly sisters. She'd never had enough confidence in her physical appearance to believe that a handsome prince would rescue her, but she had believed implicitly in her father's love, and had always expected that one day he would vanquish her enemies and they could live peacefully and happily together. Her phone call had been one last attempt to make that happen, and now it had failed so comprehensively she knew definitively that she had no choice but to engineer her own happy ending. Relying on someone else to rescue her had not worked at any time in nearly sixteen years: now was the time to subvert the happy ever after and rescue herself.

She thought for a moment. Tomorrow was her last exam, a morning one, so by 11.30 a.m. she would be a free agent. The time had come to put her careful planning into action. She pulled her rucksack out from under her bed and rifled through her cupboards and drawers, adding to the rucksack the essentials – clean underwear, a change of clothes, moisturiser, deodorant, a toothbrush. Then, heart racing and palms sweaty, she moved on to the next stage.

She slipped as noiselessly as possible down the staircase from her room to the main landing, outside her mother's room, then she stood and listened for a moment. The TV was on downstairs, so it seemed a fairly safe bet that her mum was occupied. She pushed open the bedroom door and went in, inhaling the familiar scent of Yves Saint Laurent's Opium, her mum's signature perfume. Her handbag was lying carelessly on the dressing table and Phoebe rummaged through it. Make-up bag, compact mirror, breath freshener, tissues . . . purse. Hands shaking, she unzipped it. Bingo. One of the many credit cards was quickly extracted, and then she spotted that there was a tight roll of twenties in there as well. This hadn't been part of the plan, but it was very tempting. She counted them quickly, keeping one ear cocked for any sounds from downstairs. £200. She grabbed four of the notes, then rolled the rest up and replaced them. Within moments she was out of the room and on her way back upstairs, card and cash tucked into her bra. She suppressed the qualms of guilt that arose despite herself. It wasn't really stealing – most of the parents at school seemed to be planning some kind of end of exams celebration for their child; all she was doing was taking the money her mum should have spent on her, if she was any kind of a decent parent, and using it to create that mythical happy ending.

24

For the fifth night in a row Imogen and Indigo were staying over with Alex and Molly. The girls were long since tucked up in Molly's bunk beds and Imogen and Alex were curled up on the sofa, cradling large glasses of red wine while Ella Fitzgerald crooned softly in the background. They weren't talking, but their silence was companionable and relaxed. Alex's cat, Custard, strolled nonchalantly in, surveyed the room fastidiously and then leapt onto Imogen's lap, snuggling down and purring ferociously as she stroked his head and ears. Imogen understood how the cat felt. Warm and content and secure, she felt like purring herself. Then she frowned. Unlike Custard, she did have more on her mind than which flavour food pouch would be selected for supper that evening.

Earlier that day, the head teacher of Middleton Community Primary School in Hull had phoned her to ask, in the nicest possible way, when she was going to make up her mind about their job offer. The kaleidoscope that was Imogen's consciousness had spun faster and faster at that point. She saw her dingy flat; her daughter's forlorn face as she was the last child to be collected yet again. She saw her parents' cosy house and the look of hopeful excitement on their faces when she'd popped in to see them after her job interview. She saw a sign on a polished wooden door saying 'Ms I. Daniels, Deputy Head Teacher'. All powerful reasons for taking this fantastic job opportunity. In fact, the only image that caused her to pause was the face of the man sitting next to her. She glanced covertly sideways. He was tall and broad-shouldered and muscular, with dark hair clippered ruthlessly short to hide the thinning patches. From a distance he could look almost intimidating, but close up the warmth and humanity in his dark brown eyes dispelled that impression. Gentle and sexy and kind and a good cook. She sighed deeply.

He turned and smiled at her.

'That was a big sigh, sweetheart. What's the matter?'

Reluctant to spoil the mood of blissful contentment, Imogen was about to deny there being anything the matter. Then she paused. It wasn't fair: the discussion, however difficult, had to be broached.

She shifted her position to face him properly. Custard glared at her, disgusted at being disturbed.

'Actually, there is a bit of a problem.'

Instantly his face was tense.

'What kind of a problem?'

Imogen ran her finger around the rim of her wine glass before taking a big gulp.

'The thing is, Alex, things have moved so suddenly for us, far quicker than I was expecting.'

He looked even more worried.

'You know, Imogen, I'm sorry if I've come on too strong. I can back off a bit. I know you've only just come out of a relationship and it must be difficult for you. I suppose I've just got a bit carried away because I l-like you so much.'

She shook her head.

'No, it's not that. It's nothing to do with you coming on too strong, or me breaking up with Pete.' She paused again. God, she was making heavy weather of this. There was no easy way to say it, so she just had to stop prevaricating and get it out.

'Before we became . . . close, I'd applied for a new job. Up north, in Hull, near to my parents. I thought it would be a fresh start for me and Indy, a better quality of life. And it's a promotion as well, so money would be a lot less tight, and it's a really exciting opportunity . . . Anyway, to cut a long story short, I've now accepted it. It starts in September, so I'll be moving house in the summer.'

There were a few seconds of stunned silence.

'Whew! Well, I must admit I didn't see this one coming. So, are you saying that this is the end of the road for us, then?'

'No!' Imogen was vehement. 'No, that's not what I want at all. I really, really like you, Alex. I can see our relationship going somewhere. I've agonised so much over this job, I honestly have, but at the end of the day, I have to think of what's best for Indigo, and I thought it would put too much pressure on us if I turned down the opportunity because of you, when it's still such early days for us.'

There was another silence. Imogen looked down, blinking back tears. In that moment all her reasons for accepting the job seemed obscure, and she would have given anything to be able to wind back the clock, change her answer and regain the perfect contentment of a few minutes earlier. Then she felt her wine glass being gently pulled away and Alex took both her hands in his.

'Do you mean it, Imogen? That you could see a future for us?'

She nodded, too tearful to trust her voice.

Suddenly and unexpectedly, he laughed.

'Well, that's OK then!'

She looked at him quizzically.

'Think about it. What are the really important things for our relationship? The way I feel about you – well, that's not in any doubt! You're the most beautiful, kind, generous, intelligent, caring woman I've ever met, and I'm falling madly in love with you.' He ignored Imogen's sharp intake of breath and continued. 'And your feelings for me – well you've just said that you really like me, and can see a future for us. The kids – we each get on really well with the other's daughter, and Indigo and Molly adore each other. That's the important stuff. The rest is just . . . geography.'

Imogen released the breath she'd been holding pretty much since the job offer was confirmed.

'Really? You truly think we can make it work?'

He leaned over and kissed her.

'Of course we can bloody well make it work! There're trains, aren't there? And it can't be that long a drive. As it happens, a couple of contracts have come up for me in Leeds and Sheffield, so I was going to have to spend some time up north anyway.' He grinned. 'You never know, if those contracts go well, I could set up a northern office – maybe Molly and I will move too at some point.'

Imogen laughed delightedly.

'Wow! I can't believe how relieved I feel. I've been dreading telling you.' She stopped, and frowned again. 'But what about Molly's mum? You can't move too far away from her, can you?'

'Talk about meeting trouble halfway! Honestly, you're being ridiculous. Let's just go with the flow and enjoy being together, celebrate your new job, get excited about the possibilities and don't get bogged down stressing about the what-ifs.'

Imogen looked doubtful.

'That's what Ella said as well, but . . .'

Seeing that Imogen was about to spiral off yet again into a series of guilt-ridden worries and anxieties, Alex kissed her, more passionately this time, lowering her back into the sofa cushions, causing Custard to give a chagrined yelp and leap from the sofa. They both laughed, and then Alex slipped his big hands under her T-shirt, unclasped her bra and cupped her breasts. She sighed again, with pleasure this time, and pressed herself against him, at least for the moment giving herself up to feeling rather than thinking.

Callum had dragged himself through the school day. His students found him short-tempered and irritable, totally unlike the normal, famously laid-back Mr McCraig. Some boys sent to him at break-time, after being caught smoking, were subjected to an irate rant that reduced one of them, a worldly-wise tough nut of fourteen, to extremely unusual tears. Colleagues who approached him for a casual chat were given fairly short shrift as well, so by the end of the day, staffroom gossip was rife.

'What the bloody hell's the matter with Callum McCraig today?' Anita Warberg, a Physics teacher, was asking her friend Tracey Tyndall from the History department.

Tracey shrugged theatrically. 'Search me! Did you hear that he made Kyle Spencer cry, though? That's pretty good going.'

Anita laughed. 'Yeah, I would have loved to have seen that. But seriously, it's not Callum's usual style, is it? What's going on? He's been all over the place for the last few weeks, but today it's like the devil's got into him.'

Tracey leaned in confidentially. 'Well, I did hear that he'd left his wife. Maybe it's something to do with that?'

Anita looked doubtful.

'Hmm, maybe. Thing is, though, I don't blame him for leaving her. I'm just surprised he didn't do it years ago. Have you met Liz McCraig?'

Tracey, who was a relatively new member of staff, shook her head.

'Well, she hasn't even bothered to turn up to the Christmas do for the past few years, but she used to come, and oh my God, she's such a bitch.'

'In what way?'

Anita considered.

'In pretty much every way! She's a model, you know, and obviously thinks that makes her God's gift. She was so patronising and superior – and not just to us other plebby teachers, but to Callum as well. I never knew how he put up with her, to be honest. I would have thought leaving her would put a real spring in his step, not create this mood!'

Tracey looked searchingly at her friend.

'Hmm, you haven't got a bit of a soft spot for our Cal, have you?'

Anita blushed.

'Don't be ridiculous! You sound like one of the kids. "Eh, Miss, do you fancy Sir? Do you, Miss? Do you want him to give you one?"'

Tracey looked knowing.

'I dunno, Anita. I reckon you could do a lot worse. He's not bad-looking for an older bloke, and he's dead nice. I reckon you should give him a shoulder to cry on. You never know . . .'

Anita shook her head, slightly unconvincingly.

'Nah, I'm not interested. The problem with turning forty is that all the men your own age either aren't available at all, or they're chasing some girl in their twenties, or they've just got too much bloody baggage. Even if I did fancy Callum – and I'm *not* saying I do, by the way – he's going to have a bitch of an ex-wife, a moody teenage daughter – it's just not worth the hassle.'

Unaware of the interest he was generating down the corridor in the staffroom, Callum was sitting at his desk trying to summon up the energy to phone Phoebe. He knew he ought to, had to in fact. Her exams had finished that morning, and after she had worked so hard and experienced so much disruption and turmoil over the last couple of months, he knew that the very least she deserved was some undivided attention, a bit of spoiling; and there wasn't a snowflake's chance in hell she'd get that from her mother. He was also feeling pretty bad about not taking her call the night before. He tried to formulate a plan. Maybe he could pick her up and they could go into town, down to the Albert Dock perhaps, or one of the restaurants in Liverpool One for an early dinner. He shuddered slightly at the thought of going so near the Hilton, but then steeled himself. Afterwards he could take her back to his and show her the house that hopefully would soon be her home. Now she'd officially left school and her sixteenth birthday was a matter of weeks away, Callum really couldn't see what was to stop her just moving out of the family home and in with him. Let Liz do her worst then.

He sighed. A few months ago that would have been all he could have asked for. An escape from his stale and stifling marriage without losing his beloved daughter. Now it seemed a flat and empty prospect without any chance of Ella being a part of it. However.

He pulled the phone on his desk towards him and dialled Phoebe's mobile number. It cut straight to voice-mail. Irritated, he hung up and dialled what for so long had been his own home number. After a couple of rings Liz answered.

'Hi Liz, it's Callum. Is Phoebe there, please?'

'Nope, don't think so.' She sounded bored.

He tried, with only moderate success, to control the annoyance in his voice.

'Well, do you think you could check for me, please? Her phone's not on.'

Liz sighed with exasperation.

'Okaay.' The phone crackled as she walked with it, and he heard her call, 'Phoebe! Phoebe! Are you there? It's your father on the phone.'

There was a short pause and then Liz was back.

'No, I told you I didn't think she was there.'

'Well, where is she, then? How did her last exam go?'

Liz sounded slightly guilt-stricken.

'Oh God, I'd forgotten it was her last one today. Was it this morning? She's probably gone back to Becky's, she's spent most of her time there these last few weeks.' She didn't add 'since you left her', but the emphasis in her tone was sufficiently acidic for the meaning to be crystal clear.

Callum exhaled.

'OK, I'll try and get hold of her at Becky's. I want to take her out for dinner tonight, to celebrate, if you've got no objection?'

'Oh great idea, Callum, she really needs feeding up,' she replied sarcastically and Callum banged the receiver down, relieved beyond measure that, whatever the state of his romantic life, at least he was finally able to offer his daughter an escape from this woman's toxic presence.

He checked in his mobile and found the Steins's home number.

Ruth Stein answered the phone.

'Hello? Oh, hello, Callum.' Her voice noticeably chilled. 'What can I do for you?'

'Is Phoebe there, please, Ruth?'

She was curt.

'No, she hasn't been here today. It was their last exam, as you may remember, and Becky came straight home. She was shattered, and she's had a nap, and now we're taking her out for dinner. I had rather assumed that Phoebe might be with you.'

Callum listened in silence, hurt at the obvious inisinuation that he might not have remembered it was Phoebe's last exam, and at the implication that he should have been with her that afternoon. He was also beginning to wonder, slightly uncomfortably, where exactly Phoebe was. He replied, defensively, 'I've been in work all day, but I'm trying to get hold of her now. I want to take her out as well.'

'Hmmphh. Well . . .' Ruth paused, wondering whether or not to go for it. 'Well, I know it's none of my business, Callum, and I don't want to pry into what's going on between you and Liz, but I do think you've treated poor Phoebe badly. She's been round here almost every night for weeks, and neither of you seem bothered. And all while she's going through her exams. I do think it's pretty irresponsible.'

Callum felt a wave of cold shame engulf him. He'd known Ruth for over a decade, ever since Phoebe and Becky became friends in reception class. She was warm and kind and softly spoken, and so criticism from her was particularly compelling.

'I know, Ruth. I do know I've let her down. It has been fairly difficult, though. But things will get better, I'll be less distracted, and be there for her more.'

Ruth's voice softened.

'I'm glad to hear it. It's not that I mind having her round, she's a lovely girl, and a great friend to Becky, but I just want what's best for her.'

'I know. Me too. Anyway, I'd better go, 'cos I do want to get hold of her about this evening.'

Anxious now, with a vision of Phoebe wandering alone and friendless around Liverpool, he dialled her mobile again. Still no answer. He left a message.

'Hi Pheebs, it's Dad. Congratulations on finishing your exams! Look, I really want to take you out tonight to celebrate, and then I've got a bit of a surprise for you. Give me a ring when you get this, OK?'

He hung up and then got his jacket from the back of the door. Although it was only 4.30 p.m., hours earlier than he'd normally leave school, he felt he'd had enough for the day. Worry about Phoebe and his inadequacies as a parent had temporarily driven thoughts of Ella from his mind, and he decided that he would carry out his plan from the previous evening. He'd pop to the supermarket on the way home, buy a few bits and pieces, maybe some flowers for Phoebe. He knew he'd been a catastrophically bad father recently, but he would make it up to her. Too much of the past few weeks had been about adults' bad decisions and self-absorption; the time had come to put Phoebe first for a change, and he was determined to do just that.

25

The household and childcare tasks that had seemed so effortless to Ella during the past few weeks had resumed their original, overwhelming, proportions. The same jobs needed to be done – surfaces dusted, floors vacuumed, clothes washed, ironed and put away, meals cooked, children washed, dressed and entertained – but all her joyous energy had evaporated.

Before meeting Callum, Ella had felt that she was at the bottom of a black hole, with no visible way out. The minutiae of her daily life bored her almost to tears, and she was chronically exhausted. She hadn't been able to articulate her feelings to anyone because she knew that to all appearances she was incredibly lucky. Gorgeous kids, nice home, loving and lovely husband. Every time she reflected on her many blessings, though, she felt even more miserable, because if that wasn't enough for her, then what would be? She had thought that another baby would fill the yearning emptiness, but it had turned out that passionate sex and an illicit cyber-relationship with another man had done an even better job. Ella smiled wryly as she reflected that had Greg known those were the two options he might have been more enthusiastic about a third child.

The weeks with Callum in her life had been amazing, but his absence made everything seem even bleaker than it had before, with the additional problem that her husband was barely speaking to her. The sensible, rational part of Ella knew that she had made the right decision. The wise decision. The moral and grown-up decision. But that knowledge did nothing to ease the extent to which she missed Callum. She missed texting him little anecdotes or witticisms that occurred to her throughout the day, and she missed the lifting of her spirits, the bubble of excitement when a new text message or email came through from him. She still had that little surge of optimism every time the new message symbol appeared on her phone, in case Callum had disregarded her instructions and contacted her anyway, but so far he hadn't. It had been less than twenty-four hours since she had told Callum they could never be together, but it felt like months.

In addition to her other problems, Ella was horny as hell. She and Greg hadn't slept together since she got back from Liverpool, nearly two months ago now. Until recently Ella would have said celibacy would be a blessing – shagging her husband was merely one of a long list of jobs she knew she ought to do, but could rarely muster the energy for, like cleaning out the cupboard under the stairs, hoovering under the beds and doing her pelvic floor exercises. After a night of wild and amazing sex with Callum, she had discovered that her libido was very much alive and kicking, but perversely, having sex with Greg while the memory of Callum was so persistent had felt more like infidelity than sleeping with Callum in the first place. Not that sleep had played a very large part in that night's activities. A few times Greg had tried to initiate something and she had feigned a headache, or tiredness or a period, in stereotypical fashion, and then over the last couple of weeks he had made no overtures at all. She'd been relieved in a way, as she was running out of excuses, but since Greg had confronted her about Callum's emails she was getting worried instead.

The previous evening, after getting back from dumping Callum and drinking with Imogen, she'd really wanted to make love to Greg. As well as feeling sexually frustrated, she was also desperate to reconnect with him, to seal their relationship and, hopefully, to drive all thoughts of Callum from her mind once and for all. Greg had been slumped in front of the telly when she got home and as she'd chatted to him, filling him in about Imogen's love life and about what the kids had got up to that day, he had barely lifted his eyes from the screen, and certainly hadn't made eye contact with her.

'What are you watching? Is it good?' she'd asked at last.

He'd shrugged.

'S'alright.'

She'd gone over to the sofa then and snuggled next to him, stroking his arm and back, but he felt unyielding, unresponsive.

'How about an early night?'

He'd shrugged again.

'You go up if you want. I'm going to finish watching this.'

She'd nearly given up at this point, but had made one final effort.

'What time does it finish? I'm not especially tired . . .'

He had looked at her then and she had been able to see no trace of love or warmth in his eyes.

'Go to bed, Ella. It won't finish until late, and you need your sleep.'

She'd gone to kiss him on the lips, but he moved somehow, and she ended up giving him a chaste peck on the cheek before retreating, defeated, to bed.

It was all desperately ironic, Ella reflected, as she stirred risotto now. Here they were, looking on the surface like the perfect couple – children sleeping soundly upstairs, Greg sitting with a glass of wine and the paper while she prepared supper – and yet the cracks she was trying to paper over were gaping underneath. She had no idea what Greg was thinking. Clearly he suspected her of some kind of infidelity – his checking-up phone call to Imogen had demonstrated that – and yet on the surface he had appeared to accept Ella's explanation for the email exchanges with Callum without too much questioning. But what did he feel now? In believing himself to be cuckolded, was he hurt? Angry? Sad? Or, at some point, had he fallen out of love with her and was even now planning the best way to extricate himself?

Well done, Ella, she congratulated herself. You appear to have dumped the man who adores you, the man you've been overwhelmingly in love with since the age of seventeen, the man who's made your life worth living again over the past few weeks, in favour of a husband who won't speak to you, won't sleep with you and is probably about to dump *you*. Nice work.

★　　★　　★

'Hi Phoebe, it's Dad again. Did you get my last message? Give me a call, love.'

'Phoebe, where are you? Have you lost your phone? I suppose if you have you won't get this anyway, but if you do then ring me.'

'Phoebe, where the hell are you? It's turned ten o'clock at night, and I'm worried now. Please ring me and let me know you're OK.'

Callum paced up and down his new living room. 10.15 p.m. and as far as he could piece together, no one had seen Phoebe since her last exam finished at 11.30 a.m. He'd phoned the Steins again and spoken to both Ruth and Becky. Ruth hadn't seen Phoebe at all, and Becky's story was that while after the exam she had been shattered and just wanted to go home to sleep, Phoebe had said she was going into town. Becky had last seen her walking to the bus stop.

This time twenty-four hours earlier Callum had been in a daze of despair at Ella's rejection, and had felt as though he would do anything at all to get her back, to hold her in his arms once again. It had felt like the most intense pain he had ever experienced – when Liz had forced him to cool his friendship with Ella, all those years ago, it had been difficult, but he had known deep down that a relationship with her would be disastrously inappropriate, and he had only been walking away from the promise of something rather than the reality. The actuality he'd experienced over the last few weeks had been so much better than anything he could have imagined, and losing it therefore worse. Or so he had thought. Now, Ella had receded so far into the back of his mind that he could barely recall her. Now he knew that the heartbreak of yesterday was as nothing compared to the anxiety of today. Now he knew that he would gladly bargain any hope of ever seeing Ella again for having Phoebe back home safe and well.

Talking to Liz again, he'd had the cold comfort of hearing a note of anxiety creep into her voice for the first time.

'No, I didn't see her this morning, she didn't mention anything to me about her plans. I just assumed she'd be at Becky's . . .'

'Well, has she mentioned any other friends recently?' Callum had asked.

Liz had sounded tired and hopeless.

'No, I don't think so. I'm sure she hasn't. It's just Becky, really, isn't it? Oh God, Callum. Do you think she's OK? What are we going to do?'

That was the question Callum was pondering now. What were they going to do? It was well past the time Phoebe might reasonably have been expected to be out in town, especially by herself. A couple of times she and Becky had gone to a gig or to the pictures in town, but that had always been carefully planned beforehand, on the strict understanding that a parent picked them up afterwards. He knew that if this was a pupil at school and he was being asked for his professional advice, he would probably advise the parents to call in the police at this point, if only as a precaution. He couldn't quite face doing that, though. While there were no officials involved it seemed like a minor hiccup in domestic life that he could get a handle on; describing the situation to the police would be an admission that something serious was wrong, and he wasn't quite ready to go there yet. He had phoned the A&E department of the Royal Liverpool, but either no one answering to Phoebe's description had been admitted or the exigencies of the Data Protection Act meant that they weren't prepared to confirm it. He hadn't really believed that was the solution – Phoebe would have had her phone with her and surely, if she'd been taken in unconscious, the staff would have tried the numbers stored as 'Mum', 'Dad' or 'Home'. A sudden thought struck him, and he called Liz again.

'Phoebe?' Her voice was pitifully hopeful as she answered the phone.

'No, sorry, me again. I take it you haven't heard from her either, then?'

'No. Oh God, Callum. Where the hell is she?' She sounded tense and panicked again now.

'Well, I was just wondering if she might have – run away, I suppose. I mean, things haven't been easy lately.'

'No secret who's to blame for that!' she retorted acerbically.

'Leave it, Liz. Now's not the time. We just need to concentrate on finding Phoebe. Can you check her room and see if she's taken anything?'

'OK.' He heard the muffled sound of her running upstairs.

A few moments passed, and she was back on the line again.

'I'm not sure.' She paused and then admitted, 'I haven't been up here for so long, I'm not sure what should be here.'

Callum tried to control his impatience. As he had already pointed out, this was not the moment for point-scoring.

'What about her rucksack? The flowery one?'

'I can't see it. But she uses that for school anyway, doesn't she?'

He sighed.

'That's true. Well, what about in her bathroom? Is her toothbrush there?'

Another moment, and then Liz came back, with a more optimistic tone in her voice.

'Her toothbrush isn't here, or her toothpaste. That's a good sign, isn't it?'

'Is it?' Callum's voice was grim.

'Well, yes. If the little madam's run away, then at least we know she hasn't been abducted or worse. Thank God for that; that's got to be good news. Hasn't it?'

'I suppose you could look at it that way. Or you could say that we've made our fifteen-year-old daughter so miserable that she felt she had no choice but to run away from the home we made untenable for her, and is now out, alone, in the middle of the night, and we haven't the smallest idea where, let alone how to get her back. I'm not sure that's what I'd call tremendously good news, to be honest.'

26

Following her last exam, Phoebe had jumped on a bus into town in a mood of mingled exhilaration and terror. She was a good girl. She had always been a good girl. Perhaps the fact that she had lived as long as she could remember with the bitter knowledge that her appearance made her a continual disappointment to her mother had meant that in every other way she had exerted herself tooth and nail to be the perfect daughter. She worked hard at school and always got top results. She didn't smoke, or drink, or hang out at bus stops or in pub car parks with unsuitable boys. She was polite and tidy and always remembered her grandparents' birthdays. This was, without a shadow of a doubt, the most daring and rebellious thing she had ever done.

Already she had stolen from her mum, and come into town without telling her parents where she was going, neither of which she would have previously contemplated. Now, standing scanning the departures board at Liverpool Lime Street station, she was about to go several steps further. She saw what she was looking for. The 12.07 departure to London Euston, Platform 7. She hurried over, her rucksack thumping slightly against her back, but not as persistently as her heart was thumping against her

229

ribs. She stood for a moment and looked at the sleek red and silver train, then up at the high domed glass roof, sparkling in the early summer sunshine.

She had a one-way ticket to London, booked online and collected at a machine in the station, tucked safely in the pocket of her jeans, but it wasn't too late. She could turn round, get the bus back to Allerton, sneak the money and credit card back into her mum's purse, call her dad again, pop round to Becky's – resume normal life before anyone noticed that she had stepped out of it. But no. That was the whole point. She had no normal life to resume any more. Her normal, such as it was, had been shattered when her dad walked out without a backwards glance, leaving her with a mother who ignored her at best, resented her at worst. Phoebe had no idea what her future would be. While she heard other pupils in her year chatting about their plans for the summer, the A-level options they would take, whether to stay on at school or attend sixth-form college, she hadn't been able to sketch out even a rudimentary future, because she was powerless. The last few weeks had demonstrated with crystal clarity that no one was going to consult or even consider her. She was the flotsam and jetsam on the tide of adult selfishness. This scheme, hatched over many weeks, was her way of seizing back some control, of demonstrating that in future she would need to be treated as more than a pawn in someone else's game.

She took a deep breath, switched her phone off so there was no possibility of being tracked and stepped onto the train.

She found her allotted seat and looked around. It felt smart and futuristic, although she found the overly high seat backs somewhat claustrophobic; and she was glad there was no one sitting next to her, because the armrest between the seats dug into her hip until she raised it and let her generous flesh spill comfortably onto the seat next to hers. She looked out of the window as the train wound its way through the terraced rooftops. Somewhere in that sea of red brick were both her parents – her dad at school, probably meting out lunch-break discipline, her mum maybe at the gym, or meeting a friend for a 'salad, no dressing please'. At the moment they were oblivious, but before long they would hopefully be learning their lesson.

Thinking of what her parents would be up to at lunchtime reminded Phoebe of how hungry she was herself. As the train rounded the curve onto the Runcorn railway bridge, alongside the dramatic greenish-white curve of the road bridge over the muddily industrial Mersey, she lurched her way down to the buffet car. A smoked salmon and cream cheese sandwich, large bag of salt and vinegar crisps, Mars bar and bottle of Diet Coke gave her hardly any change from £10 and she gulped slightly. If everything was this expensive, she worried, the cash supply that had seemed so generous as she worked it all out in her bedroom at home would dwindle alarmingly quickly.

Back at her seat and munching away, she ran through the details of her finances once more. Her mum's credit card had booked the train ticket, and she'd also used it to book herself into a hotel for a couple of nights. When she'd looked online, there were some Travelodges on the outer edges of the Tube map that seemed fairly good value, far more so than central London hotels, and so she'd thought that was the best bet. She had the reservation details for one tucked in her wallet, and once she'd found her bearings she was sure that she'd be able to find it easily enough. Of course, that depended on her mum not having the credit card stopped, but she wasn't too concerned about that eventuality; Liz had several cards, and this one had been right at the back of her wallet, so probably wasn't one she used that frequently. Even if she did discover it was lost, it would probably take her a few days, and even then she might not associate it with Phoebe.

She had the £80 cash she'd taken as well, and about £25 left over from that month's allowance – luckily revision had meant that she and Becky hadn't been out much and she'd been eating all her meals with the Steins. In her own savings account, for which she had a debit card, there was a healthy balance of £220. It would just have to do. She wasn't sure quite how far things would go anyway. She supposed that for the rest of today her parents would assume she was with Becky and not worry. Would her mum notice when she didn't return home that night? Doubtful. She'd been spending more and more time in her own room, and her mum hardly ever ventured up there. It would be interesting – in fact, a higher-stakes game of the daisy petal rhyme 'He loves me, he loves me not' – to see exactly how long it would take for her parents to realise that she'd gone at all, and from that deduce how much they really cared for her.

She and Becky had worked out that she shouldn't use her mobile as it might be trackable – Phoebe only had a very hazy idea as to whether this was true or not, but had decided not to take the risk. She had therefore set up a new email account, the address of which she had given only to Becky, so that Becky could keep her informed as to what was going on back at base. Their plan was a two-stage one, beautiful in its simplicity. First of all Phoebe's parents would discover (at some point) that she was missing. She hoped that this would give them – or at least her father, as she wasn't convinced Liz gave a damn one way or another – the fright of their lives. There would be a poetic justice in Callum having his life turned upside down in a way he couldn't control, just as he had done to her. Then when they discovered where she was – Becky was going to make a judgement call as to how long to leave it – they would see that she had taken control of her own life and was making her own plans for the future.

Becky's cousin, Elisa, was in her early twenties and lived in Clapton in east London, sharing a flat with her boyfriend and two other couples. Becky had been down to visit a couple of times and said it was really cool and a great area. Elisa was broke and planning on turning her little box room/study into a bedroom, and had said that Phoebe could live there if she wanted. True, Becky hadn't mentioned that Phoebe was only fifteen, but seeing as her sixteenth birthday was only a matter of weeks away that surely couldn't be terribly relevant. Unfortunately, Elisa was in Berlin for work for the next few days, hence Phoebe needing a hotel, but after that she could move in. It would cost the slightly eye-watering sum of £75 a week, but that included all bills and Phoebe knew she had enough money for the first couple of weeks, by which time she would need to have found a job. Elisa might be able to help there as well; she'd emailed, slightly vaguely, about her office needing 'admin cover' over the summer, and if that worked out Phoebe would be paid £7 an hour for a thirty-five-hour week, so even after paying her rent and travel she would still have more money to spend than ever in her life before. Come September, of course, something would need to change again – Phoebe had looked up various sixth-form colleges in east London, and there was a huge choice, but she wouldn't be able to study for her A-levels and work full-time. However, that was several weeks away, and in the meantime Phoebe was just revelling in the fact that stage one of her plan was successfully completed.

Arriving at London Euston was rather overwhelming. Phoebe had never been to London before, although she'd long dreamed of doing so, and it was bigger and busier than she could ever have imagined. Station announcements seemed to be saying something about a delayed departure to Manchester Piccadilly now ready for boarding, and suddenly Phoebe was nearly knocked over in the surge of people heading for that train. She panicked slightly, but then took some calming breaths, hitched her rucksack more firmly onto her shoulders and reminded herself of her plan.

She'd brought hardly any clothes with her – nothing she'd owned as a schoolgirl in Liverpool seemed quite right for her new role as a woman about town in London. She'd done her internet research on this as well, and discovered that the large H&M on Oxford Street stocked a range called BiB – Big is Beautiful – and that the Primark on Oxford Street sold plus-size clothes as well. She was hoping that between the two she'd be able to kit herself out with a new wardrobe without busting the limit on her mum's credit card. That was probably a task for tomorrow, though. First, before burdening herself with carrier bags, she wanted to explore some of London, and her primary objectives were Covent Garden and Soho. She spoke to the helpful man in the Transport for London information booth and discovered that she needed something called, rather surreally, an Oyster card in order to be able to travel by Tube or bus. She sorted that and then, with the instructions that she needed 'Northern Line, Charing Cross Branch, southbound – get off at Leicester Square' ringing in her ears, she headed off in the direction of the signs marked Underground, and prepared to have an adventure.

27

Greg sat at the kitchen table, watching Ella stirring a pan on the stove, as he had on countless previous evenings. Ella had always been a good cook, and had always enjoyed cooking, so he'd never made much effort to move beyond his student staples of fry-ups, toasties and Pot Noodles. On the rare occasions he needed to cook for the kids, some combination of cheese, baked beans and toast usually hit the spot, and, in nine years of living together he'd never once been required to cook for Ella. He took a sip of wine and considered this point. Of course, before the children were born they'd eaten out regularly. Not usually anything fancy – maybe meeting a big group of friends at PizzaExpress, or it might be just the two of them at a nice local gastropub. One year, their New Year's resolution had been to try the cuisine of at least twenty-five different countries, and they'd had such amazing fun doing that. The first few were effortless – Thai, Japanese, Chinese, Italian, Mexican, French, British. Then they'd had to challenge themselves a little more, and had explored some remote corners of London as they did so, eating Portuguese in Stockwell, Turkish in Dalston, Polish in Hammersmith, Vietnamese in Hackney, Somalian in Wembley. It had been so enjoyable – a joint project to research the types of food and the places they could go, and then a mini adventure hopping on the Tube to somewhere they would never normally go, to taste something they'd never normally taste.

It wasn't as though Ella never got a break from cooking any more, though, Greg thought defensively to himself. They normally got a takeaway on a Friday night, occasionally had Sunday lunch out with the kids, and then his parents were always happy to babysit for an evening so they could go out for a birthday or anniversary dinner. Somehow though, somewhere along the line, it had ceased to be either spontaneous or fun. Rather like their sex life, in fact. Greg had another mouthful of wine. The glimmerings of an idea were beginning to form in his mind.

For days he had been sunk into a torpor of depression. Knowing that Ella was either having, or contemplating having, an affair with another man, he'd felt powerless to react. If he confronted her angrily, which was exactly what he felt like doing half the time, then she might call his bluff, walk out on him, leave him and take his kids with her. On the other hand, carrying on as usual, maintaining the illusion of a happy marriage, which was the line he had intended to take, was proving almost impossible. He winced at the thought of his behaviour the night before. Firstly, phoning his wife's friend to check up on her as though she was an errant teenage daughter, and then rebuffing her tentative attempts at seduction so boorishly. He castigated himself inwardly. Way to go Greg, two nice examples for Ella of why she'd probably be better off with Callum Fucking McCraig, whoever he may be.

But now this idea, which had just occurred to him and was now hovering teasingly in his consciousness, challenging him to make something of it, now *that* could just be the answer.

He looked up from the newspaper he had been pretending to read and caught Ella's eye as she turned away from her cooking for a moment. She smiled, and he smiled back.

'Ella?'

'Yes?' She looked so eager, and hopeful, and beautiful despite her beat-up jeans and threadbare T-shirt, that his heart clenched.

'D'you remember when we did that ethnic food thing? A few years ago, pre-Aidan?'

Her eyes danced delightedly. As much, he suspected, because he had initiated a positive topic of conversation for the first time in weeks as it was because of her recollections of curries past.

'God, yeah, of course I do. That was so much fun, wasn't it?' She sounded animated but slightly wistful, and as she served mushroom risotto into two bowls and placed a rocket salad on the table and he refilled their glasses, they continued with an animated series of reminiscences and shared one of the most enjoyable meals they'd had for a long time.

Phoebe had studied Wordsworth in her English classes, and had found him to be frankly overrated. Compared with, say, the starkly moving First World War poetry they'd looked at, or the heartbreakingly perfect couplets in *Romeo and Juliet*, their set Shakespeare text, Wordsworth had seemed clichéd and overblown. However, walking across Hungerford Bridge from Embankment station to the South Bank, his line, 'Earth hath not anything to show more fair,' popped into her head, and although this was a different bridge and it was dusk, not dawn, she couldn't help but feel he'd been on to something after all. She was in a mood of total exhilaration, in love with London and the unique sense of energy and excitement it exuded. She felt calmly certain that she had done exactly the right thing in coming here – the hugeness and possibility of London seemed to contextualise her own problems.

She was glad she'd worn her comfiest trainers, because she knew she must have walked miles that afternoon, her rucksack clinging damply to her back. She'd bought a London A–Z at a little newsagent outside Leicester Square station, and had planned a route to take in every street and landmark she'd read about and dreamed of. She looked longingly at the brightly lit theatres, but knew rationally that to buy a ticket, even from one of the tempting half-price booths which were everywhere, wouldn't be wise given she had no real idea how long she had to make her money last. She'd wandered through Seven Dials, picturing the adventures of the 1920s aristocrats in Agatha Christie's eponymous novel. She'd strolled through the Covent Garden piazza and looked admiringly at the Opera House, remembering with a bitter twinge how she had imagined this building constantly when she was ten years old, reading Lorna Hill's Sadler's Wells books and dreaming of being a ballerina – until, that is, her mother had punctured her dream by laughing derisively when she'd asked if she could have ballet lessons and pointing out that they probably didn't make leotards in her size. Inevitably, her father had jumped in and said that of course she could have lessons, but by then her fragile self-confidence had been punctured too severely for her to be able to face them.

She'd pictured Soho as seedy, sexy and dangerous, and so was slightly disappointed that walking down Old Compton Street on a sunny June afternoon didn't really feel like anything out of the ordinary. There were a few sex shops, but there were also branches of Caffè Nero and Costa, for every punk or goth there was a middle-aged Home Counties couple on their way back from a matinee, and she didn't see a single drag queen. Piccadilly Circus had enthralled her; approaching it from a little side street she could see the famous Eros statue, framed by an archway, with the red and blue London Underground logo in the edge of the frame. A shiver of pure delight ran through her. She climbed onto the steps of Eros with all the other tourists and gazed up at the bright adverts, then down towards Westminster. She crossed the road and walked up Piccadilly, this time imagining Peter Wimsey living the 1930s bachelor dream and solving a few mysteries while he did so. She'd then been enchanted to discover the biggest Waterstones she'd ever seen, and had spent a blissful few hours browsing the eight floors, buying herself, courtesy of Liz's credit card again, a *Time Out* guidebook to London. Then, feeling very grown up, she'd ordered a latte and a chocolate brownie in the fifth-floor coffee bar and sat, alternately gazing out of the window at the rooftops and spires of London and browsing through her new book for ideas about what to do next.

Finally, she had decided to walk down to Trafalgar Square, then to Embankment, and cross the bridge before heading to the British Film Institute. That felt suitably sophisticated, and according to the guidebook, there was a café-bar there that sounded perfect for a light supper before she had to start the mission to find her hotel.

And so here she was, walking lingeringly over the river, wishing for the first time that there was someone – Becky or her dad – here to share all this, to whom she could comment and exclaim and then talk it all through with over a meal. She paused her train of thought. No. The whole point of this was to demonstrate her independence, and it was working. She mentally congratulated herself on doing a great job: everything she had planned had come off. She'd braved the London Underground and survived, and had found her way around all afternoon, having some of the most memorable experiences of her life in the process. This was the time for celebrating, not for weakening and pining for company.

The BFI was everything she hoped it would be. Phoebe allowed herself to imagine that she was five stone lighter, with her hair cut into a pixie crop, perhaps with some geek-chic, chunky-framed glasses to set off her delicate femininity. She'd wear simple skinny jeans with ballet pumps and a black cashmere roll-neck, a leather satchel flung casually over one arm. She'd be studying something intellectual yet cool, and would regularly spend time at the BFI watching original French films, without subtitles. It was a pleasing vision, and one she continued to indulge in as she found a seat and went to the bar to order. One benefit of her weight was that she knew she looked at least five years older than her real age and was constantly being mistaken for a university student; she decided to take advantage of this and, along with her charcuterie plate, sourdough toast and olives, ordered a large glass of red wine. It felt like the kind of thing her alter ego in the skinny black roll-neck would do.

Actually taking a sip made her mouth screw up with involuntary disgust. When she'd had wine before, occasionally, it had been white wine in a spritzer diluted with lemonade – this was very different. She persevered though, and when the food arrived she found the pungency of the garlic and spices helped the wine to go down a lot more easily. So easily, in fact, that it was gone in no time, and she ordered another. She sat, gulping more than sipping, people-watching and letting the pleasantly woozy feeling the wine was creating wash over her. It was so enjoyable that she lingered longer than she had intended and was stunned when she realised it was after 10 p.m. Finding her hotel for the night had to be a priority, but red-wine-induced recklessness whispered that it would be fun, first, to nip back over the river and see if Soho was more what she had imagined at this time of night. She consulted her guidebook and map again, aware that the words and lines looked slightly fuzzy now. From Tottenham Court Road station she could get the Central Line to Snaresbrook on the outskirts of east London, where the Travelodge she'd booked was located. She contemplated phoning ahead to tell them she'd be there in an hour or so, but was still worried about turning her phone on. When she'd checked on the website it had said that late check-in wasn't a problem. True, it hadn't specified how late, but it wouldn't take her long to have a quick wander around Soho and she hazily thought it would take about half an hour on the Tube. She'd be tucked up in bed by 11.30 p.m. for sure.

After going to the loo she set off again, retracing her footsteps along the South Bank, over the bridge, through Trafalgar Square and Piccadilly Circus and into Soho. It did indeed feel like a different place by night. Some of the sights were familiar from Liverpool: large crowds of giggling women on a hen night, the bride decorated with a pink sparkly tiara and a condom-bedecked veil; Essex boys in for a night on the town – smart shirts, slicked-back hair and lots of pushing and shoving – Phoebe had seen *Gavin and Stacey*, she knew all about that. But there were other things she hadn't noticed earlier that day, and which were completely outside her experience so far – phone boxes encrusted with pictures of nearly naked women offering all kinds of services. 'Massage' shops with blacked-out windows and red neon lights – even Phoebe wasn't naïve enough to think that's where you went to get your RSI sorted out. It was past 11 p.m. now, and Phoebe suddenly started to panic that she had left it too late for the hotel. How long would it actually take to get there on the Tube? Where was Tottenham Court Road, anyway? And what time did the Tube stop running? Maybe she should have booked a hotel in the centre of town, just for tonight. Feeling panicky now, her head pounding from fear and tannin, she tried to calm down and think sensibly. There was a little café over there, she could go and get some water, which she felt she badly needed, sit down, check her map for the best way to get to

Tottenham Court Road and maybe her guidebook would say until what time the trains carried on running. She could even get a taxi to the Tube station if she needed to, or possibly all the way to the hotel if the trains had stopped already. Yes, it would cost money, but she did have plenty of cash; she had been mercilessly abusing Liz's credit card all day.

She sat down rather gingerly at a slightly sticky plastic table, and ordered a bottle of water from the surly waitress who came over. Then she took off her rucksack to find the map – and froze with horror. The zip pocket on the front, where she'd been keeping her wallet, phone and map, was open. She plunged her hand inside – it was empty. Her stomach lurched and she yanked open the zip of the main pocket, hoping and praying that somehow they would be there instead. No trace. She felt clammy and nauseated, and her hands were shaking as she tipped her bag upside down on the table, beyond caring about hygiene standards now, and rifled through her things – pyjamas, clean underwear and clothes, washbag, books, but no money, no map, no phone, no Oyster card and no credit card.

28

Callum was enduring the worst night of his life. It wasn't just the horrific images tormenting him – of Phoebe alone, lonely, frightened, kidnapped, raped – it was the crushing remorse that he was responsible for having driven her to whatever situation she now found herself in. What had he been playing at these last few weeks? Love and lust for Ella had blotted out everything else, and although he had told himself that he was doing the right thing for Phoebe by focussing on setting up a new life for them both, rather than spending time with her there and then, in his heart he knew that he'd been doing it for Ella and himself more than for Phoebe.

She'd been in the middle of her GCSEs, for heaven's sake, and he'd barely seen her, let alone been there to help her with her revision timetable, test her on her notes, reassure her that she was going to do brilliantly. He'd done far, far more for his students than he'd done for his own daughter. Any pricking of conscience had been stilled by a reflection that he'd done more than his fair share of this kind of thing over the years, and it was Liz's turn to pull her weight – especially as she was so insistent that as a 'full-time' mother she deserved custody of Phoebe. The thing is, though, he'd known that Liz wouldn't step up to it and that, far from bolstering Phoebe's confidence, conversations between them only undermined Phoebe further. Goodness knows where Phoebe would have been without the Steins – reading between the lines of their phone conversations earlier that day, he could see that Ruth Stein had been pretty much singlehandedly responsible for all the physical and emotional succour Phoebe had received over the past few weeks, and Callum felt simultaneous waves of frank gratitude and burning humiliation at the thought.

Worst of all, though, was last night. Phoebe had phoned him, on the eve of her last exam, and he hadn't even bothered to take the call because he preferred to indulge in an evening of drunken self-pity about his girlfriend dumping him. Perfect father of the year behaviour.

After pacing the floor for what felt like hours with these reflections spinning in his head, Callum decided that if he hadn't heard from Phoebe by midnight then he would call the police. As so often in crisis situations his mind then seized on an inessential, and he started obsessing about logistics. Should he phone 999? Or call the local police station? The first seemed rather melodramatic, but the second was what you did when you lost your dog, not your precious only child. Just as he was coming to the conclusion that it would be 999 and be damned, his phone rang.

He threw himself across the room and picked it up, swiping manically at the green button on the touch screen. It wasn't a number he recognised and he prayed desperately that the voice on the other end wasn't going to be a professionally sympathetic one asking, 'Are you the father of Phoebe McCraig?'

It wasn't. There was a moment of silence when he answered, and he repeated, 'Hello? Hello? Callum McCraig here,' until a small, scared voice said, 'Daddy? It's me.'

His knees went weak with relief and he sank onto the nearest chair before they could give way entirely. His hands were shaking, but he concentrated hard on keeping his voice warm, steady and reassuring for Phoebe's sake.

'Phoebe! Darling. Where are you? Where have you been? We've been so worried, sweetheart.'

'Oh, Dad, I'm sorry. I'm so sorry.' She started crying, and he could feel his own throat close up.

'Don't be silly, pet. You've got nothing to be sorry for. I'm sorry, I'm so sorry about not being around for you after your mum and I broke up. I will make it up to you, I promise. Now, where are you? I'm going to come and pick you up.'

At this she sobbed harder than ever, and at first he couldn't make out what she was saying.

'Sorry, love, where did you say?'

'Picca . . . dilly . . . Cir . . . cus,' he made out at last.

'What?! In London?'

'Yes. And Dad, I'm in a phone box, and the money's about to go, and I haven't got any more.'

'OK, don't panic, I'll phone you back on your mobile.'

'You can't, I've lost it,' she wailed.

He heard the telltale bleeps and shouted at her urgently.

'Listen Phoebe, stay there. Stay in that phone box. I'm going to get the number and call you back there. And if I can't, phone the operator and make a reverse-charge call to our home number. Have you got that?'

He didn't hear her reply before the line went dead.

He fumbled with his phone – never particularly technically able at the best of times, he now felt completely inept
as he tried to retrieve the incoming number and call it
back, praying that that system still worked. Thankfully it
did, and moments later he heard Phoebe's voice.

'Hello? Is that you, Dad?'

'Yes, love. Now tell me what's going on.'

It all came out then. Her loneliness and resentment, the
grand plan to run away, the excitement, and then her
panic when she realised she'd lost everything and was
completely stuck.

'And I just didn't know what to do, Dad. I couldn't face
phoning Mum, I just couldn't. And I couldn't remember
Becky's number, but I thought I knew your number off by
heart. Then I thought I couldn't phone 'cos I didn't have
any money, but I found I did have a bit of loose change in
my jeans pocket, so I found a phone box and called you.
But I don't know what to do now.'

'It's alright, love, we'll sort it out,' Callum soothed, with
a calmness and certainty he was far from feeling. The
thought of his precious, beautiful, naïve daughter out on
her own in Soho, at midnight, without any money or a
phone, when he was a four-hour drive away, was enough
to make his blood run cold. He forced himself to keep
cool. Luckily, twenty years' experience as a teacher in a
comprehensive had given him plenty of practice of thinking on his feet, improvising and not letting anyone suspect
he wasn't totally in control.

'Listen, the café you were in when you found your
things were gone, is it nearby and still open?'

'Yes, just across the street. I can see it from here. And it's a twenty-four-hour one.'

Callum breathed a sigh of relief.

'OK, and is it nice? I mean, did you feel safe there?'

Phoebe reflected for a moment. The shabby little café and grouchy staff didn't exactly feel like a haven, but, on the other hand, compared to the inside of the phone box with its peeling paint, stale urine tang and adverts for Thai babes, it seemed pretty promising.

'Umm, yes. It was fine.'

'Do you know the address?'

'Yeah, it's called The Big Cuppa, and it's on Denman Street, at the end nearest Piccadilly Circus.'

Callum scribbled frantically.

'OK. Right, now listen to me, Pheebs. This is the plan. Go back to the café now – have you got enough money for a drink?'

She shook her head.

'No, I don't think so. I've got about forty pence in five-pence pieces I think.'

'Alright, not to worry. Go back and order anyway, and just sit there. I've got a friend who lives in London – do you remember Ella, who used to babysit for you?'

Phoebe cast her mind back to a dim and distant memory.

'Yes, I think so. She was really nice.'

'Yes, she is. Well, I'm going to phone her and ask her to come and meet you at the café. I don't know how long it will take her, but she'll come. And then she'll stay with you, somewhere, until I can get there. I'll leave as soon as I can, but it's going to take me a few hours.'

Phoebe started crying again.

'I'm so sorry, Dad. I know I've been a nightmare, and caused this whole problem, but please don't bring Mum with you. Please. I just can't stand having her shouting at me.'

'It's alright. I won't, I promise. Just me. Now, listen Pheebs. If I can't get hold of Ella then I'll try and get a phone number for the café and call you there. Otherwise, just stay there. It's not ideal, but you should be safe. And if you don't feel safe, in any way, then phone 999. You don't need money to do that from a call box.'

Phoebe laughed through her tears.

'I know that, Dad. Stranger Danger stuff, I've been hearing it for years.'

'Yes, well, it's important. Do you promise me?'

'Yes, I promise.'

'Good girl. I love you, Phoebe.'

'I love you too, Dad.'

29

Ella finished brushing her teeth and started cleansing her face. Even bare of make-up there was a certain glow about the woman looking back at her. She and Greg had had their best evening together for months, if not years. They'd shared a bottle of red wine over dinner, and then sat for hours chatting. He'd loaded the dishwasher, but instead of automatically going through to put the telly on or heading up to bed, Ella had stayed and they'd carried on chatting. They hadn't talked at all about their recent problems, or about the kids, or about their friends. Instead, they'd talked about themselves, reminiscing, reminding each other of when they were a couple instead of just parents. Now they were both getting ready for bed and Ella was quietly confident that if she tried to seduce Greg tonight she wouldn't be rejected, and that was only if he didn't make a move on her first.

She was about to rinse her face when she heard what sounded like the phone ringing. Slightly worried – after all, it was nearly midnight – she ran through to the bedroom, hoping there was nothing wrong with her parents, or Greg's, or Immy, only to see that Greg had already taken the call and was standing with a face like thunder. Less worried now, as he looked angry more than distressed, she was just deciding it must be a crank caller when Greg said frigidly, 'Very well, if you insist, I will pass the phone to *my wife*.'

Her eyebrows shot up and she looked at him enquiringly.

He made no attempt to cover the phone, but stood holding it out to her.

'It's for you.' His voice was flat and cold. 'Callum McCraig.'

Ella's stomach flipped over backwards and she felt a film of icy sweat break out on her forehead. What the hell was Callum playing at? Unsure how best to get out of this, she took the phone.

'Callum? Why on earth are you phoning me at this time of night?'

Callum's voice was urgent and insistent.

'I'm sorry, Ella. I know you asked me not to contact you again, and I wouldn't have, but you HAVE to help me. It's Phoebe.'

'Phoebe? What's the matter with Phoebe?'

Ella was still feeling sceptical, convinced that this was some ploy of Callum's to cause trouble between her and Greg and so drive her into his arms. The thing was, though, with Greg standing there looking fractionally less friendly than the Terminator she couldn't let what she said to Callum betray that they were, or ever had been, any more than friends, which ruled out a lot of the extremely irate things she wanted to say to him. And she could hardly take the phone out of the room to speak privately; with Greg's current mood that would be tanta-mount to asking for a divorce.

Callum's tone when he replied, however, was convincing. He sounded totally desperate.

'She's run away, to London. She's in some dodgy little café in Soho, with no money or phone – they were stolen. I've just got in the car now, but it's going to take me hours to drive down. Please, Ella, you have to go and find her and look after her for me.'

'Callum! What are you talking about? It's the middle of the bloody night.'

Now he sounded every inch the deputy headteacher.

'Exactly. It's the middle of the bloody night, and my fifteen-year-old daughter is totally alone and penniless in the middle of one of the biggest cities in the world. You're a parent, Ella, imagine if that was your kid. Even if you won't do this to help me, please, do it to help the little girl you used to look after.'

Ella sighed. When he put it like that, there was no way she could say no to him. She grabbed a piece of paper and jotted down the details Callum gave her. Then she assured him again that she would go as soon as possible and hung up, turning trepidatiously to face Greg.

'What the fuck is going on, Ella?'

She had never heard him sound so angry.

'I'm so sorry, Greg, it's a total nightmare. Callum's daughter, Phoebe, who I used to babysit for when I was a teenager, has run away. She's in Soho, on her own, and she's had her bag snatched or something. Callum's driving down, but anything could happen to her, so I've said I'll go and meet her, check she's alright.'

She thought Greg was going to explode.

'Oh come on, Ella. This is a bit much, even for your recent standards of behaviour. Your lover, or whatever he is, phones you, in our home, at midnight, and you jump to attention and go running off to meet him with some sorry excuse of a story? I'm not totally stupid, you know.'

Ella was rifling through her wardrobe as they spoke, looking for a thick sweater. She pulled on a shabby but warm hoodie and her trainers.

'Listen, Greg. I understand why you're angry. I'm so sorry about this, but I promise, cross my heart, on the children's lives, that the reason I'm going now is to look after Phoebe, like I said. I know we need to talk properly, but now I need to rush to get to her.'

She fell back on Callum's line.

'Imagine if in a few years' time it was Hattie – wouldn't you hope that someone would help her?'

Greg harrumphed.

'I'd better get myself a mistress now then, in preparation, hadn't I?'

Ella decided to ignore this and reached for the phone to book a minicab, taking her emergency supply of cash from the little china jar on her bedside table. As an afterthought she took another warm sweater from her cupboard in case Phoebe was cold. Then she went over to Greg, who was sitting on the edge of the bed, head in hands.

'Greg, I love you. I love you so much. You have to trust me and let me do this, and then we'll sort it all out. I promise.'

She kissed the top of his head and, getting no response, turned and ran downstairs to wait for the taxi.

It came within a few minutes and she slipped out, closing the door with exaggerated care so as not to wake the children.

Sitting in the back of the taxi as it rumbled along, she could almost laugh at the slings and arrows of outrageous fortune. Of all evenings for this to happen, just as she and Greg were getting on so well, when she was beginning to think that he might forgive her after all, that her marriage might just be salvageable, despite the mess she had made of everything.

Her nanna had always said that old sins have long shadows, and that truism came back to her now. If she hadn't cheated on Greg with Callum, then she wouldn't be sitting in this taxi now. She wondered what would have happened to Phoebe in that case, but then realised with horror that, probably, without their affair, Callum wouldn't have left Liz and Phoebe wouldn't have felt the need to run away. When you came down to it, the fact that this girl was alone and vulnerable, two hundred miles away from home, was her fault. She shuddered, and asked the taxi driver if he could go any faster. She thought about her own children, innocently sleeping while their mother made such a mess of her own life that she was seriously jeopardising their future happiness. If Greg couldn't forgive her for this, if the truth of her affair with Callum came out, then what kind of emotional wrecks would her kids be by the time they reached *their* teenage years? Her selfishness and irresponsibility struck her afresh.

She forced her mind back to practical considerations. What the hell was she going to *do* with Phoebe until Callum turned up? Taking her home and having Callum, in heaven knows what mood, turning up there at 4 a.m. didn't really bear thinking about. There was no way her emergency cash supply was going to cover the taxi fares and a hotel bill, and putting a hotel, however innocently, on her joint credit card was clearly not an option tonight. She grimaced to herself and hoped that the café was salubrious enough for them to stay in while they waited for the cavalry, otherwise known as Callum McCraig, to arrive.

30

Phoebe sat down, shivering slightly, at the same table in the café she'd occupied earlier. The surly waitress glared at her and Phoebe wilted, but knew she had no alternative but to brazen it out and pray that Ella wouldn't be long. She ordered a cup of tea and then went to the little toilet off the back of the room, more to escape the waitress's hostile gaze for a moment than because she particularly needed a wee. She surveyed herself in the mirror. Not good. Her face was blotchy and red from all the tears, and her hair tousled – it turned out that tearing your hair out wasn't a metaphor; in her panic she had been tugging at handfuls of hair, running her fingers through it as she desperately tried to think what to do.

Normally Phoebe didn't make much effort with her appearance. She had a miserable conviction that when you were as fat as she was, there was no point. In fact, making an effort with clothes or make-up might make things worse, because she imagined people sniggering behind her back – 'Look at that fat cow, does she really think a bit of lipstick is going to help?' Besides, make-up was Liz's domain and sometimes Phoebe felt that the only way she could assert her identity was by doing the opposite of what Liz wanted her to do.

Now, though, Phoebe suddenly wanted to make an effort. She had only been a little girl the last time she'd seen Ella, and a spark of pride made her determined that Ella wasn't going to think what a wreck she'd grown up to be. With this in mind she washed her face, feeling instantly better as the cool water soothed her tear-swollen eyes. There was no way she could contemplate drying her face on the grimy roller-towel, so she pulled out her pyjama top – the pink gingham one Callum had bought her in the Lake District the day before her world fell apart – and dried herself on that. Then she cleaned her teeth, rubbed in some moisturiser and lip balm and brushed her hair until it was straight and smooth once more. A quick spritz of the Marc Jacobs Daisy perfume Callum had bought her for Christmas, and she felt slightly more confident again. Bloody freezing though; she really wished she'd brought something warmer to wear than her long-sleeved T-shirt, but the weather had been gorgeous when she'd set off that morning.

Even now it probably wasn't really that cold; she was shivering partly out of a shock reaction. Back at her little table she wrapped her hands gratefully around the mug of tea and tried not to think about how she would pay for it if Ella didn't turn up. She supposed, ironically, that if she was arrested for non-payment of her bill then at least she'd have a roof over her head in a police cell. God, this was all so humiliating. Her big adventure, her gesture of independence, her stand to show her parents that she could manage without them, and less than twelve hours after leaving she'd been on the phone begging to be rescued.

She really hadn't wanted to phone Callum, had gone through every possible alternative in her mind, but there simply wasn't any. The only person she knew in London was Elisa and she was abroad, and Phoebe didn't know her phone number anyway. She couldn't even remember Becky's number to call her for some advice and support – that was the problem with mobile phones, according to her father, no one ever bothered to learn numbers any more. So he had insisted that she memorised his mobile number in case of emergencies. Of course, she knew her home phone number too, but there was no way she was going to call Liz. She honestly felt that she would rather have slept on the street or walked back to Liverpool than phone her mother and explain what had happened. So really that meant it had to be Callum's mobile.

Despite the humiliation, Phoebe couldn't help but feel cheered by the warmth and love in Callum's voice when she'd spoken to him. He *had* noticed that she wasn't there, he had been worried, he did still care about her. It didn't really help, though, she thought in frustration. When they got back to Liverpool she would have no choice but to move back in with her mother and hardly see Callum, and she felt physically sick at the thought.

Ella paid the taxi driver and then paused to look around. It was a very long time since she'd been in Soho by herself at turned midnight and, despite everything, she felt a small thrill of excitement at being out in the world. To her huge relief she quickly spotted the café Callum had described and hurried towards it. There didn't seem to be much demand for an all-night greasy spoon, even in Soho, because there only appeared to be one customer, a girl sitting in the brightly lit window nursing what looked to be a mug of tea. It had to be Phoebe.

Phoebe had only been five when Ella last saw her, so she had been slightly worried that she wouldn't recognise her. Callum had talked about her a lot, that night in Liverpool, on the phone, in emails, but although he had said that she was beautiful, and that she struggled with her weight, he hadn't been specific in his description. Ella had slightly dismissed his raptures about Phoebe's beauty because, after all, all fathers thought that their daughter was the most beautiful girl in the world. In this case, though, Callum had not been biased. The girl Ella could see in the window was extremely pretty. She was very definitely overweight, but that didn't detract from her long, golden-blonde hair or delicate features. Of course, Liz had been ridiculously good-looking, from what Ella could remember, and Phoebe had definitely got her looks from her. But to Ella's mind she was even prettier. Whether it was the extra weight or simply her personality that took the edge off Liz's slight hardness, it was difficult to tell.

Ella walked briskly to the door and opened it, and the girl stood up and moved towards her.

'Ella?'

Ella nodded. 'Phoebe?' She opened her arms and gave her a warm hug. 'Wow! I can't believe how grown up you are! And how gorgeous you are!'

She felt Phoebe shaking with sobs and, guiding her gently back to the table, sat her down and handed her a clean tissue. Then, noticing that Phoebe was shivering, she pulled out the spare sweater she'd brought with her and handed it over.

'There you go, pop that on, you look as though you're freezing.'

Phoebe pulled the sweater on, crying even harder.

'Oh Phoebe, what is it, love?' Ella asked.

Phoebe blew her nose and visibly tried to pull herself together.

'Sorry, you must think I'm a complete nutcase. It's just that you hugged me, and my mum never hugs me, and I haven't seen my dad for ages, and then giving me the top – well, that's the kind of thing mums do, isn't it?'

Seeing that Ella looked puzzled, she tried to explain.

'I mean, mums try and think of things that will be good for their children, like having jumpers or snacks with them. My friend Becky's mum is like that. And my mum never has been, so no one has ever done that for me, 'cos I just don't think dads are as good at it. So it made me cry that you thought of it for me, even though you don't really know me.'

'Oh Phoebe.' Ella squeezed both her hands. 'It does sound like you've been having a rough time. I tell you what. Let's order some hot chocolates, and something sweet and carby, and then you can tell me all about it.'

After he heard the front door shut Greg lay back on the bed, pulling the duvet tightly around him. Suddenly the pieces had all fallen into place, and the picture they made terrified him. When Ella had said that she used to babysit for Callum's daughter something had clicked, and he had realised exactly who Callum McCraig was. When he and Ella were first together, they'd shared the obligatory stories about past loves and relationships. As they were only twenty at the time, these weren't exactly long sagas. Greg had had a steady girlfriend at school from fifteen to seventeen – she was the girl he'd lost his virginity to, and they'd had a comfortable if not very exciting relationship, which had fizzled out amicably through the pressures of A-levels and the excitement of going off to university. He'd had a brief but intense relationship with a girl called Lizzie in his first year at uni, but that had ended in (his) tears when she told him that she was gay, and in love with her flatmate. Then he'd met Ella, and had understood what all the fuss about this love business was really about.

Ella's history was even briefer. She'd had a handful of one-night stands, and before that had been in love with one of her teachers at sixth form. Greg had been ready to dismiss that as a silly crush, until he saw the pain that still came to Ella's face when she talked about it and realised that, requited or not, this had been the real deal for Ella. She'd never told him his name, but he remembered that she had said she'd used to babysit for his daughter. It couldn't be coincidence. Callum McCraig and that older married man who had broken Ella's eighteen-year-old heart had to be one and the same person.

That put an entirely different complexion on things. Greg had been relatively confident that, although Ella may have been tempted, had definitely been flirtatious, she wouldn't actually have cheated on him. She just wasn't the kind of woman who would put her marriage and family at risk for the sake of a fling with some guy she barely knew. But this was different. This wasn't 'some guy', this was Ella's first love. This was the man who'd messed her up so badly that she'd not actually been in a proper relationship until she met Greg. This was the ultimate example of The One Who Got Away. It was all so clear now. Ella had met Callum, presumably accidentally, when she was in

Liverpool for that confounded hen night. They'd slept together and had been maintaining a relationship by email, and presumably phone, ever since. That explained Ella's exhilaration combined with emotional distance, it explained the warm intimacy of the emails that had troubled him, and it explained her eagerness to rush to the rescue tonight.

Despite Greg's protestations he did believe that Ella was going to rescue the daughter, and was not using it as an excuse for a clandestine meet-up. After all, it was hardly subtle to have your lover phone the house at midnight and then dash off in a taxi to meet him; she could have come up with a hundred better cover stories if she'd tried. But the fact that Callum had known he could rely on her, the fact that Ella had gone instantly with barely a backward glance, it all spoke of a familiarity and confidence between them that was far more disturbing than a relationship based solely on lust.

What the hell was he going to do? It felt completely hopeless. Earlier that evening he had allowed himself to believe that it was all going to be alright. Ella had been experiencing some version of a seven-year itch, but she'd come through it, they'd come through it, and he had a plan that would hopefully make their marriage and family stronger than ever. Something had shifted as he and Ella talked that evening. He had suddenly felt that he was able to see her side of the story, to see how things had got to the point where she might look outside their marriage for something she was no longer finding within it. He had looked at the past four years through Ella's eyes rather than his own, and had been shocked at how bleak the landscape appeared. Sure, his life had changed since having children. There were many more nocturnal interruptions, far less spontaneity. But from 8.30 a.m. to around 7 p.m. every weekday his life hadn't changed at all. He travelled on the same Tube line, to the same workplace, where he interacted with the same colleagues. He enjoyed his work – it was challenging and stimulating and he liked and respected the majority of the people he worked with. And, crucially, they still saw him as the same person. He was still Greg Casey, solicitor-at-law, or Greg in Legal, and so although his sense of identity had expanded to encompass the role of father, he was still fundamentally sure of himself and his place in the world. Not so Ella. She hadn't had a lucrative professional career like his in the first place, but she had very much had an identity and a sense of self. She'd been deeply involved with student politics at the LSE, had spent weekends on protest marches, or volunteering with the Howard League for Penal Reform. Ella's small contribution to the bills had come through her part-time job as a waitress at a quirky little coffee bar just off Lincoln's Inn Fields, where she could barista with the best of them, flirt with the regulars and would frequently take a turn baking their signature carrot cake or chocolate cheesecake.

Of course, when Aidan was born there had been no question that it would make sense for Ella to stay at home and look after him. After all, there was no way her salary would cover even the subsidised childcare provided by the university. Probably, with hindsight, they should have waited a little longer before having children, but Ella had been desperately broody and he'd been too much in love to say no. After all, he knew they'd have kids together at some point, so starting a few years earlier than he'd planned hadn't seemed to be a particularly big deal. They'd moved out of their little rented flat when Ella discovered she was pregnant and the new mortgage was a big stretch, although it helped that Greg was promoted at around the same time. The promotion, though, had come with its own price in terms of extended hours and responsibility, leaving Ella stuck at home with first one and then soon two small children and no adult company for hours on end. The contrast between her life as an urban intellectual and as a suburban stay-at-home mum could hardly have been greater, and Greg had never fully appreciated just how hard that shift must have been for her. He'd had glimmers of insight of course, had frequently suggested she got a job of some kind, but he hadn't been able to appreciate just how trapped she must have felt and how eroded her self-confidence must have been.

He ground his teeth in frustration. He could see exactly how bumping into Callum – who had only known her as an idealistic teenager and had no image of the downtrodden mum – must have been intoxicating. Especially coming on top of that silly row they'd had about a third baby. He punched the wall angrily, wishing it was Callum's face. Of course, he'd never seen Callum's face, but in his mind's eye he was some sort of improbably good-looking, suave, self-satisfied George Clooney–Sean Connery hybrid. The intolerable image of Ella, his Ella, naked with this man snaked into his mind to torment him and he punched the wall again, almost relishing the pain in his hand as it provided a split second's relief from his mental agony.

He and Ella had been so good together, could be so

good again, and although they'd lost their way a bit he knew he just couldn't stand it if she was going to throw their fantastic relationship away.

Shoulders slumped in despair, Greg, aware that real life wouldn't stop for his emotional crises, resignedly continued getting ready for bed and then popped in to check on the children. Aidan was lying, as he always did, on his tummy with his bottom sticking up in the air, not much of him visible under the light summer quilt but some fluffy blond hair. Harriet was lying on her side, her teddy bear clutched to her, looking like an advertiser's dream image of a child asleep. Soft brown curls tumbled on forehead? Check. Long dark lashes sweeping rosy cheeks? Check. Pursed rosebud lips? Check. Greg knelt down next to her cot, heart throbbing with the intensity of his love for her. She looked just like Ella, and that thought made his heart ache more. Then suddenly he thought of that girl, Phoebe, who Ella had gone out to meet this evening. 'Imagine if it was Hattie,' Ella had flung at him as she left, and imagine he did. Imagine if it was this precious girl, out on her own in a city far from home, and he had no idea where she was or even if she was safe. The tears that had been building for weeks finally came, and he curled up in a ball on his daughter's fluffy pink heart-shaped rug and wept until the pile was wet through. Finally, he stopped crying and levered himself to his feet. Cold now, he went back to the bedroom, pulled on his dressing gown and then climbed into bed with his iPad. The recognition of his children's vulnerability had stiffened his resolve. He was not going to have his life and his children's lives ruined by Ella running off with her teenage love. He was going to fight for her. He was going to make a plan to save his marriage, starting right now.

31

Ella and Phoebe sat facing each other, both holding large mugs of hot chocolate topped with synthetic cream and implausibly coloured marshmallows. Ella looked at her drink warily and took a cautious sip. It was surprisingly nice. Probably not Green & Black's organic, but warm and sweet, which was what seemed to be required right now.

Phoebe was gazing down at her own mug, having seemingly lost her appetite for confession. Ella cleared her throat.

'So, Phoebe, we could make polite conversation about my children, or your favourite subjects at school, and bore ourselves to tears. Or we could cut that crap and you could tell me what on earth you're doing on your own in London in the middle of the night.'

Phoebe gave an involuntary giggle and looked up shyly. What she saw was comforting. Ella was really pretty, she thought, but sort of ordinary-looking too. She wasn't wearing any make-up, her curly hair was pulled back in a rough ponytail with lots of bits escaping and she was wearing a plain, navy-blue Fat Face hoodie. She also looked smiley and kind, and interested, and although Phoebe had been regretting her initial outburst and planning to be much more reserved for the rest of their time together, something about Ella was so reassuring that she decided to throw caution to the wind and tell her the whole sorry story.

Beginning, middle, end, her English teacher had drummed into them in creative writing classes. The problem was always when the beginning was. Was it when Phoebe was born to a mother who'd never seemed to want her? Was it when she left her cosy, friendly primary school where she'd been so happy and started at St Augustine's, where she'd been mercilessly bullied since day one? Was it when her dad left her mum, and seemed to leave her into the bargain? It was very hard to know.

'Do you remember my mum?' she asked.

Ella nodded, cautiously.

'Well, you know that she's a complete bitch, then.'

'Errmm . . .' Ella knew that she was on very shaky ground, and momentarily cursed her decision to start this conversation.

Phoebe grinned.

'Don't worry, I won't make you agree with me. But it helps if you remember her, because you'll be able to picture what I'm saying more easily.'

Ella nodded again.

'The thing is, I've always been a disappointment to my mum. Too fat, not pretty enough, not interested in fashion or make-up or anything. The exact opposite of what she would have wanted in a daughter. And that's been horrible, but it was never too bad, because I think my dad was a disappointment to her as well.'

Ella raised her eyebrows enquiringly.

'Yeah. She would have liked to be married to someone rich and successful and cool, not to a teacher. She was always pretty horrible to Dad. But, like I said, it wasn't too bad, because Dad and I had each other, and' – her voice choked slightly – 'I really love my dad. And he likes reading and all the stuff I'm interested in, so we just got on with things, and kept out of Mum's way as much as possible.'

Ella was thoughtful. This account of Callum and Liz's marriage corresponded very closely with Callum's own story, suggesting that his 'my wife doesn't understand me' line had been genuine. Interesting.

Phoebe was talking again.

'I always used to pray that Mum and Dad would split up, and Dad and I could live on our own and be happy, but they never did.'

Ella asked softly, 'Why do you think that was?'

Phoebe shrugged.

'I dunno, really. I don't think Mum wanted them to split up – she doesn't actually earn that much as a model any more, and I think she liked the stability of Dad's salary, and our house, even though she didn't like me and Dad much.'

Ella felt terribly sad for Phoebe. She was far too young to have such a cynical, though probably accurate, view of the world.

'I'm sure your mum does love you, Phoebe.'

She shrugged again.

'Hmm, maybe. I don't know. But she definitely doesn't *like* me, she doesn't enjoy spending time with me, she isn't interested in me. And she's not very good at being a mum, like I said.'

She stared hard at Ella.

'How old are your children?'

'I've got a little boy, Aidan, who's three, and a girl, Hattie, who's just turned eighteen months.'

Phoebe nodded.

'Well, they're a bit young, it's not quite the same, but I can just tell that you'd be a different kind of mum. A better mum.'

'Better in what way?'

'Well, for example, imagine Hattie grew up to be overweight and got bullied at school. What would you do?'

Ella thought for a moment.

'I'd try and sort it out, I suppose. I'd go in and talk to the teachers. I'd talk to Hattie about whether she wanted to lose weight, and try to help her if she did. I'd encourage her to have her friends round so that she had positive experiences with girls her own age. And, I suppose, if none of that worked then I'd think about her moving schools.'

Phoebe nodded, satisfied.

'I knew you'd be a better mum than mine!'

'Why, what did your mum do?'

Phoebe sighed.

'Well, first of all, she's always blamed me for being bullied. Saying that if I would just lose some weight, I wouldn't be an easy target.'

She started pleating the paper napkin, looking down and avoiding Ella's eyes again.

'I know I'm too fat. I really want to lose weight, I know it would be healthier. But I just don't know how to. Every time I get upset I eat to make myself feel better, and then either everyone at school is horrible to me again, or my mum has another go, so I eat more, and I just go round and round.'

Ella prayed briefly for wisdom before replying.

'Oh Phoebe, it's such a classic catch-22 situation. Believe me, you're not the first person to go through this, and you won't be the last. I think the thing is, you need to learn to recognise when you're eating for a reason that isn't hunger. There are loads of reasons people overeat – because everyone else is, or because they're sad, lonely, stressed, tired, bored . . .'

Phoebe grinned.

'Yep, I eat for all of those reasons. But I'm always starving too!'

Ella thought again.

'What do you eat at mealtimes?'

Phoebe pulled a face.

'Low-cal ready meals. Or cottage cheese and salad. Except recently I've been eating at my friend Becky's house loads, and her mum cooks really nice things, casseroles and pizza and stuff.' Phoebe frowned. 'The funny thing is, since I've been eating there, I actually think I might have lost a bit of weight, even though Becky's mum doesn't make anything low-fat.'

Ella said gently, 'I'm not surprised. I wouldn't have thought that low-cal ready meals would have all the nutrients and calories you need at your age. So you'd be permanently hungry, and then there's a big temptation to fill up on junk food.' She paused again. 'You know what, Phoebe? I've always struggled with my weight. I'm a size 14–16, which isn't huge, but isn't skinny either, but I only stay this size because I've spent ten years figuring out how to control my weight.'

Phoebe was wide-eyed.

'God, I'd love to be a size 16! How do you do it?'

Ella smiled.

'There's no magic formula, I'm afraid. What works for me is trying to spot when I want to eat for an emotional reason, and then doing something else that makes me happy instead – like having a bath, or treating myself to a new magazine. I cook pretty much all our meals from scratch, and I make sure that vegetables make up at least half of them. I *never* drink fizzy drinks or squash, just water.' She grinned. 'And wine. And hot chocolate. And I go running, which is great. But if I want some cake or some chocolate I eat it, because actually, life is for living. I want to be healthy, but I'm not going to starve myself for the sake of a model figure that I don't even want.'

Phoebe was nodding vigorously.

'Yes! That's exactly it! My mum wants me to be a size 8, like her, and I kind of know I'm not ever going to be, so I lose the will to try and be any smaller at all.'

'Yes, I think that's quite common too. There's so much pressure on women to be stick thin that they either make themselves ill to get there, or give up completely and don't do themselves any health favours. Anyway, is that why you ran away, because of the bullying, and the problems with your mum?'

Phoebe shook her head.

'No, not really. That had all been going on for ever, and I could sort of put up with it. It was my dad leaving that really ruined things.'

Ella's stomach felt as though she'd just descended twenty floors in a very fast lift. Throughout their conversation she had been consoling herself with the thought that, actually, the reasons Phoebe had run away didn't have anything to do with her and Callum, that she wasn't responsible for this girl's pain. That was now exposed as a comforting fiction.

Luckily, Phoebe was staring down at the remains of her toasted teacake, and didn't see the spasm of guilt pass across Ella's face.

'I still don't understand it, Ella. When I used to pray for my parents to split up, it was because I wanted me and Dad to get away from my mum. I knew he wasn't happy either, but I never in a million years thought that he'd leave without me.'

Ella tried very hard to keep her voice calm and level.

'Did he have anywhere to take you to? 'Cos the thing is, Phoebe, I know he would have wanted to take you with him, more than anything, but he couldn't take you to sleep on his mate's sofa, could he? I think, I mean, I'm sure he was just trying to get things sorted out a bit so that he was ready for you to live with him if you wanted to.'

Phoebe frowned.

'But why couldn't he just have waited? Even if it was just until after my exams?'

Ella tried to negotiate the tightrope between defending Callum and not losing Phoebe's confidence.

'Erm, well, I suppose it must have been an incredibly difficult decision for him to make. Once he'd plucked up the courage to do it, maybe he just felt he needed to get on and do it straight away, that he might lose his nerve if he didn't.'

That sounded plausible enough, surely?

'Ye-ees.' Phoebe didn't sound convinced. 'But what *made* him suddenly decide?'

Damn. This girl was too perceptive for Ella's liking.

'Didn't you say that your parents had a huge row the day before Callum left? Maybe that was the trigger.'

Phoebe nodded.

'Yes, that's true, they did. It was the first time they'd ever really rowed openly in front of me, and in fact . . .' She trailed off, and looked accusingly at Ella.

'Hang on. I *didn't* tell you they had a row the day before Dad left. I know I didn't. So how on earth do you know that?'

Oh, bloody hell. Ella felt panicked. If Phoebe found out her father had cheated on her mother it might damage their relationship irrevocably. And there was the hideous possibility that Phoebe would storm out of the café, leaving Ella to chase her impotently around Soho. And it was hardly her place to tell her anything anyway. On the other hand, she only had split seconds to concoct a suitable cover story, and Phoebe was looking straight at her with those disconcertingly clear turquoise eyes.

'I guess your dad must have told me, then.' She smiled, with her best attempt at nonchalance.

Phoebe nodded slowly, clearly turning things over in her mind. Unfortunately for Ella she started to rapidly draw some very unhelpful conclusions.

'Hang on a minute. The last time you babysat for me was years ago, when Dad was your teacher. How come you kept in touch? Dad's never mentioned you until just now.'

Ella made one last attempt at a cover story.

'No, we haven't been in touch all this time. I was up in Liverpool a few weeks ago for my friend's hen do, and we ran into each other by chance. We had a catch-up, and swapped numbers. I told your dad then that I lived in London, and so obviously he thought of me today.'

That sounded entirely reasonable, to her ears at least. But she hadn't reckoned on Phoebe's Miss Marple tendencies.

'When you ran into Dad, was that before or after he split up with Mum?'

'Ummm . . .' Ella stalled.

Phoebe stared hard at Ella. All her instincts were screaming that there was something she was missing, something she wasn't being told. This story about Ella and Callum running into each other after so many years, but then Ella being the person he turned to tonight, just didn't stack up. She liked Ella a lot, and her natural inclination was always towards deference, but this evening was bizarre in so many ways that she felt strangely empowered. After the terror of her situation earlier, suddenly asking a grown-up a question didn't seem like such a big deal. Especially as she felt that being kept in the dark about the workings of adult relationships was what had led to her current crisis.

'Is there something going on with you and my dad?' she asked bluntly.

32

Phoebe watched the red flush spread across Ella's face. There was the real answer, whatever Ella said now. Phoebe smiled inwardly. Things were suddenly making a lot more sense. Falling in love with Ella was what had made her Dad leave so suddenly. And she could totally see why he had, because Ella was lovely. For a moment Phoebe felt hopeful – imagine living with Dad and Ella! It would be like having a proper mum. And then maybe they'd have a baby and she would have a little brother or sister like she'd always wanted! Her mind raced ahead for a second, but then the recollection that Ella was already married with children brought her fantasy to an abrupt halt. It wasn't going to be quite that easy.

Ella was still sitting in silence, pressing her hands to her red cheeks to try and cool them.

Phoebe smiled at her.

'I wouldn't mind, you know. If you were. You'd be a great stepmum.'

'Oh, Phoebe.' Ella could feel tears prickling her eyes. 'You are so lovely, and I'd be proud to have you as my stepdaughter. But it isn't going to happen, darling.'

Phoebe's heart sank a little, but she nodded stoically.

'So, what *is* happening then?'

Ella wrestled with her conscience, and then decided. Sod it. She wasn't this girl's parent, or step-parent. The only thing she had promised Callum was that she would keep Phoebe safe until he arrived. It wasn't her fault that his daughter's interrogation skills would put the FBI to shame. Anyway, it seemed like enough damage had been done by a total lack of communication; maybe this was the time for full disclosure.

'OK, Phoebe. I'm going to treat you like the adult you almost are, and tell you the whole story – or what I know of it, anyway. But you have to promise me that you will remember one thing throughout.'

'What's that?'

'That your dad loves you more than life itself. He absolutely adores you, and I know he will do everything he possibly can to make things right for you.'

Phoebe nodded. The relief in Callum's voice when she'd called him earlier had already told her that.

'Right. Well. When I first met your dad I was only a year or so older than you are now. He was one of my A-level teachers. I fell madly in love with him at pretty much first sight.'

Seeing Phoebe's mouth form a moue of disgust, Ella grinned.

'I know it's revolting thinking of your dad like that, but try and get over it. Anyway, nothing ever happened of course, despite me wanting it to. I was his student, he was married – but we did get on really well, and sixth form is much more informal than ordinary school, so we got a chance to chat quite a lot, and were friends, I suppose you could say. That was why he asked me to babysit you, I guess. Anyway, eventually I finished sixth form, and left, heartbroken that he didn't love me back.'

Phoebe was listening intently.

'I met my husband, Greg, at uni, and that was that. Until I bumped into Callum, like I said, when I was on a hen do a few weeks ago.'

She took a deep breath. This was the tricky bit.

'Greg and I had been having quite a tough time, a bit of a bad patch, and you know that your parents weren't very happy.' Ella shrugged. 'Not that that excuses it, but it might explain it . . .' She paused again. Honesty was one thing, detailing her father's sexual exploits to a teenage girl was quite another. Best to draw a discreet veil over that aspect of things.

Phoebe clearly shared her view, because she looked up with a mischievous twinkle.

'Yep, OK. I think I can fill in the gaps. As much as I want to, anyway. But what happened then? Did my dad leave my mum for you? But you haven't left your husband, have you?'

Ella shook her head.

'I don't know exactly why your dad did what he did, Phoebe. He'll probably kill me for saying this, in fact, he'll probably kill me for saying any of this, but you'll have to ask him. I think that meeting me maybe gave him the impetus he needed to leave an unhappy marriage. He did want me to leave Greg, for us to be together, but that wasn't ever really an option.'

'Why not? I thought you said you were in love with him?'

Ella cringed.

'Oh god, Phoebe. I don't come out of any of this very well, do I? I was in love with Callum when I was seventeen, eighteen. But I've changed a lot since then, grown up, got married, had children—'

'None of that stopped you sleeping with him, though!'

Phoebe was embarrassingly direct, and Ella decided to use that approach herself.

'No, it didn't. But it absolutely should have done. I did a really bad thing, and I think I might have wrecked my own marriage in the process, as well as causing this nightmare for you. I'm so sorry, Phoebe. If I could turn back the clock and not make the same mistake then I would.'

Phoebe sighed disconsolately.

'So you and Dad aren't going to get together?'

Ella shook her head.

'Definitely not, Phoebe. But you and I can still be friends, you know. We can email and text. Maybe you could come and stay with me in London at some point.'

Phoebe's eyes lit up.

'I'd love that. I really love London. Although it's pretty scary being on your own here with no money.'

Ella shuddered.

'Yeah, I can imagine it would be.'

They lapsed into a companionable silence until Phoebe broke in with, 'So, does your husband know about you and my dad? What about the bad patch you said you were having, is that all sorted now?'

Ella shrugged dramatically.

'Who knows? I really messed up, Phoebe. Greg doesn't know for certain about Callum, but he definitely suspects.

I don't know whether to tell him the whole truth or not. And as for the bad patch . . .'

Phoebe's eyes were wide.

'Did he have an affair?'

Ella laughed.

'No, it wasn't like that. Basically, we fell out because I really wanted a third baby, and he didn't.'

'Oh.' Phoebe's face fell. This was considerably less interesting.

'Why didn't he?' she asked, politely.

'Lots of reasons, but mainly because he thought that I wanted another baby so I could hide from the fact that I wasn't happy with my life in general, that I haven't got any real focus.'

Phoebe looked slightly uncomprehending.

'Oh.'

Ella smiled ruefully.

'Do you know what the really annoying thing is? I think he might have been right all along. And to be honest, I think the thing with your dad was trying to fill the gap as well.'

Phoebe still looked slightly blank, and Ella tried to explain.

'I've never really had a proper career, and the last few years I've been at home with the kids, and I've got into a rut, I guess. I was bored and lonely, and feeling like that for a long time made me depressed.'

Phoebe gave her another clear-eyed glance.

'Well, why don't you get a job then?'

Ella started to rehearse all the reasons why this was impossible – the cost of childcare, the difficulty of flexible working, her lack of training or experience – but then stopped. Phoebe was right. Greg was right. She should stop whinging and making excuses, and just bloody do it.

'You're right. Everyone's right, except me. Which makes it all the more ironic, really, that the thing I think I might really like to do is to train as a counsellor.'

Ella waited a moment for Phoebe to start laughing, and to point out that someone so adept at messing up her own life, and other people's lives, was scarcely in a position to counsel other people, but she didn't.

'Wow, that's a really good idea, Ella. You'd be brilliant.'

Ella strained to hear a sarcastic note in her voice, but there didn't seem to be one.

'Really?'

'Really. You can start now – practise on me. Help me sort my life out.'

Ella smiled.

'I don't know much about it yet, but I don't think counsellors are supposed to offer advice exactly, more listen while you talk through what's bothering you.'

'Hmm, well, personally I'd like some advice.'

'About what?'

Phoebe made a dramatic gesture.

'Everything! My life is just a complete mess in every way you can possibly imagine!'

Ella suppressed a smile at Phoebe's slight lapse into melodrama, but no one knew better than she did how teenage crises could cast long shadows, and she also knew from Callum's depiction of his family life that Phoebe had endured a far harder time than many girls her age.

'The first thing is, I genuinely think things are going to get much better for you. I shouldn't tell you this because I think Callum wants it to be a surprise, but he's rented a little house now, with a bedroom for you, so hopefully you should be able to go and live with him when you go back.'

Phoebe exhaled, feeling as if she could breathe properly for the first time since the nightmare of that overheard conversation.

'Are you sure?'

Ella nodded.

'That's what he's been trying to sort out. Clearly, he hasn't communicated with you as well as he could have done, but, as I said, he really loves you.'

Phoebe let her mind run with some images of a future in which she didn't have to hide out in her room, in which she wasn't tiptoeing around the eggshells of Liz's mood swings, in which she wouldn't have to eat in secret.

As though reading Phoebe's mind, Ella continued. 'So, if I'm being bossy, instead of just listening, then I reckon there's a few things you should do. One, learn to cook. I seem to remember that Callum was never much of a cook, and it won't do either of you any good to live on takeaways, so learn how to do it yourself. Buy a book by someone like Jamie Oliver, or Ainsley Harriott's pretty good, and just work your way through it.'

Phoebe was gratifyingly enthusiastic.

'Yeah, I'd been thinking about that, because my friend Becky cooks with her mum a lot. And I reckon her mum would help me, if I asked.'

'I'm sure she would.' Ella felt grateful that Phoebe had a mother figure in her life, because however much she may yearn to fulfil that role herself she knew that there was no real way she would be able to.

'So, what are the other things?'

Ella hesitated. It was one thing for Phoebe to criticise her mum, but someone else wading in to do so could be taken very badly.

'Well, I know from what you said that your relationship with your mum isn't good.'

Phoebe snorted.

'I think you should just relax and let it not be good. The more you either fight with her or try to please her, the worse you make it for yourself. I know it feels like the be-all and end-all now, but, Phoebe, you have your escape route all planned. You're going to be living with your dad, then in a couple of years you'll be off to university, and your horizons will expand immeasurably. I'm not saying your parents will cease to matter, but your relationship with them won't be so all-consuming. And I have a hunch, anyway, that you and your mum might get along a lot better when you're not living together.'

Phoebe was trying to take all this in. Although she had fantasised for years about escaping, it was hard to grasp that she was within such easy reach of that escape actually being possible.

'And what about everyone at school? I'll still be fat; they'll still be horrible.'

'Sixth form is really different to school. Lots of the girls who make your life miserable now won't go on to sixth form – they won't be clever enough to get the grades in their GCSEs. You don't even have to stay on at the same school if you don't want to, you and your dad could look at sixth-form colleges if you wanted a really fresh start. And, Phoebe, being overweight isn't the worst thing in the world to be. I think when you're a bit happier, and eating proper food instead of alternating diet food with junk food binges, you'll lose some weight naturally anyway. But you have to stop defining yourself as fat. You're lots of things – you're clever and perceptive and sensitive and funny and beautiful, and they're all things that no amount of dieting could change, and which no amount of weight can hide. Just repeat all those things when you're feeling down, because honestly, you've got such a lot going for you.'

Phoebe blushed with pleasure. She was trying to think how to respond when Ella's phone rang.

'Hello. Yes, we're still in that café. Yes, all fine. OK, great, see you soon. Bye.'

She turned to Phoebe.

'That was your dad. He's just finding somewhere to park, and thinks he'll be with us in ten minutes or so.'

33

Callum locked the car, consulted Google Maps and then strode as quickly as he could in the direction of the café where his daughter and the woman he had thought was the love of his life were waiting.

He'd made it down from Liverpool in just under three and a half hours, which was pretty good going. The motorways had been quiet and so he'd put his foot down, never dropping below eighty. He knew that Phoebe was safe now she was with Ella, but he was just desperate to see her, to hug her, to reassure her, and himself, that it was all going to be OK. He felt more ambivalent about seeing Ella. A couple of days previously he would have sold his soul to be going to London to meet her, but now his predominant feeling was embarrassment. Last time he'd seen Ella she'd been naked in his arms, and now he had to make polite conversation with her in front of his daughter, knowing that in large part it was their relationship that was responsible for Phoebe's current situation.

The café door jingled as he opened it, and Phoebe looked up. She was in his arms in seconds. He hugged her tightly to him and stroked her hair while she sobbed into his familiar bulk. After a few minutes she calmed down and stepped back. He placed his hands on her shoulders, holding her at arm's length, and surveyed her. It was only a week or so since he'd last seen her, but they'd both been through such momentous, life-changing events since then that he half expected her to look totally different. She didn't, of course. As always, looking at her lovely face, he could trace all the Phoebes he'd known – from the tiny red-faced baby to the chubby-cheeked toddler, the earnest little schoolgirl, and now the beautiful young woman. He felt the same overwhelming wave of love that he'd experienced for the first time when he held his baby daughter a few moments after her birth, and he berated himself yet again for having failed her so badly in recent weeks. It was too easy with kids – once they could deal with their own practical needs and didn't require you to change their nappy, puree their food, get them dressed and undressed and walk them to and from school – to forget that the job of being a parent wasn't over. In fact, their emotional needs are all the greater, and far harder to meet.

'I'm so, so sorry, Dad,' Phoebe was saying, her face tear-stained.

'Oh Phoebe, sweetheart, it's OK. You shouldn't have run away, and I think you know now that you put yourself in a potentially very dangerous situation, but I do understand why you did it, and the blame for that lies with me, and, to an extent, your mum. Not you.'

'But, Dad, you having to come all the way down here, and I've lost my phone and Mum's credit card – and what about your job – how are you going to get into school tomorrow? I've messed everything up!'

He shook her slightly.

'No, you haven't. Now I've got you safe again, there's no problem we can't solve. When I realised you were missing, I phoned the Head and explained that there was a family crisis and I wouldn't be in tomorrow, which is now today, so she's not expecting me at school. You're far more important than work, sweetheart. So, this is what we're going to do. I've booked a hotel, just round the corner, and we're going to go there now and try and get some sleep for what's left of the night. We'll deal with everything else in the morning. Including, when we get back to Liverpool, showing you my new house.'

Phoebe had relaxed a bit, now that she realised there really wasn't a massive telling-off in store.

'Oh yes! Ella said you had a house, and that she thought I'd be able to live with you.'

'Did she now?' Callum's mouth curved in a wryly amused smile, and he looked over to where Ella was hovering sheepishly in the background, not wanting to leave without saying a proper goodbye to Phoebe and exchanging a few words with Callum, but equally not wanting to intrude on the family reunion.

'And what else has Ella said?' he asked drily.

'Oh loads! She told me about the house, and about you and her having an affair but that you're not going to get together properly, and that I should learn to cook, and—'

'What?!' Callum was horrified now, the colour drained from his face.

Ella took her courage in both hands and stepped forwards, inwardly lamenting Phoebe's loquaciousness.

'Hi, Callum. How are you? You made good time coming down.'

Unsurprisingly, he refused to be deflected.

'*What* did Phoebe say you'd told her? What are you playing at, Ella?'

Phoebe looked anxious again now, glancing between Callum's thunderous face and Ella's apprehensive one.

'Look, Callum, I'm sorry. I know it's not my place to have told her, but Phoebe's a very smart girl, as I'm sure you know. She'd guessed half of the story anyway, and I had to make a judgement call. I thought it was better to be honest with her, and give her the facts. After all –' Ella's voice was more confident now '– not telling her things hasn't proved a particularly successful strategy, has it?'

Callum rubbed his hand across his eyes. The woman standing opposite him, in faded jeans and a hoodie, dark circles under her eyes and no make-up, wasn't a goddess. She wasn't his salvation. She wasn't even necessarily his dream woman. What she was, and always had been, he saw in a moment of unexpected clarity, was the exact opposite of Liz in almost every way. That was what had attracted him to her all those years ago, and that was what had set off such an explosive chain reaction of desire and longing when he met her again. Ella O'Connor – Ella Casey rather – was bright and witty, passionate and warm, and had seemed a perfect refuge from his sterile marriage. She was even Liz's physical opposite – dark instead of fair, short instead of tall, curvy rather than slim.

She had represented to Callum an escape, a fresh start, a safety net – but really she was none of those things. She was a person in her own right, who had made her own messes, who came with her own baggage. With the prospect of a custody battle with Liz still to come, with sorting out Phoebe's life both practically and emotionally, and maintaining his own demanding job, the idea of a relationship with a woman fourteen years younger than him and who had two young children of her own simply made him feel old and exhausted.

He was extremely irritated that she had told Phoebe about their relationship, although, thankfully, Phoebe didn't seem particularly perturbed by the revelation. She was talking now.

'Sorry, Ella, I shouldn't have said you told me. Dad, don't be mad with Ella – it wasn't her fault, it was me asking loads of questions. She kind of had to tell me.'

Callum sighed wearily.

'Don't worry, Pheebs. I'm not mad with Ella, she's right, it is better to be honest, I suppose.'

'And is she right, Dad? Are you definitely not going to get together?'

'Absolutely not!' Ella and Callum spoke as one.

Callum put his arm around his daughter's shoulders and turned to Ella.

'Thank you so much, Ella. Seriously, I just don't know what we would have done without you. You've been a complete star tonight, and I'll be grateful for ever.'

She smiled, and he felt a sharp pang. He could see now, very clearly, that there couldn't be, shouldn't be, a future for them, but the thought of what might have been in some parallel universe was very bittersweet.

'It was nothing, Callum. Anyone would have done the same. It was great to meet Phoebe again, and to be honest, I think she's helped me at least as much as I've helped her.'

She hugged Phoebe tightly.

'You take care, darling. Remember what we've talked about, and remember, you've got my number. If you need a chat, I'm here.'

Phoebe hugged her back.

'Thank you, Ella. You've been amazing. Your kids are *so* lucky.'

There was a brief and awkward pause as Ella and Callum looked at each other. To hug or not to hug? They both lurched forward at the same moment, clashing slightly, and then she felt his stubble graze her cheek as they held each other tightly for a moment. This time she was relieved to note no flutters in either heart or groin.

'Thank you, Ella. You've been amazing. Your husband is *so* lucky,' Callum parroted, breaking the tension as they all laughed. And then he and Phoebe were gone. Ella watched them walk down the street for a moment, arms linked, chatting as they went, before collecting her bag, settling the bill and heading for home herself.

34

It was nearly 5 a.m. when Ella let herself in and crept up the stairs. At least Greg hadn't bolted the door against her, she reflected. That had to be a good sign, surely? She checked on the children first, wincing at the knowledge that they'd be awake for the day in less than two hours and she had had no sleep whatsoever. Never mind, times like this were what CBeebies was invented for. Greg was asleep too, propped up against the pillows, still wearing his dressing gown. She surveyed his familiar face lovingly. It was all going to be alright, it had to be. She was still feeling buoyed by the adrenaline of having decided on both a new career and what to do about her future with Greg, and it took a considerable effort of will not to wake him there and then.

She undressed quickly, letting her clothes fall to the floor where she stood, pulled on the oversized T-shirt she slept in and slipped into bed, unfortunately waking Greg despite her best efforts. His gaze was unfocussed at first, and then she could see realisation dawning.

'Whatimersit?' he asked blearily.

'It's just gone five. Phoebe's safe now. Sorry I woke you.'

'S'OK.' He was more wide awake now. 'Listen, tomorrow – later – I've taken the day off. You can't cope with the kids all day with no sleep.'

Ella was surprised and touched, and didn't feel tempted to point out, as she might have done, that she'd frequently looked after the kids all day with scarcely any sleep. Greg hadn't finished yet, though.

'You sleep in, in the morning. I'll get them up and sort breakfast, and then I'm going to take them round to my mum's and ask her if she'll have them for the day.'

Ella raised her eyebrows questioningly.

'Now's not the time, Ella, but we need to have a serious talk, and it would be much easier if we didn't have to look after the kids at the same time. Now, get some sleep.'

With that, he turned away from her and snuggled down, apparently falling asleep again within moments.

Ella had already thought that she wouldn't be able to sleep after the emotional dramas of the night, and Greg's dramatic pronouncement did nothing to change her mind. In fact, though, she was so tired that she fell asleep almost instantly. She stirred when Hattie called, but didn't open her eyes as she felt Greg get up and go to her. There were various muffled mumblings, but Ella just pulled the duvet over her head and let herself sink back into a blissful oblivion.

When she woke up again the sunlight was streaming in through the gap in the curtains. She squinted at her phone. 10 a.m. She felt slightly groggy, but five hours was a lot more than she often got, and she knew that she wouldn't be able to go back to sleep now. She got up and stretched. The house felt eerily quiet, and she realised how little time she spent in it on her own. Presumably Greg was out taking the kids to his mum's, as he'd promised.

Butterflies crept into her stomach. What had Greg meant about them needing to talk? Last night, with Phoebe, Ella had felt so confident of the way ahead. She would tell Greg the whole unvarnished truth so that there were no more lies and deception between them, and then tell him how much she loved him, how much she wanted their marriage to work – and also share with him her new career plans. Now, though, she was scared. What if she was planning that, just as Greg was getting ready to tell her he was leaving?

She pulled herself together. Whatever Greg wanted to say, she was going to look her best while he said it. She took a long shower, relishing the feeling of the warm water running over her face, hair, body. Then, after rubbing in scented body lotion, she dressed carefully, picking a flowery summer dress she'd had for years but which Greg had always liked. A little cardie over the top, and then her Birkenstocks. She blow-dried her hair and put on a bit of make-up, wondering ironically to herself if she should have chosen waterproof mascara. When Greg arrived home she was in the kitchen sipping a strong coffee.

He smiled at her a little shyly.

'Hiya. Did you get some more sleep?'

'Yes, I did. Thanks so much for sorting the kids. Were they OK?'

God, they were being agonisingly polite to each other.

'Yes, they're fine. Ate good breakfasts, and pretty excited about having a day with Grandma.'

'Oh, that's good. And your mum didn't mind?'

'No, she loves having them. I think she's finding the days a bit long since she stopped work, so it's good for all of them.'

Ella nodded, and then an awkward silence fell.

'Have you eaten?' Greg asked at last.

Ella gestured at her mug.

'No, I needed some coffee first. I'm starving now, though. Shall I make us something?'

Greg shook his head firmly.

'No. This is a day off for you. I'm taking you out for brunch.'

Ella's heart lifted. Surely, surely this couldn't be the precursor to being unceremoniously left? Could it?

They walked in silence through the narrow villagey streets of terraced cottages that comprised their area of Walthamstow. After a little while, Greg took Ella's hand, and she wondered when they had last walked together like this. Now, whenever they went anywhere together, their hands were full of toddlers, buggies and changing bags and there was no chance to hold hands with each other. Quite a metaphor for the way life in general had become.

They came to the café Greg had in mind and took a table outside in the sunshine, both placing orders of a bacon butty, a latte and freshly squeezed orange juice.

Which one of us is going to start now? Ella pondered. Do I launch into my confession of adultery and plea for forgiveness, or do I wait and see what Greg has to say first? Before she had decided, Greg started to speak.

'Ella, I want to start by saying I'm really sorry.'

'*You're* sorry? What on earth for?'

'I don't think I've been nearly as empathetic or supportive or understanding as I could have been over these last few years. Being at home with the kids, the way our lives have had to change, has been really tough for you, and I haven't appreciated that enough.'

Ella was silent, guilt pounding inside her. Three months ago she would have been so thrilled to hear Greg say that, to have an indication from him that he still saw her as a person, that he had some understanding of how she felt. Now it just made her feel awful. Greg was apologising to her for not being understanding enough, and she'd slept with another man. She couldn't let him carry on like this – loving her, liking her, sympathising with her – when he didn't know the truth.

'Oh, Greg.'

Her eyes filled with tears and she blinked them back desperately, determined not to give in to them and to look as though she was employing emotional blackmail, and then she blurted out in one breath, 'Greg, it's me who should be apologising. I did something awful. I don't know why, really, and I regret it so much, but when I was in Liverpool I slept with Callum. I'm so, so, so sorry. It was a terrible mistake. I love you so much, Greg. I'll do anything to make it up to you, I promise. I'm *so* sorry.'

She paused. Greg wasn't looking at her, but gazing intently at his bacon sandwich. Every detail of it, down to the blob of brown sauce oozing down the side, felt as if it was imprinting itself on his consciousness. He had known what Ella had just told him, or thought he had, but hearing her say it out loud, having his suspicions confirmed, still came as a blow to his solar plexus, and he felt nauseated.

'Greg? Say something. Please?'

He reached over to take her hand.

'I already kind of knew, Ella.'

'You did?'

He nodded.

'Yeah. Obviously I suspected when I found those emails, but I tried to convince myself it was just flirting. But then last night – I realised who he was. He's that teacher, isn't he? The one you were in love with at school.'

'Yes.' It came out as a whisper. 'I think that's maybe why it happened. I'm not trying to make excuses, just give you the reason. I think that a tiny part of me had always wondered what if, and then meeting him again when I was feeling so low anyway . . .'

Her voice trailed off, but then she gazed straight into Greg's eyes and said adamantly, 'But listen, Greg. This is the important bit. There is no "what if" any more. I'm not in love with him, with Callum. I love you. I only love you. And I've been so bloody scared that I've ruined everything.'

Greg was shaking his head. This was hard, harder even than he'd imagined it would be when he'd thought things through last night. However, loving Ella was both the reason he was feeling so much pain and the reason he knew he had to overcome it.

'No, you haven't. Listen, Ella. I'm definitely not saying you can cheat on me every time we go through a bad patch, but I think I do understand what happened and why. And I love you too, so much, so I really think we can work things out.'

Ella was crying openly now, and he grimaced at her.

'Good God, woman, stop making a public show of yourself. Dry your eyes. Blow your nose. Eat your breakfast.'

Giggling through her tears, Ella complied as best she could.

Greg continued.

'You see, Ella, I love you, and I do know you love me too. But this Callum thing, it wasn't the start of the problem, was it? Somehow it had already started going wrong for us. But I think we can solve it. I have to ask, first, though – do you still really want another baby?'

Ella didn't need to consider.

'Definitely not at the moment.' She took a deep breath. 'I want to go back to college.'

'Really?' Greg seemed surprised. 'To finish your PhD?'

'Oh my God, no! I don't think that's ever going to happen! No, I want to train to be a counsellor.' She was talking faster now, trying to get all the words out before he had a chance to criticise or pick holes.

'I think you can do it part-time. Aidan will be eligible for fifteen hours' free nursery time when he turns three, and I thought maybe your mum might have Hattie – like you said, she's been moaning a bit that she's bored, and she does love having them. By the time I qualified, Aidan would be at school, and Hattie at nursery. And I could work really flexibly round them. What do you think?'

A broad smile had spread across Greg's face.

'I think it's a bloody fantastic idea! You'd be amazing. But you're going to need a course that starts in January, not September.'

'Oh? Why's that?'

'Because, my darling girl, I have big plans for this autumn.' He paused dramatically.

'I'm going to take a sabbatical, and we're going to spend three months travelling across America together.'

With that, he stood up.

'Just going to pay the bill, won't be a minute.'

Ella sat in stunned silence, her mind racing. Of course, Greg's company did have a policy that employees with five or more years' service could apply to take a sabbatical of up to three months' unpaid leave. They'd talked about him using it when Hattie was born, but had decided they just couldn't afford it. Wow. America. It had been one of their dreams as students to hire a camper van and make their way across the USA from east coast to west. New York, Boston, Washington, Chicago, Las Vegas, Seattle, San Francisco, Los Angeles . . . All those places she'd read about, watched in films – how mind-blowing it would be to see them for real.

For a few moments she was in a daze of happy excitement, but then, inexorably, cold drips of reality began to penetrate. How could they afford it? What about Aidan starting nursery? Would it be too disruptive for the children?

Then Greg was back, taking her hand, and without really discussing it they headed for Epping Forest, talking constantly.

'We'll use the money Uncle Harry left me,' Greg said.

'But Greg, that's our rainy-day money, our emergency fund. We can't spend it on a holiday!'

Greg's voice was serious.

'Ella. You had an affair. We've grown so far apart, come closer to breaking up than I ever thought possible. If this isn't a rainy day, isn't an emergency, then I don't know what the hell is! We need time to reconnect, to have fun together, to remember what we were like and what we enjoyed before we got onto the treadmill. I want to spend more time with the kids – they grow up and change so fast, and I hardly see them during the week. They'll be at school soon, and we won't have the opportunity for anything like this. Now's the time – me being able to take a sabbatical, you not having started your course, the kids not being in school, having the money. It's meant to be. We're going. I haven't actually booked it yet, but I've planned loads of it. The big difference from what we've talked about before is that I think we should do west coast to east – get the end of summer in California and have some beach trips, and then finish up with Christmas in New York. What do you think?'

35

Phoebe couldn't really believe the way the day was turning out. She and her dad had gone to an absolutely gorgeous hotel – he'd booked a junior suite, which meant that there was a small living room off the bedroom, and as she was still technically a child, a single bed had been set up in there for her. Callum had chivalrously offered her the double bed, but she'd taken one look at his six foot three inches and broad shoulders and another at the narrow single bed and opted to take that herself. It had been unlike anywhere she'd ever stayed before – right in the heart of London, ultra-stylish décor with a basket of designer toiletries and a big, futuristically designed bowl of fresh fruit. None of the charming staff had seemed the least bit fazed by them showing up at gone 4 a.m.; they'd just courteously shown them to their room and explained that breakfast would be served until noon.

Phoebe had fallen into a deep and dreamless sleep almost instantly, feeling a childish sense of security knowing that her dad was just next door. When they woke up the next morning they had to rush to have showers and get dressed to make it down to breakfast in time. It had been worth hurrying though – Phoebe's mouth watered at the recollection of the delicious smoked salmon and scrambled eggs, with freshly squeezed orange juice, which she'd chosen. Callum had had the full English, of course, and they'd chatted amiably throughout the meal about nothing very important.

Phoebe kept feeling her stomach clench with tension at the prospect of the telling-off that, despite everything, she felt was surely coming soon, but it had never materialised. Then, however, Callum had suggested she called her mum.

'I obviously let her know that you were safe, but she'd love to talk to you, Phoebe. I think you should give her a ring.'

Phoebe had gone instantly rigid, shaking her head vehemently, but Callum had gently persisted and Phoebe eventually agreed. To her intense astonishment, Liz had actually apologised.

'I haven't focussed enough on you with these exams, and I am sorry.'

Of course, she'd also given her a homily on dishonesty and irresponsibility, but it could have been a lot worse. Phoebe, in fact, had endured much worse lectures, for crimes such as a trip to McDonald's for a burger, fries and milkshake, so getting only a mild admonishment for having stolen money and a credit card from her mum's purse and run away to London seemed, frankly, bizarre.

She said as much to Callum.

'Why are you and Mum both being so nice to me about this? I don't get it.'

Callum had patted her arm.

'You gave us the fright of our lives, Phoebe. I can't speak for your mum, but it made me do a lot of thinking about what kind of parent I'd been, and how I wanted our relationship to be in future. And then I was so bloody relieved and grateful that you were safe and sound, the last thing I want to do is start shouting at you. If you *ever* do *anything* like this again, however—'

He broke off, making a throat-slitting gesture, and Phoebe grinned up at him.

'Don't worry, Dad. There's no way I'm ever going to do this again, I promise. I do love London, though,' she'd added wistfully.

And that was the point at which Callum suggested they went shopping, before having an early supper out somewhere and leaving after that to drive back.

Now here they were, bombing up the motorway to the sounds of *Queen's Greatest Hits*, after a companionable afternoon mooching around London together. Phoebe teased Callum about his musical taste, calling it dad-rock, but she had to admit that there was nothing quite like a bit of Queen for a road trip. In the boot of the car sat several carrier bags, filled with some trendy clothes she'd been thrilled to find in her size, a new mobile phone and a couple of cookery books.

By the time they arrived back in Liverpool they were both shattered. Phoebe had been eager to see Callum's new house – *her* new house – but suddenly she just wanted to be back in her familiar little bedroom. After Liz had been so friendly on the phone, she'd got over her sick feeling of dread at seeing her again, and there seemed a lot to be said now for being back with her own things and her own books to try to process everything that had happened. The next day was Saturday, so she had the whole weekend to see the house and, Callum had said, to decide what colour she wanted her room to be and what furniture she would need.

Callum parked outside his old home and helped Phoebe up the path and the three front steps with her multitude of bags. As she was fumbling for her keys, the door opened and Liz stood there, already in her pyjamas, hair pulled back, face make-up free. Callum watched, unable to believe his eyes, as she reached out and hugged Phoebe.

'Oh sweetheart, I'm so glad to see you. Thank God you're safe.'

Phoebe felt her inner ice queen begin to melt as she returned the hug. She turned to kiss her dad goodbye, and then between them she and her mum dragged all the bags inside. Liz glanced at the big wall clock in the hall.

'It's late, Phoebe. You need to get to bed. I'll give you a hand up with all these things, and then shall I make you a hot chocolate and bring it up?'

Phoebe nearly fainted. Her mum being maternal, and offering her sustenance! Wonders would never cease. She agreed in a slightly dazed tone and then changed into her pyjamas while her mum was downstairs making the hot chocolate. When she reappeared Liz was carrying two mugs, although Phoebe was amused to note that her mum's, in contrast to Ella's the previous evening, contained herbal tea of some kind – she wasn't letting her hair down to the extent that she'd consume a fat- and sugar-laden beverage.

Liz sat tentatively on the edge of the sofa and looked around the room. Phoebe was curled up on her bed, a pillow wedged behind her, sipping her hot chocolate appreciatively. Everything else felt strangely unfamiliar for a room in her own home – this was not somewhere Liz had ever felt welcome, or spent a lot of time. She had been shocked, though, at how terrified she had been when she thought Phoebe might be lost, and how guilty she had felt at her own part in that. She'd resolved to herself that, if Phoebe was found safe and well, she would do her utmost to build bridges. Ironically she knew that the first bridge would have to be rescinding her objections to Phoebe living with Callum. If she didn't do that, the toxic resentment would poison any chance she might have of establishing some kind of a relationship with her daughter.

And when she'd thought it through calmly, it hadn't seemed so bad after all. She'd spent a couple of hours that afternoon looking on Rightmove, and had been amazed at how much houses like theirs were selling for. It was immaculately, stylishly decorated, and her research suggested that with her half of the proceeds and some of the modelling earnings she had squirrelled away, she'd be able to afford a lovely modern apartment in the city centre. She was suddenly quite excited at the prospect of life as a single, child-free girl about town, something she hadn't been for nearly twenty years.

'So, what have you been buying, then?' she asked, more to break the silence than for any other reason.

Phoebe looked wary, as well she might, given some of her mum's previous comments on her clothes and style, but she could sense that Liz was trying, and so duly started lifting clothes out of the bags.

'There's this jacket, that's my favourite thing, I think.'

It was bright red needlecord, and would make even

jeans and a plain T-shirt look something special. Liz smiled and nodded, and continued to do so as Phoebe showed her a pair of jeans, some new Converse, two T-shirts and a dress. The dress was knee-length stretch jersey, a black background with a ditsy floral print, and although Phoebe normally played it safe in jeans and baggy tops, she loved the way this dress draped flatteringly over the problem areas of her tummy, thighs and bum. Even Liz seemed approving.

'They're all really nice, love. I must admit I didn't know you could get such fashionable things in your size.' She paused, realising the clanger, and then tried, unsuccessfully, to row back.

'I mean, it's just that if you were a bit slimmer you'd have even more choice, and there'd be loads of different styles you could wear, but these are great, they really are.'

Phoebe took a deep breath. It would be so easy to start crying, to throw her mum out of her room, and to eat a Double Decker to make herself feel better, but a lot of what Ella had said last night had really resonated with her.

'Being overweight isn't the worst thing in the world to be, Mum.' She echoed Ella's words.

'No, I know. But it does make life more difficult, you must see that.'

'I'd like to lose some weight so I was healthier. But what makes life really difficult isn't me being fat, it's how other people respond to that. I'm going to learn to cook, and I'm going to eat proper home-cooked meals, stop snacking so much, and see what happens. But it's not the be-all and end-all.'

Liz was quietly impressed at her daughter's maturity. Only a few weeks ago Phoebe would have been crying, sulking and stomping if she criticised her weight. Just as she was trying to decide how to respond, Phoebe continued.

'Anyway, Mum, thanks so much for the hot chocolate. I'm really tired now, though, so I'm going to get into bed. Night night.'

Liz found herself on the landing, holding her now-empty mug of tea, with no real idea of how she had been dismissed. She shrugged philosophically. Phoebe was safe, and they hadn't had an argument. That would have to do for now. Aware that it was past midnight, and she was going to have a series of busy days negotiating with Callum, estate agents, solicitors and heaven knows what else, she decided to go to bed herself.

On the other side of the door, Phoebe was hugging herself in triumph. She'd done it. Her mum had started with the criticism and she had managed to keep calm *and* have the last word. She drained the last of her hot chocolate, decided that she was far too tired to clean her teeth, turned her light off and curled up to go to sleep.

36

Ella sighed reluctantly, and wriggled out of Greg's reach.

'No, I'd love to, but the kids—'

He reached out for her again, tracing the curve of her face, neck, breast, until she shivered delightedly.

'The kids are downstairs with a double length *Octonauts* episode. So we've got – ' he checked his watch ' – eighteen minutes, get your kit off!'

Seventeen minutes later Ella was pulling her clothes back on after a fast, furious and extremely satisfying quickie. Sex on a Saturday morning – practically unheard of. Everything seemed to have changed between her and Greg, though. Ella had joked to Imogen that if she'd known having an affair would be so good for her marriage she'd have done it years ago. They couldn't keep their hands off each other. Aidan was frankly disgusted that Mummy and Daddy were being 'so kissy', but she and Greg were also talking in a way they hadn't done for years.

Some of that was the excitement of planning their trip – discussing routes, stop-offs, campsites, the merits of various camper vans – but they were also just sharing more of the minutiae of daily life. Ella would text Greg at work with something funny one of the kids had said, or just to say she loved him. Greg had got his mum to babysit one night a week for a couple of hours, so he and Ella could go to their local to share a carefree bottle of wine.

Hattie and Aidan came charging up the stairs.

'Daddy! It's finished! Mummy – when's Indigo getting here?'

It was Ella's turn to look at her watch.

'Bloody hell, Greg, they'll all be here in less than an hour! I've got loads still to do!'

She was aware that she didn't feel nearly as stressed as she probably should have done – that was what the after-glow of an orgasm did for you – and Greg smiled lazily at her.

'Tell you what, I'll take the kids to the swings for half an hour or so, give you a chance to sort things out, how about that?'

'Yay, swings, yay swings!' the children chorused, and Ella gave Greg a grateful smile.

'That would be perfect, thank you.'

Imogen, Alex, Indigo and Molly were all coming round for lunch, and, as Imogen was due to start her new job the following week, it was a bit of a farewell celebration, so Ella wanted it to be perfect.

The weather was gorgeous blazing sunshine, of the kind you always associate with late August but rarely actually get, so Ella had decided they should eat outside. There wasn't much to do for the food now. A chicken, rosemary and thyme stuffed under its buttered skin, was roasting in the oven for the meat-eaters, and she'd made a roast tomato and goat's cheese tart for Imogen and Indigo. An enormous bowl of chive-studded potato salad, home-made mayonnaise and all, was ready in the fridge and her pavlova base was made, the cream whipped, just waiting to be assembled and topped with raspberries at the last minute. She'd also made an enormous chocolate fudge cake, shakily piping 'Good luck' across the top in sugar-pink icing, which Indigo, at least, would love.

Now she just had to throw together a salad – spinach, avocado and pine nuts for the adults, with bowls of cherry tomato and chopped cucumber for the kids – and decorate the table and garden.

Half an hour later, as she heard the kids erupt back into the house, Ella stood back to admire her work. The salads were made and the table looked like something out of a posh magazine – under the shade of the big old apple tree, covered in a white linen cloth, with jam jars of roses in all shades of pink everywhere. She'd strung floral bunting from trees and bushes, and there was an enormous plastic crate filled with ice and several bottles of rosé. Perfect.

Ten minutes later, Imogen arrived, bubbling over with excited laughter and closely followed by Alex, Molly and Indigo.

Imogen embraced Ella warmly and handed over a bottle of champagne.

'What are we celebrating?' Ella asked, giggling more because Imogen's excitement was infectious than because anything was particularly funny.

Imogen and Alex exchanged glances, and then Imogen burst out, 'We've bought a house! We literally just exchanged contracts half an hour ago!'

Questions started pouring out of Ella – 'What? How? Where? Are you not going to Hull then? Do you mean you've bought it together?' – while Greg calmly shepherded everyone through to the garden, collecting champagne flutes en route. The children, of course, had disappeared off to play in Aidan's room, contrarily ignoring the sunshine, when Ella knew that had it been pouring with rain they would have been begging to play in the garden. She mentally shrugged. That was kids for you.

Imogen started to explain.

'Well, as you know, I start the new job in Hull next week, but Alex runs a company based in London. We'd planned to do everything very sensibly – I'd rent a flat in Hull, we'd see how things go, Alex and Molly could come up at weekends, or Indy and I could come down here.'

Ella nodded. Last she'd heard this had been what was going to happen.

Alex took up the tale.

'But then I got awarded a couple of big contracts for firms based up north – one in Leeds, one in Sheffield, so I knew I'd need to spend a lot of time up there.'

Imogen was talking again, words tripping over each other in her excitement.

'So we just thought, sod it, let's buy somewhere! I know we haven't been together that long, but neither of us can imagine not being together for ever, so we just thought it made sense to buy a family home – for all four of us, and any other children we might have at some point.'

'Wow!' Ella was almost stunned into silence. She'd been so preoccupied with her own dramas over the past few weeks that she really hadn't seen this one coming. Thinking about it now, though, she could see that it made total sense. She'd never seen Imogen look this happy before, and, although she didn't know Alex well yet, he was clearly absolutely besotted.

'That's amazing – congratulations! So, what's it like?'

Imogen launched into a vivid description.

'It's gorgeous! And enormous! You just wouldn't believe the contrast to my grotty little flat! It's in a lovely little village a few miles outside Hull, a fifteen-minute drive for me to get to work, and only half an hour from my parents. Five bedrooms, and an acre of garden! There's this huge kitchen, complete with Aga, of course, and a living room, a study, a playroom . . . You'll definitely be able to come and stay, 'cos there's loads of room – Molly and Indigo are inseparable, so they're insisting on sharing a room, even though there's plenty of space for them to have one each. But that's great, they've both acquired a sister, and it gives us lots of space for our London friends to come and see us.'

Ella laughed.

'Well, once we get back from our travels you won't keep us away! It sounds wonderful. Have you got any pictures?'

Imogen pulled out the estate agent's pamphlet from her capacious tapestry bag and dragged her chair over to Ella's.

The two men exchanged glances and eye-rolls.

'Oh God,' Alex groaned, 'they could be doing that all day, couldn't they?'

Greg nodded.

'Yep, I would say so. Forget any hopes of lunch, it's all going to be Farrow and Ball colour charts. Seriously, though, congratulations. It's amazing news. Immy really deserves it – I guess you already know, but she put up with a lot of shit from Indigo's dad.'

Alex nodded.

'Yeah, you know what Imogen's like – she's far too nice to bitch, but I had definitely got that impression. But that's all over. I'm going to look after her and Indy now.'

Greg nodded.

'I can see that. But tell me, how's the practical side going to work?'

Alex grimaced.

'The truth is it's probably going to be a bit tricky to begin with. Molly and I will be in Hull Tuesday to Friday, and then come back down here for the weekend so Molly can see her mum, and I can do some time in the office here on a Saturday and Monday. But then next year, when Molly starts school, she'll be full-time in Hull we think, and so will I, and just make trips down to London as and when I need to.'

He pulled another face.

'My ex-wife wasn't exactly thrilled at first, as you can imagine, but she's come round now. She'll have Molly for most of the school holidays, we think.'

Greg raised his eyebrows.

'And is Pete going to see Indigo?'

Alex started laughing, and glanced over at Imogen. She looked up from the paper she and Ella were poring over.

'Greg was just asking about Pete and Indigo, darling.'

Imogen started to laugh as well.

'Oh God, you'd never believe it. All these years I thought I'd never get him to move out of London, and now he's actually talking about moving to Leeds!'

'What?!'

'I know. It's all pretty ironic. I think we must have just rubbed each other up totally the wrong way. I was desperate for him to settle down a bit more, get a proper job, be a better father, and he constantly pushed back against that. Now we've split up and no one's nagging him, he's talking about doing a law conversion course in Leeds – he'd flat-share with a mate of his who lives there. Apparently he wants to train as a solicitor and then specialise in immigration and asylum issues. Although I'll believe it when I actually see it – he's not really one of life's completer-finishers.'

She paused and pulled a face.

'He's been much keener on seeing Indigo too, I think that's partly why he's thinking about Leeds. I'm really torn, though, because although on one hand I do want Indy to have a positive relationship with him, I also know I'm going to struggle to trust him with her.'

Ella patted her hand reassuringly.

'I wouldn't worry too much. For one thing, like you said, it hasn't happened yet. Pete's always a great one for plans, but how often does he actually follow through? But when he does see her, I'm sure he'll have learnt his lesson, Immy. After all, although he'd never admit it, Indy's accident and knowing he was responsible must have given him a hell of a shock. Don't let worrying about him spoil it anyway – it all sounds perfect, and I'm so happy for you.'

Imogen hugged her.

'I know you are. And me for you, too.'

Greg took this as an opportune moment to pop the champagne cork.

'Here's to Alex, Imogen, Molly and Indigo, and to new beginnings.'

'To new beginnings!' they all echoed.

37

From: phoebe.mccraig@jamesroad6thform.org
To: ella1985@mailbox.org

Dear Ella

Sorry it's taken me so long to reply to your email. It was great to see you too, and to meet Aidan and Hattie. They're so sweet! I can't believe how much Hattie looks like you. I love that video of them trying surfing, like little Californian beach dudes. They won't want to come back to Britain!

It sounds like you're having an amazing trip. I think it's New York I'm most jealous about. New York at Christmas might just be the most exciting thing ever.

Actually, Dad was talking about us going away for Christmas (but not to NY, unfortunately). It's just going to be the two of us, 'cos Mum's got this new boyfriend she wants to be with (don't ask, he's a bodybuilder and nightclub DJ, cliché or what!). I quite like the idea of Christmas in our little house though. It's so nice now. I've been doing some decorating at weekends, and it looks really cool – Ruth, Becky's mum, had all these old   magazines, and I tried to copy things out of there. And my room is gorgeous! I thought I was going to really miss my old room, but I don't at all. This one has lovely wooden floorboards, and a genuine old Victorian cast-iron fireplace, so I've kind of gone with that as the theme. I got a fab handmade patchwork quilt at a craft fair, and I've got tea-lights, and fairy lights all round the fireplace. Anyway, like I was saying, I'm quite excited about getting a Christmas tree here, and decorating everything. Cooking Christmas dinner might be a bit scary, but I made roast chicken last weekend and it was really nice, so it's not that different, is it? And if I get too freaked out by it we can always just buy stuff from M&S. I'm trying to persuade Dad to invite Anita, who's one of the teachers at his school, for Christmas. She and Dad have been friends for ages, so I've known her since I was a little girl, and she's really nice. I think she's got a bit of a crush on Dad, and I really wanted him to meet someone, so I thought Christmas might help things along! What do you think??

The other thing I meant to tell you about the house is that Dad's bought it now, it's not just rented. The lady who owned it before is getting married, and she's going to live in her new husband's house. They want the money to pay for the wedding, which seems like a pretty expensive wedding to me, but what do I know? I'm just glad we can stay here, 'cos I don't really want any more change for a while.

Sixth form is just fab! I'm so glad you suggested going to a sixth form college, it's loads better than school. We get to call the teachers by their first names, and there's no uniform, and when you get free periods you don't have to stay in college, so a group of us hang out together all the time in a coffee shop across the road. Becky loves it too, and we've got a big group of friends now, which is much better than it just being the two of us, although Becky is still my best friend. You were right, being 'different' isn't such a big deal as it was at school. I've lost a bit of weight, although I'm still what people politely call 'curvy', but I'm not nearly so stressed about it. And Mum is too busy with DJ Carl to care much about what dress size I am. (18 now, for the record!)

Anyway, I've kind of saved the most exciting thing for last. I've got a boyfriend! I literally never thought that would happen to me. I've never even said this to Becky 'cos it makes me sound so pathetic, but I used to see mums pushing babies round in their prams, and then go home and cry because I thought I was too fat and ugly for anyone to ever want to have sex with me, so I'd never have a baby of my own. Not that Justin and I are thinking of having a baby, mind you!

So, he's called Justin, and he's in Year 12 too. He came from an all-boys' school, and so he was probably as shy with girls as I was with boys. He's really tall (even taller than Dad, I think), and really skinny. I was a bit worried we'd look weird together, but as I said, no one seems that bothered by things like that. He's got dark hair, and glasses – he said he used to get skitted at school for looking like Harry Potter, and he kind of does, a bit! But I've always fancied Daniel Radcliffe . . . He's really clever, doing FIVE A-levels (Chemistry, Maths, Further Maths, Biology, and Physics!!), and he wants to be a doctor. When you're home from America and come to Liverpool to see your parents you have to meet him. I think you'll really like him!

Right, I need to go and start making tea. I'm trying steak fajitas tonight, wish me luck!

Lots of love, and big kisses to Aidan and Hattie

Phoebe xxxxx

From: imogend@teachnet.com
To: ella1985@mailbox.org

Hi Ella

Wow, it all sounds fabulous, I'm so jealous.

Everything totally manic here – settling into new job, new house, new way of living. We're getting chickens – fresh eggs every morning! I'm so happy. I just feel as though everything's come together at last. Indigo loves it here, loves seeing more of my mum and dad, LOVES living with Molly. She really misses her at the weekends. And Alex . . . I just didn't know men like that existed!

Right, gotta go, there's a million different things I should be doing . . .

Loads of love

Immy xxx

Ella read her emails with a smile on her face. Imogen seemed to have found a lifestyle, as well as a relationship, that fitted her personality in a way that living with Pete in London could never have done. Phoebe's email was utterly typical of her, and Ella was so glad that things seemed to be going well for her at last. It had been lovely to spend the day with her in Liverpool when she'd taken the kids up to say goodbye to her parents before the start of their trip. She'd been a bit worried about how Greg would feel about her seeing Phoebe, but he'd been fine.

'Look, I can't say I'd be happy with you seeing much of Callum – it's not that I don't trust you, but I'm buggered if I know why I should trust him. Any bloke who thought he had half a chance would try it on with you, it's a natural male reaction. But of course I don't mind you seeing Phoebe, she sounds a really nice girl.'

Ella took a slurp of her latte. She was in a café in Boston that had free Wi-Fi; living in a camper van meant that they'd learned to take advantage of any free facilities they could get their hands on, and Greg had volunteered to take the kids to a soft play centre for a morning to give her a chance to catch up with emails, and with the blog of their trip she'd started, if she returned the favour the next day.

She started typing her replies.

From: ella1985@mailbox.org
To: imogend@teachnet.com

Hi Immy,

Ha, keeping chickens! That is you. It's going to be goats next, isn't it? And probably a beehive . . . Seriously, it all sounds great, and fantastic that Indigo is happy.

We're still loving our trip. I think Greg and I both felt that we missed out on a lot of our twenties because we were knee-deep in nappies, and although we wouldn't change the kids, it's great to be getting a bit of it back. Aidan and Hattie loving it too, especially living in a camper van!

Can't wait to see you at New Year – can't decide if 2013 has been the best or worst ever year for us – what do you reckon? Either way, def think we need a few bottles of champagne to welcome in 2014. And some boiled eggs . . .

E xxxxx

From: ella1985@mailbox.org
To: phoebe.mccraig@jamesroad6thform.org

Dear Phoebe

Happy Thanksgiving! Well, for yesterday. It's so nice to hear from you, and I'm so glad that everything seems to be going well.

Great news about Callum buying the house – after all the work you've put in, it would be such a shame to have to move out, wouldn't it? I think you should definitely stay at home for Christmas, I never think a house feels like a proper home until you've had a Christmas there. And how would Father Christmas find you in a hotel, anyway? That's Aidan and Hattie's preoccupation at the moment. We're ditching the camper van when we get to New York and renting a serviced apartment. There's no way I'm trying to cook Christmas dinner on a two-ring camping stove, and NYC isn't exactly famous for its campsites anyway. I can just see us trying to find a spot in Central Park. Anyway,

Greg's come up with an elaborate story which involves the elves fitting Rudolph with satnav, and I think the kids are happy enough with that for the time being!

As for Christmas dinner, for two (or three!) of you, you only need a chicken anyway, so you've already done it. Just stick a few chipolatas in too, and my best piece of advice is to use Auntie Bessie's roasties.

I think I might know Anita. Is her last name Warberg? There was a Miss Warberg who taught Physics when I was in sixth form, and I'm pretty sure she was called Anita. I didn't take Physics, but I remember she seemed really nice. I wouldn't push your dad, though, Phoebe. He's had a tough year one way and another. I know you want him to be happy with someone soon, and I'm sure he will be, but he needs to do it in his own time.

Justin sounds lovely! To be honest with you, I quite fancy Daniel Radcliffe too – which is very embarrassing given he's about ten years younger than me – so lucky you! You really deserve someone nice, Phoebe, I'm so happy for you. I don't think you're pathetic at all for wondering if you'd find someone, I think most people think that at some point. But also he's a lucky guy to have met you, remember that. Just make sure that you do make sure there aren't any babies yet! I think 26 was on the young side to be a first time mother, 16 would really be pushing it. And, just in case you haven't heard this enough from other people, don't do anything you're not completely happy and comfortable with. And be careful whatever you do. There, surrogate mother bit over.

We're still having a fantastic time, it really is the trip

of a lifetime. A bloke Greg was at school with married an American woman, and they live in Boston, so we celebrated Thanksgiving with them yesterday. It was fun being with a proper American household for a proper American festival. Quite weird having turkey and trimmings when it's not Christmas, and sweet potato with marshmallows is just WRONG (although the kids loved it – turns out melting sweeties on to their veg is the way forward!). Pumpkin pie is delish though, definitely a lot nicer than Christmas pudding.

Anyway darling, I'd better go. I've got loads more catch-up emails to send, and Greg will only be able to stand the soft play centre for so long.

Lots of love

Ella xxx

Ella pressed send and then, Greg's plight in KidzWorld not withstanding, she allowed herself a few moments of contented contemplation. After an incredibly tumultuous few months, during which life had thrown them more than a few curveballs, she, Imogen and Phoebe all seemed to have come out the other side happier than they could ever have imagined. Fresh from a Thanksgiving celebration, with the 'counting your blessings' ethos still resonating, Ella silently added her friends' delighted enjoyment of their new lives to her own list of things to be thankful for.

ACKNOWLEDGEMENTS

Huge thanks to my amazingly talented editor, Francesca Best, and the fantastic team at Hodder, particularly Emilie Ferguson and Naomi Berwin. I'm very lucky to have such a great group of people to work with.

Thanks also to my brilliant agent, Sheila Ableman, for her incredible belief, commitment, enthusiasm and some really fun working lunches.

A big thank you to Charlotte Connor for her advice on family law – I may have got it all wrong anyway, but that's definitely my fault, not hers!

My parents, Sue and Nick Chandler, have been so support-ive, and so proud of my writing – I should probably apologise to all their friends, colleagues and chance-met acquaintances who've been route-marched to a bookshop and forced to hand over their credit card . . . sorry about that.

On a similar note, my gorgeous girl, Anna, is also very proud of me and has great fun spotting *Two for Joy* on the shelves in bookshops. She's too young to read my books yet and is a bit disappointed that I don't do my own illustrations, but is still very keen to tell everyone that her mummy's an author.

I didn't have the easiest year while writing *To Have and to Hold*, but I have been unbelievably lucky in the huge amounts of love and support I've received. My husband and parents have been rocks, but so have a group of friends who've put up with me crying on the phone, at playdates, in the park, in cafés, in the toilets at a wedding (etc. etc. etc.), and have also stepped in to deal with practicalities like cooking and childcare when I needed them. Esther, Haf, Helen, Holly, Jenny, Kate, Rachel and Rosalind – you make my world a better place, thank you!

Most of all, thank you so much to the readers of my books and blog. There'd be no point without you, and I love your comments, feedback and reviews.

Read on for the first chapter of Helen Chandler's brilliant debut novel, shortlisted for the RNA Contemporary Romantic Novel Award . . .

TWO FOR JOY

Julia and Toby have been friends for years, but apart from a couple of drunken snogs in their university days, there's never been anything more than friendship between them. It's only when Toby goes through a dramatic break up with his gorgeous ballerina girlfriend, Ruby, that he and Julia realise they're meant to be together.

Then Ruby drops a bombshell – she's pregnant – and though he feels torn in two, Toby feels he has to give their relationship another chance.

Heartbroken Julia is left to lick her wounds in her little Walthamstow home, thinking she has lost Toby forever. But things soon become much more complicated . . .

'This is a pure delight . . . beautifully handled with some unexpected, humorous and emotional moments, all thrown into a fast-moving plot. I loved it.' *Lovereading.co.uk*

Out now in paperback and ebook

HODDER

I

As Julia raised her eyes to Toby's face she realised that he had been waiting for her response, probably for some minutes. The noise of the busy restaurant seemed to have receded: it was just the two of them, and she had to think of something to say. Her hand groped instinctively for the trusty goldfish bowl of Pinot Grigio on the table in front of her and she took a restorative gulp before attempting anything as complicated as the formulation of a sentence.

'Wow, Tobes, that's . . . that's amazing. Wow. It's . . . erm . . . incredible.'

Even to her own ears her voice sounded forced and unnatural.

'Incredibly good, or incredibly bad?' Toby raised his eyebrows quizzically and she could sense that he was a little hurt by her lack of enthusiasm.

She rallied, and willed herself to control the myriad complex emotions which were whirling around her head and concentrate on being a good friend to Toby. But what did 'good friend' mean in this context? Did it mean offering unconditional support? Was she being a good friend if she encouraged him in this insane plan to marry a woman he barely knew and had nothing in common with? Or would a truly good friend try and talk him out of it, point out that marriages were likely enough to fail without the odds being stacked against them to the extent they would be here?

Maybe she could compromise. 'Well, incredibly good, of course. It's amazing that you feel so strongly for Ruby, that you're so happy together.' She paused, and frowned. 'The only thing is, I suppose, that you haven't been together that long. Wouldn't it be better to at least live together for a while first before getting engaged? It's such a big step.'

Toby gave Julia a funny little half-smile. 'That's why I love you, Julia. Your romantic impulsiveness. Listen, it *is* a big step, I am aware of that, but that's not automatically a bad thing, you know. Ruby is so beautiful, so exciting, she makes me feel so alive. I don't want to risk losing that now I've found it – now I've discovered the person I can be when I'm with her. Asking her to move in with me would feel routine and functional. Actually proposing won't leave her in any doubt about what I feel.'

Julia sighed. Surely by this time she was old enough to know that compromise rarely worked. She hadn't, in any way, achieved her objective of making Toby think twice about his rash decision. All she had succeeded in doing was to ensure that she herself appeared in the worst possible light as an unromantic killjoy. 'Well, proposing to her should certainly give her an indication of how you feel.'

Oh God. That sounded sarcastic and bitter as well. 'Sorry, Toby. I don't want to spoil things for you. I just want you to be happy, and it's a bit of a shock, that's all. I had no idea things were so serious between you and Ruby.'

Toby's face lit up as he began to eulogise. 'Honestly, Ju, I've never felt like this before. She's literally all I can think about. She's so beautiful, so passionate. I can't concentrate when I'm not with her because I'm thinking about the next time I'll see her, and I can't concentrate when I *am* with her because I'm just mesmerised looking at her. Do you understand what I mean? All I want to do is look at her.'

Julia couldn't decide whether her feelings of slight nausea were caused by downing half a bottle of wine in five minutes flat, or by Toby's saccharine sincerity. She did understand, though. She herself had experienced very similar feelings in the past. The trouble was, she had been thirteen years old, and the object of her affections was the student teacher assigned to her French class. And while she would happily have proposed to him, always supposing she had been able to muster something more eloquent than a nervous giggle in his presence, with the benefit of seventeen years' hindsight she couldn't help but feel that the relationship might not have lasted. Luckily a spark of feminine intuition surfaced, somewhat later than it might have done, but nonetheless in time to prevent her sharing the comparison with Toby.

She looked at him affectionately. He had changed remarkably little in the time she had known him, and as he sat now, elbows on the table, leaning forward, eyes alight with eagerness, he could still have been the passionate student activist she had first seen holding forth in the college bar, twelve years previously. 'Come on then, Romeo. Let's order some fizz to celebrate. And don't worry, I understand it's top secret until you actually ask her on Friday. My lips are sealed.'

The rest of the evening passed with their normal mix of banter, teasing, chatting and joking, and if Julia felt the need of a little more alcoholic lubrication than might otherwise have been the case, well, at least The Proposal wasn't referred to again.

It was only when they said goodbye in the Tube station at Oxford Circus that things felt any different. They stood together for a moment in the crowded-even-on-a-Sunday-evening ticket hall, and Julia was suddenly aware of how tall he was. At five foot eight herself, Julia liked tall men and the way they always made her feel so deliciously feminine and protected, but she had never really considered Toby in that category and he had certainly never had that effect on her. She knew he was well over six foot, of course, and she was in flat ballet pumps that night, which emphasised the difference, but suddenly there seemed to be something else as well. Some awareness of him as a man, of her as a woman. Some slight frisson when he bent to kiss her cheek and his stubble grazed her slightly.

'Well, bye then,' she said awkwardly as they stepped away from each other. 'Maybe see you next weekend, to celebrate?'

Toby appeared faintly embarrassed, but pleased. 'Yeah, that'd be great. I'll talk to Ruby, see what her plans are, and give you a call.'

There was another moment of slightly strained silence and then he was off, loping towards the escalators without a backward glance.

Julia stood for a minute, fancying she could still feel the pressure of his hands on her upper arms. She gave herself a mental shake. Bit of a coincidence that the first time she found herself going all Mills and Boon about Toby's height and the set of his shoulders was the evening he told her he was proposing to someone else. Talk about the unobtainable being more attractive . . .

Back in her own little house later that night, Julia threw herself luxuriously full length onto her purple needlecord sofa and began drinking the pint glass of water which would hopefully stave off hangover hell in the morning, wincing at the thought of the budget meeting starting less than nine hours later. She knew, though, that there was no point going to bed just yet. Her mind was still buzzing from the champagne and from Toby's news.

Now she was alone in her sanctuary and didn't have to pretend anything for Toby's sake, she tried to analyse honestly how she felt. Not good, she decided. She curled up and cradled a patchwork cushion on her lap. Why was this so hard?

Was it turning thirty that had made the difference? Julia didn't think she was an inherently selfish person. She had willingly, even enthusiastically, submitted to having her hair contorted into unnatural curls and squeezing her curves into unflattering pastel satin at both her younger brother's and best friend's weddings, and was just delighted that people she loved were so happy.

She had been equally enthusiastic a year or two later to return to the scene of the fashion crime, this time hoping that a hasty lunchtime purchase of the best Debenhams had to offer in the way of linen jackets and big hats would say 'responsible, caring yet independent-minded godmother and aunt' rather than 'desperate broody singleton'. She wasn't at all sure that she had succeeded in the latter; there had been, at least to her paranoid gaze, far too many sympathetic glances, although it was only her teenage cousin who had actually voiced what she suspected the rest of the family were thinking: 'Doesn't it make you feel weird, Ju, that your little brother's married with a baby and you haven't even got a boyfriend at the moment?'

Julia was determined not to fulfil the Bridget Jones stereotype (although if it could involve Colin Firth and Hugh Grant fighting over her in a fountain she would be prepared to reconsider), but she was uncomfortably aware that circumstances, not to mention her own unspoken but compelling longing for a baby, were conspiring against her.

Newspapers and magazines were constantly full of articles about the growing number of single households, of women reaching the peak of their careers and then turning forty and producing strings of beautiful babies, and rationally Julia knew that the world had moved on from the days when you married the boy next door aged twenty, popped out a baby every two years until you had your perfect little family, and then got your hair cut and permed, bought a mid-calf-length floral skirt from Marks and Spencer and settled back to wait for grandchildren.

It was just that no one appeared to have shared the news of this demographic shift with her closest and oldest friend Rose – married at twenty-seven, mother to the divine Sebastian at twenty-eight, and be-Bodened stay-at-home mum in her comfortable four-bedroom detached house in an affluent Berkshire commuter village. Or with her younger brother Harry – married at twenty-two to his childhood sweetheart Angela (Julia strongly suspected that Angela's adherence to a branch of Christianity which forcefully advocated no sex before marriage had more than a little to do with that) and now father to adorable Sarah and Ruth.

Or with her mother and father. Eddie and Pat Upton had been happily married and contentedly installed in their suburban Manchester three-bedroom semi for thirty-two years. They were at a loss to understand why their only daughter had moved to London, paid six times the national average wage for a Victorian terrace that only the very kind-hearted (or the polar opposite, an estate agent) could describe as two-bedroomed, and didn't even have a boyfriend.

None of that had really bothered her before, though, and she had been quite content with her little house, her demanding but satisfying job and her role as group mother to a wide circle of friends.

Was Toby just the final straw? He was the last of her closest friends to meet his other half. He was also an ex-boyfriend, if you counted a few half-hearted snogs and gropes at the university bops which sometimes seemed another lifetime ago. Maybe it was that despite making different decisions from her parents, she came from a warm, close, loving family and had enjoyed an idyllic childhood; watching her brother recreate that with his girls sometimes made her feel that she had somehow managed to miss the boat, and Toby's forthcoming engagement just underlined the point further.

One thing which really did bother her was how little she had seen of Toby during the last few months since he had been dating Ruby. Perhaps a key reason why she had never particularly minded being single was that the traditional 'couple times' – Sunday nights, holidays, work Christmas parties – had never held any terrors for her because there had always been Toby, and she had more fun with him than she had ever had with any of the blokes she had been in so-called relationships with. Presumably Ruby wouldn't be too keen, though, on her husband spending his weekends and holidays with another woman, which meant that singledom was going to mean something very different in future.

And then there was Ruby herself. There were no two ways about it: Julia just didn't *like* Ruby, and at the thought of Ruby as Toby's wife this dislike seemed to swell to the point where Julia thought she might burst with angry outrage. Ruby seemed to be Julia's complete opposite – dark where Julia was fair, size 8 to Julia's size 14, petite where Julia was tall. Julia was a hospital manager, Deputy Director of Operations at St Benedict's NHS Trust, one of London's most prestigious teaching hospitals, a relatively well-paid job high on responsibility but low on glamour. Ruby was a ballet dancer, currently performing in what she described as a 'retro yet avant-garde interpretation of *Swan Lake*', working for almost nothing but funding her stylish existence through a generous allowance from her parents. Julia's parents worked in middle-management roles in local government; Ruby's father was a baronet and had the country estate to go with it. The only thing the two women had in common was Toby, and that didn't provide them with much in the way of conversation at dinner parties. At first Julia had been paranoid about referring too much to her and Toby's shared past, and she was scrupulous in avoiding the 'do you remember' anecdotes that she worried could lead to Ruby feeling insecure or excluded. She quickly realised, however, that there was no need to worry at all. Ruby was supremely self-confident. Self-absorbed, even, thought Julia bitchily, and it was only too clear that it had never entered Ruby's head to consider Julia as either threat or competition.

Rose, in a fit of G&T-induced honesty, had once said that Julia was jealous of Ruby; jealous that she was the only one of Toby's girlfriends who had ever seriously threatened her position as number one woman in Toby's life. She had also said that Julia was in danger of being a dog in the manger – not wanting Toby for herself, but not wanting anyone else to have him either. Julia's response back then had been dismissive. 'I've got no reason to be jealous. Just because Toby happens to be shagging some nubile bimbo, it doesn't change our friendship. After all, he's not about to marry the woman.'

Now, facing the prospect of an engagement she had not even allowed herself to consider as a possibility, and filled with something which did feel horribly like jealousy, Julia considered whether there was any truth in what Rose had said. She supposed, uncomfortably, that she *had* always considered Toby to be hers, and had always felt that given any encouragement he would be more than happy to make the transition from best friend to boyfriend. They had made the obligatory agreement at university – 'if we're not married by the time we're thirty-five, we'll marry each other' – and while Julia had never really considered that there was any spark of sexual attraction between them, on her part at least she loved him very much as a friend, and her thirty-fifth birthday no longer felt the impossibly distant event it had at nineteen. Maybe she *had* felt subconsciously that Toby was her back-up option.

Julia cringed at her own arrogance. Why had she imagined that Toby – tall, dark, handsome, successful – was going to be left on the shelf, willing to be her reserve choice should Mr Darcy/Rochester/de Winter not make an appearance in time? After all, no one ever bemoaned the plight of single thirty-something men – if men were single in their thirties, she thought cynically, it was only because they were trying to decide which twenty-something babe to shag next.

Maybe this was just the wake-up call she needed. Looking round her kitchen as she went to get yet another glass of water before heading off to bed, Julia concluded that with her well-stocked spice cupboard, her full range of Nigella cookbooks and her small but perfectly formed herb garden, she was living the Smug Married life, but had somehow neglected to provide herself with that ultimate Smug Married accessory: a husband. She needed to stop spending all her free time having cosy dinners with either Toby or her coupled-up friends, and start getting out and meeting people. As of tomorrow, Things Must Change.